# Definitely Against Policy

## by

## Renata North

The Wild Rose Press, Inc.
PO Box 708
Adams Basin, NY 14410-0708
Visit us at www.thewildrosepress.com

Publishing History
First Edition, 2024
Trade Paperback ISBN 978-1-5092-5585-6
Digital ISBN 978-1-5092-5586-3


Published in the United States of America

# Dedication

To Andy

Chapter One

Stephen's teeth were straight and square and bright yellow, his smile a double fence of lemon Chiclets surrounded by fleshy, pink lips. Mary Rose sank into a seat near the rear door of the streetcar, wiped the fog from the window with her sleeve, and peered through. If this wasn't a one-off misprint and her boss looked the same in the other ads, she would be so dead. Or worse. Unemployed.

She caught a glimpse of the university express as it rushed by in the left lane with the ad on its starboard side, "Stephen Hill, Realtor, Matching people with property!" in true blue Baskerville font, nary a hint of green, Stephen's collar as white as a virginal Yuletide snowdrift. Why, then, were his teeth so yellow? And not "overdue for hygiene" yellow, but full-on bingo-dabber yellow.

It was Stephen's fault for never smiling a warning, never revealing the problem with even so much as a mild chuckle. Except it wasn't his fault. It was all on her. She should've opened the attachments to see the proofs before she approved them with a distracted thumbs-up. Photoshop could've worked a miracle, if only she'd known.

She was so very, very fired.

Heart pounding, temples thrumming, consciousness evaporating from her body into the ether, she shrank into the seat for refuge. Breathe, goddamn it! In for the count of three and out for five. Or was it the other way round? Expel the bad to make space for the good. Just breathe.

"Mary Rose! Golly! Is that you? Both of us on the same streetcar? Imagine!"

Mary looked up. The face and voice were vaguely familiar, like spotting a minor celebrity in a café. The young woman was already wedging herself onto the bench. Mary squeezed over.

"I'm Dr. Silverstein's student? Philosophy 307? Theories on Justice?"

"Of course." The talkative personal trainer who thought Kant's categorical imperative was 'a brilliant game-changer.' "Umm…"

"Megan. Like the princess!"

"Megan. Right." Mary looked sideways at her seatmate. "May I ask you a question? As a student of philosophy."

"Shoot." Megan mimed a pistol aim and trigger pull, then elbow-nudged Mary's ribs. "Don't be a bashful Bonny. Go on."

"What would you do if you made a mistake at work and accidentally humiliated your boss?"

"That's easy. I'd confess and apologize. Like Jocko Willink, the motivational guru? Extreme ownership?"

"Even if you were only half responsible? And it wasn't on purpose?"

"Mary, you know the Challenger disaster? Back in the 80s? That wasn't 'on purpose.'" Megan flashed air quotes with bedazzled fingernails. "The engineers still manned up and took all the blame. One hundred percent. People respect that."

2

A dubious assertion. In Mary's experience, people who accepted blame wore the mantle of the scapegoat. Anyway, maybe she was catastrophizing. A mistake at the wheel, a mechanical failure, they could actually kill someone. A poster, on the other hand—

"Would you still confess and apologize for something really minor?" asked Mary. "Like an unfortunate printing error?"

"You mean a typo?" Megan's gaze flitted to the window. "Or that hilarious ad with Stephen Hill?" She graced her giggle with a snort. "My Gawd. Those teeth!"

"Yes. Something like that," Mary said weakly.

"Same diff. The only way out of a mistake is through. An apology...maybe bring a cake for the office with a humungous, ginormous 'Forgive me' in pink frosting. A heartfelt *mea culpa*. That means 'I'm sorry' in Greek."

"And if your boss was Stephen Hill?"

"I'd buy him a gift certificate for tooth cleaning." Snort, snort.

The streetcar turned onto Lakeshore, pitching standing passengers into wide stances.

"Almost me," lied Mary. She could use a walk in the cold air of late February.

"See you on Thursday evening?" Megan shifted sideways as Mary squeezed by.

"As always." Mary staggered to the door.

\*\*\*\*

Though taxonomically classified as boots in the kingdom of footwear, her suede desert boots were leaky, stain-prone, and ill-suited to the slush of a northern city sidewalk in winter. They were boot in form but not in function. Mary hopped over salty puddles and dodged the soiled packaging and wet dogshit that spontaneously generated as the snowbanks melted in freezing drizzle. Who cared about shoes, anyway? Might as well be late and fired in ruined boots.

As she skirted an ill-parked utility van, Mary spotted Eli Klassen, Hill Realty's top-selling agent, further up the street. She stopped dead in her tracks and stepped back. Too late. He'd seen her. He pushed something into a homeless man's hand and loped toward her in long strides, a goofy, Stephen Hill-imitation grin on his face, all teeth and lips. Though unfailingly cheerful, Eli unbalanced her. She'd pegged him as a wily lone wolf who used charm to get whatever he wanted, but she suspected she wasn't being fair, not really—

"Well, if it isn't the semi-buoyant Mary Rose!" Eli called on approach. He never missed a chance to tease her about her nautical name. "What are you doing so far from the office at this late hour?"

"Walking to work. And an equally pressing question is, 'How can you be so happy at this early hour?'"

Pivoting to walk alongside, he replied in a deep, oily tone. "Simple. After you get fired in fifteen minutes, I can ask you on a date. Workplace anti-harassment rules shall no longer stand against the prospect of our love."

Ugh. He pronounced 'harass' to rhyme with 'ferrous' and 'love' like something greasy. She couldn't stop herself from smiling. "What makes you think I'll be fired?"

Eli's handsome face twisted into Stephen Hill's leering countenance, and Mary shuddered.

After a brief silence, Eli said, "I was only joking, Mary. They won't fire you. Stephen will hide out in that Soviet-style, concrete box they call their 'city nest' and anesthetize his embarrassment with lines of coke, and Claudia will call you into her office and flay you with her tongue, but you'll survive this."

"You think so?" Mary looked up at Eli to be sure he was serious.

His dark eyes were earnest. "I know so. You're competent when you don't have your nose in a book and the unemployment rate is two percent. For exactly five minutes, Claudia will wish she could fire you, but she can't. Then she'll be all 'future-focused' and this whole beaver-tooth scandal will blow over like a bald man's haircut."

Eli flashed a smile and high-fived the homeless man as they passed, then answered the curious lift of Mary's brow.

"That's Dino. Best source of information in the downtown core. Like a freaking seismograph for predicting sales trends—which blocks will gentrify, which are stagnant. Who's scouting what for redevelopment."

"Your spy."

"My inside edge."

Minutes later, they turned onto Fountain Street and gained the front steps of a solid, red sandstone building that was once an armory. The Hill Realty offices occupied the northwestern corner of the second floor. Eli pulled open the heavy glass door and Mary stepped into the overheated lobby.

As they wiped their footwear on the bristle mat, a wave of dread washed through Mary's stomach.

Like a mother on the first day of kindergarten encouraging a child, Eli brushed the rain from her tweed-clad shoulders. "Just batten down the hatches for heavy seas and you'll sail through this storm just fine, Mary Rose."

"Less said the better?"

"Yeah. Apologize and shut up. If I were you, that would be my survival strategy."

\*\*\*\*

Mary knocked on the door, nudged it ajar, and peeked into the corner office. "Jonquil told me you wanted to have a word, Claudia?"

"Please. Sit down." Claudia karate-chopped toward the straight-backed chair opposite her.

Mary slid into the naughty seat.

"Have you seen the posters for Stephen's ad campaign?"

Mary nodded.

"Do you have any idea what you have done to my husband?"

Deciding the question was rhetorical, Mary clasped her hands contritely over her lap and waited.

Claudia's voice quivered like an over-tightened violin string. "Answer me."

Mary swallowed hard. "Umm, perhaps I have an idea, Claudia. It's likely that this incident has affected Stephen's self-esteem. I mean, he probably didn't realize that he has, umm, such fascinating dentition. Until he saw the ad. Many of us suffer from self-delusion when we look at ourselves in the mirror. It's the human condition to view ourselves subjectively

than objectively, which is, after all, impossible.
of us would crawl under a proverbial rock if we
how others really saw us and unfortunately—"

"This morning, my husband was so traumatized by
that he saw that he was forced to return to our
residence. Now he cowers at home because it's the only
place he feels safe. He certainly doesn't feel safe in
your presence."

"I understand—"

"Really, Mary? I doubt you're capable of
comprehending how Stephen must feel. Last week he
finally emerged from rehab, hopeful yet fragile,
cautiously optimistic about taking clients again, only to
find photos of his face with a gruesome, gauche,
cartoon grin plastered on the side of every streetcar in
the core. Stephen may have neglected his appearance—
he was *ill* after all—but he was *improving.* When he
saw the ads, he *wept.* I had to drive him home and tuck
him into bed with not one but *two* Ativans. I only pray
he doesn't relapse because of your negligence."

"I'm sorry."

"Sorry?" Claudia stood abruptly, propelling her
office chair into the bookcase behind her. She stalked
back and forth across the rug behind her desk, rubbing
her temples all the while. "Sorry? No, no, no, Mary.
That will not do."

"I'm truly, really, very sorry."

"*Truly, really, very.*" Claudia turned and glared.
"Puh-lease."

"If there's anything I can do...for Stephen."

Mary was about to offer the loan of her text of
Stoic philosophy with the section on "locus of control"
helpfully bookmarked when she remembered Eli's

advice. She pursed her lips and directed her eyes Claudia, who was now darting back and forth across the room like a piranha in a bowl. No wonder the woman was so skinny. She moved in a constant staccato on high heels, her internal metronome set at a relentless allegro, and Mary wondered if Stephen weren't the only Hill with a cocaine habit. At last, Claudia shoved her chair back to her desk, sat, and stared across the shiny woodgrain expanse between them. The stare was unnerving, but Mary kept her silence and stared right back.

"Your performance has been uneven," Claudia said flatly. "You had one job to do, and you failed to do it."

Actually, she had several jobs. Answering the phone, sorting mail, deleting spam, making coffee, buying gifts…

"Working with Out-of-the-Box Communications should have been your priority. Instead, let me guess"—again Claudia rubbed her temples theatrically— "you were absorbed in Nietzsche, and you approved the entire campaign without so much as a glance, without running it by me, let alone floating a test ad."

A remarkable guess. It'd been Schopenhauer, not Nietzsche. Anyway, she should've been able to trust Brad to do his job. He was the graphic designer, wasn't he?

"This was your chance to take on more responsibility. To shine. Now I wonder. I waver. I question."

Mary shrank under the heat of Claudia's intensifying stare. "It won't happen again," she blurted. "If I'm lucky enough to be given another chance, I won't let you down."

Claudia fake-chuckled. "Marking incoherent essays and giving dull PowerPoint lectures doesn't cover the bills, does it? You're smart, Mary, but not smart enough for a full scholarship. I'm sure you have a big, fat unpaid tuition bill and, if I fire you, I have a big, fat staffing gap."

*Big? Fat?* Everyone was big and fat compared to Claudia, who was once more on her feet, pacing frenetically.

"We manifest what we *do*. Where we *place our energy*. That's key." Claudia smiled with teeth so white, so diametrically opposed to the condition of her husband's, that they positively shone, though her eyes didn't crinkle up. In fact, they looked frozen.

As Mary pondered the reasons for the weird facial expression—insincerity? Botox? A neurological condition?—Claudia's attitude shifted from anger to stridency.

"Hill Realty is future focused. We succeed because we keep our *eyes on the prize*." Claudia turned on her spiked heel. "After you leave my office, you'll call Out-of-the-Box and have the offending images removed and destroyed immediately."

Mary nodded and rose.

"Have I given any indication that I am through?" Claudia scolded.

Back into the naughty chair.

"If you hope to have a future at Hill Realty, your performance must improve, Mary. But with a sick husband, I haven't the time or, frankly, the patience to mentor you. Eli is taking over sales at In-Spire."

"*Inspire?*" Forehead knit in confusion, Mary

mouthed the word.

Claudia looked disappointed already. "It's the new condo development at Lakeshore and Navy. I'd like you to assist Eli. Shadow him. Copy him. Take notes. Whatever it takes to up your game."

"Eli Klassen?" Mary squeaked.

"The one and only." Claudia smiled, this time eyes included, albeit faintly.

Mary nodded and gulped. Working for Eli directly would be...peculiar.

\*\*\*\*

Eli usually went to Roasters to flirt with the baristas and answer email over a double espresso after checking in at the office. Not this morning. Not yet. He rolled his office chair to the wall side of his worktable, opened his laptop, and settled in to enjoy the show.

Jonquil Herrington floated up in a cloud of patchouli and diaphanous drapery and parked her matronly butt on the next table.

"Have a moment?"

"For you, always, Jonquil," he replied sweetly. She hovered so near he could see up her nostrils.

"A little birdy told me that you'll be handling sales at the condo development on Lakeshore and Navy," she said in singsong.

"That's funny. I heard the same thing." Eli suppressed the urge to gloat.

"It's what, nearly three hundred units?"

"Three hundred sixteen."

"For someone who's fairly new to the game, that's a big job."

"You mean a big pie."

Jonquil shrugged. "If I were Synergy

Developments, I'd want someone with experience leading the sales team. Someone with gravitas. Someone who can relate to boomers. Understand their needs. Speak their language."

"English?"

"Humph. Always the jokester, aren't you, Eli? And that is precisely where intergenerational misunderstandings can seep in and damage a relationship with an older buyer."

"The project is attracting younger people, too."

"Exactly. Boomers and millennials. We'd work well together. As complements. Diversity of experience, of age. My fingers on the pulse of the relatively wealthy, older buyer while you seduce the up-and-comers with your wit. Your charm."

"Jonquil, are you flattering me?" He winked.

She exhaled heavily. "No. I'm merely pointing out your strengths and offering to help if you find yourself out of your depth."

"Thank you." Eli tapped the touchpad and focused on his screen.

As Jonquil drifted back to her worktable, Claudia's door opened. A very pale Mary made a beeline for the reception desk. Despite her plain office attire, she was smoking hot and completely, charmingly unaware of it.

She woke up her screen, typed and scrolled, then made a call. "Brad? This is Mary Rose from Hill Realty...Yes...Fine...Actually, not fine...Yes, I've seen them. Claudia wants them all taken down...As soon as possible...Yes, all of them...I'm sure she's aware of the terms of the contract...Can't you send a crew out?...Not even at the end of the day?...Listen, Brad. I'm in some serious hot water here...You have to help me…Oh. Fine. Bye."

Mary slammed the receiver onto its cradle, slumped back in her chair, and made a noise like a wounded animal. Then she spun in her chair to face him, a furious scarlet blush coloring her cheeks. "What I don't understand is how the ads can go up overnight, but it'll take a few days to take them down."

"Poor Stephen. And Claudia," said Jonquil. "She'll be so upset."

Mary stopped Jonquil's gush of sympathy for the Hills with a glare, then turned her chair to face her screen and placed another call. "Yes, good morning…I'd like to order a cake…A humungous, ginormous chocolate hazelnut…Yes, large is fine…That's an option? Then yes, gluten-free, keto…Yes. Put, 'I'm sorry.' In pink, please. Pickup for noon…I can pay then?…Pardon?!…Oh…Wow…No, no, that's okay. I'll stick with large…Lovely…It's Mary Rose. Thanks."

Eli was surprised by Mary's gesture of apology. He was about to compliment her originality and depart for the concentration-enhancing din of the coffee shop when Claudia messaged him.

"Summoned to the principal's office," he announced with a wry smile. After a languid stretch, he strolled across the room and knocked on Claudia's door.

"Come in."

Claudia was agitated. Full robot-toy mode. Back and forth she went, trudging a furrow in the carpet with her sharp heels.

"Eli. Thank God. Sit, sit."

He plunked himself onto the leather sofa and

extended his legs.

"You owe me a big one for giving you In-Spire," she said. "And I'd like to call in the favor."

An icy chill ran down his spine. Visions of following Stephen into the men's room invaded his mind. Eli was a negligent babysitter, especially when his charge was a fifty-year-old drug fiend.

"You'll need help with In-Spire," Claudia said casually. "Handling presales, communications, setting up the sales office, the model unit, that sort of thing."

Suspicion confirmed.

"I'm a forgiving person," she continued. "I believe in second chances. Learning from mistakes."

Yup. There would be Stephen, wound up like a cuckoo in a little wooden clock, riding shotgun, demanding they make a detour behind a boarded-up strip mall.

"I came this close to ending a relationship this morning." Claudia brought her index finger to her thumb in the air. "But something stopped me. Compassion, I suppose...." She looked through the window with her head cocked to the side, as if newly aware of her astonishing generosity, then turned. "How would you feel about working with Mary? On In-Spire?"

"Mary?"

"Yes. Mary. I realize she's not the easiest person to get along with, but I need her out of the office before Stephen returns. Keeping her in reception would be toxic. An impediment to Stephen's recovery. After this morning's debacle, I should've fired her, but she looked at me with those huge, homely eyes, like an innocent baby lamb, and I couldn't bring down the knife."

"You're a softy, Claudia." Eli chuckled. "Tough as nails with a heart of gold."

"Don't I know it. She gets one more chance, and if she blows it?" Claudia snapped her fingers. "Anyway, keep me apprised and if she gives you any trouble, I'll take immediate, corrective action. Jonquil has experience in condo sales. She can pitch in if need be."

"Who'll replace Mary at reception?"

"Well, our niece Felicity has been doing some minor clerical work for pocket money and she's looking for an internship. Until she starts, we can all take turns at the desk. It'll only be a couple of weeks."

Eli murmured his noncommittal support for Claudia's plan.

"So, are we even?" asked Claudia.

"Even Stephen," replied Eli.

"Now skedaddle, before I change my mind about Mary," said Claudia.

****

Mary stood in line at La Noisette, two blocks from Hill Realty. The trendy bakery's customers looked like the sort of people who would live in a luxury condo, judging by the photos on In-Spire's website. Healthy, well-dressed, rich, and multi-ethnic.

Fifty dollars for a bloody cake. None of these people would think twice.

She had to stop behaving impulsively. Claudia, the person she aimed to appease, didn't eat cake. Jonquil would accept a "teensy weensy" slice and then secret-eat several more. Eli would scarf down a chunk without even tasting it. Bill, Lori, and Alex, agents who came to the office sporadically, would ask about the strange message piped in pink. Maybe she should scrape it off after Claudia read it.

"Yes?" A young, mauve-haired woman flashed a customer service smile.

"Um, I'm here to pick up a cake. Mary Rose."

The smile broadened. "Large, chocolate hazelnut torte?" She retrieved a cardboard box taped shut with a pale green sticker and set it on the counter. "Here you go. Enjoy!"

"On Mastercard please."

"It's already paid for."

"Paid for?"

"A guy came in about an hour ago, asked if we'd taken your order for a cake, and paid for it."

"Oh, thank you," Mary stammered.

"Thank *him*," corrected the woman.

Despite lashing sleet, her precarious employment, and it being a Tuesday, Mary felt inexplicably happy as she hurried back to the office. Well, not inexplicably. Eli had been very, very kind to her. Perhaps she wouldn't mind working with him after all.

Chapter Two

With her pajama-clad legs folded under her and a glass of Chateau Plonque in hand, Mary watched her roommate, Dominic, savor a forkful of cake.

"Darling, this humungous, ginormous apology torte is to die for!" he enthused with his mouth full. "Every bite literally screams 'job security.'"

"Not literally. Figuratively," said Mary.

"I can't believe Claudia didn't even taste it, the ingrate."

"Or bring any home for Stephen."

"The Hills are such bores." Dominic shoveled a rosette of pink icing—the head of the apostrophe—into his mouth and waved his fork. "Now Eli, on the other hand…"

"Here we go—"

"You must bring him home to Daddy. I'll do a little party. Nothing much. Some oysters, champagne, and you vamoose before dessert."

"He's straight, Dominic."

"How do you know? He drives a BMW roadster. That's kind of gay."

"Is it?"

"And his LinkedIn photo is totally gay. Smart clothes. Fit. Facial hair trimmed close. Glossy chestnut mane and straight teeth."

"Actually, you've described a horse."

"A stallion who wears tailored shirts and drives a nice car." Dominic gazed dreamily into middle space and sipped his wine.

Mary knocked on the coffee table. "Earth to Dominic. Eli Klassen is straight."

"I could test your hypothesis," Dominic said mischievously.

"Like how we tested whether you're gay or bi? And the only way you could get it up is if I smeared mascara all over my chin and put on your suit."

"Honey, you're gorgeous, but I thought of Timothée Chalamet through the whole ordeal."

"You even had to take a Cialis."

"In my defense, we were drunk."

"And you were not, and are not, bi."

Mary embraced her best friend in a loose hug and they descended into helpless laughter until Dominic spoke gravely. "Enough about me. We must discuss your future."

"Oh?"

"Yes. Even though you fucked up today, you weren't fired, Mary. You were promoted."

"Was I?" She took a gulp of wine.

"Yes. You were." Dominic spoke in the low tone of a funeral director. "Goodbye, old Mary Rose. That ship has sunk. The new Mary Rose requires new clothes for her new job."

"*Requires?*"

"Yes. It means the same thing as 'needs.' Honestly. A liberal arts edumacation ain't what it used to be."

"I don't require anything of the sort," Mary protested as she refilled Dominic's glass.

"Mary, Mary, Mary. Yes. You. Do. Your

17

upholstered jackets and pilled sweaters and boxy footgear do not *inspire.*" He laughed at his joke. "You dress like an elderly dog trainer."

"I can't afford a new wardrobe."

"You can. A few nice but inexpensive pieces will make all the difference."

"But I hate shopping."

Dominic rolled his eyes. "We'll visit all the downtown thrift stores on Saturday, after you've finished your homework."

With a pang of guilt, Mary glanced at her desk in the corner. A leaning tower of books threatened to fall onto an empty coffee mug. Post-it notes with go-nowhere ideas fringed her computer screen. She still hadn't nailed down a dissertation topic that met Gabriel Silverstein's expectations, and now he was pushing her to take over his classes entirely. Well, tonight was for recovery after surviving Claudia's tirade, not schoolwork. With another swallow of wine, Mary evicted her acerbic academic advisor from her mental real estate and wondered aloud if the clothes made the woman or the woman made the clothes.

"Definitely the former," said Dominic. "A well-made, fashionable wardrobe and a good haircut are the foundation of success in love and career."

"Setting aside your definition of success," said Mary, "would you argue that a well-groomed poodle in a designer jacket, fancy collar, and booties has a better foundation for success than an unclothed, ungroomed mutt?"

Dominic replied impatiently. "The aphorism applies to humans, not dogs, because dogs conceptualize success differently from humans."

"And so do humans from each other," countered Mary.

"All right. Let's settle on a simple definition. Success for you would be a boyfriend who loves you, a fulfilling career, a decent night's sleep six days out of seven, and a bosom buddy with a sturdy, waterproof shoulder for emotional times."

"I score one out of four on your success-o-meter, Dominic, and I'm grateful for your shoulder."

"One out of four is a start. After we shop on Saturday, we'll update your dating profile."

"No way. Please recall, I've taken a vow of celibacy until my dissertation topic has been approved."

"Fine," he shrugged. "Have it your way. Delay your gratification until Gabriel gives you permission to pursue it."

"I don't consult Gabriel on my love—"

"Zat vas joke," Dominic interrupted in an atrocious Russian accent and smiled sardonically. "By the way, the designer collar you mention…"

"Red leather. Definitely not vinyl." Mary took a wild stab. "Maybe Hermès? The wearer was drinking a tea-colored mixture from a collapsible dog bowl outside of Roasters on Lakeshore."

"Woof!" barked Dominic.

\*\*\*\*

It was dark when Eli returned to his cold, sparsely furnished condo. He dumped a week's worth of mail, his jacket, and his laptop onto the dining room table and went to the fridge. Empty except for last night's pizza crusts, which he'd saved for reasons unknown even to himself. Laziness? Guilt? Composting? Sustenance for the coming apocalypse?

Whatever his folks back home imagined, if his evenings were a sitcom plot, it would be the most boring show ever. The TV execs could call it "Success in the City" and the pilot would feature a hapless hero who eats, jerks off, and sleeps. The end. He closed the fridge door.

Ten minutes later, he pushed through the navy curtains of the Takamatsu Sushi Bar.

"*Irashaimase!*" Kenji Ikeda grunted in an approximation of a welcome. "The usual?"

Before Eli could reply, Ikeda hollered, "Yuka! Eri-kun is here."

Ikeda's wife peeked through the kitchen curtains. "*Chotto*, Eri-kun. Sit, sit. I bring your favorite." Eli took his usual spot, and a moment later she reappeared carrying a steaming bowl of soba with vegetables and pushed it in front of him. "*Douzo*. Eat! I get you a fork?"

"That's okay, Yuka-san." Eli smiled gratefully as he took up a pair of chopsticks. "*Arigato*."

"*Jouzu, ne!*" She laughed. "You speak Japanese and use chopsticks very well!"

"You taught me everything I know." Eli rewarded Yuka's kindness with a boyish grin and slurped the noodles under her motherly gaze.

Pouring green tea from a small celadon pot, she praised his appetite while Ikeda formed clumps of vinegared rice into tiny logs for *nigirizushi*. Every meal at Takamatsu warmed Eli's heart, and late suppers, early in the week when there were fewer diners, were the best.

Soon Eli had wolfed down enough soba and nigiri to feed a small family. As Yuka bustled back to the kitchen, Ikeda looked at the clock and pushed a pitcher of sake across the counter.

"On the house," he said gruffly. "We share."

"Thanks."

Eli poured the warm, clear liquid into tiny cups and they toasted, *"Kampai!"* Ikeda drank his first cup of sake in one swallow and exhaled in noisy contentment.

Eli refilled the older man's cup. "You ever miss home, Ikeda-san?"

"Osaka? I suppose, but I have Yuka and the twins, so I'm not lonely. Parents are dead. Brother and his family are in Vancouver. Now I belong here. And you?"

"Yeah. It's too quiet in the condo. I'm the middle child of seven. Grandma living with us, nieces, nephews, and cousins visiting. So many Klassens round the supper table. It's still weird to eat meals alone."

"You're homesick."

"Maybe I am. And I'm idealizing. We weren't exactly the Waltons. I can't go home to the crazy religion, church, and Bible study, all the rules and the bad haircuts."

"A homesick refugee," pronounced Ikeda.

"From the nonsensical Church of the Evangelical Brethren." Eli shuddered. "You religious?" He asked the nosy question less from curiosity than from a wish to change the subject before he succumbed to maudlin self-pity.

"I'm Japanese," Ikeda replied, as if his ethnicity explained everything.

"He means he's part-time Buddhist, part-time Shinto, and full-time superstitious," Yuka called from the kitchen.

21

"Not superstitious," Ikeda objected.

Yuka whooshed through the curtains and gestured toward a shelf holding a ceramic cat with its paw raised to beckon money, to a calendar with tiny print under each date, and to a colorful amulet hanging by the cash register.

"They make the place feel like Japan. For authentic customer experience," Ikeda said to his wife's back as she returned to the kitchen. He gazed fondly at the cat. "Business is better when I remember to dust my *maneki neko*. Anyway, everybody has a lucky charm of some kind. It's normal."

"I don't," said Eli. "The Brethren believe that talismans and amulets and charms are idolatry and go against the first and second commandments. They're sinful."

Ikeda regarded Eli with narrowed eyes. "You can't be serious."

"I am. They're very zealous on that point, and they'll pray for you to mend your evil ways if you're caught with so much as a lucky baseball card."

As Ikeda shook his head in disbelief, Eli closed his eyes, contorted his face into the earnest smile-frown of a missionary, and placed his hand above Ikeda's head. Voice breathy and fervent, Eli intoned, "Lord Jesus, we pray that you take up your heavenly shepherd's crook and pull thy lamb Ikeda-san into the flock of the righteous so that he may be spared the eternally licking flames of Hell for his idolatry. Please hold him in your loving arms as he discards his satanic artifacts and his sinful notions. We pray, Lord, that you guide him in begging your forgiveness so that he may be born again in you, his Savior. Amen."

Eli opened his eyes to the rare sight of a grinning Ikeda, who said, "You should be a TV preacher."

"I'll consider it if I get tired of real estate. There's crossover in the skillsets—connecting with customers, creating an experience to close a sale, money management." Briefly pensive, Eli sipped his sake. When had he become so cynical?

Ikeda poured a cup of sake for Yuka as she flipped the sign on the door to 'closed'. She perched on the stool next to Eli and squeezed his elbow. "We had Mormons in Japan. Boys in white, short-sleeved shirts and black trousers, visiting from America. They sound like your people. The Mormons tried to convert people in the train stations. They told about God and the Bible and how Jesus Christ loves everyone in the world, even people in Asia."

"The Mormons sound very similar to the Brethren." Eli's face darkened with shame for uninvited North American evangelists who foisted their delusions on others. "I refused to confess my faith, let alone proselytize, so I was forced to leave the church. Anyway, selling condos is way easier than selling Christianity. At least the product is real."

Yuka smiled. "Some of the Mormons must have lost their faith on their travels. Pretty Japanese girls, beautiful temples and shrines, the glamor of Shinsaibashi..." Her voice trailed off wistfully.

"You're homesick, too," said Eli.

"No, no." She shook her head. "I have Kenji. He's my Japan."

The trio sipped the warm, sweet sake until Yuka broke the silence. "I think you need a girlfriend."

"What?" Eli squawked. He remembered his

manners. "I mean, pardon?"

"A girlfriend," Yuka repeated. "How old are you?"

"Twenty-nine."

"Five years older than the twins. Saori is already engaged. Emi has a serious boyfriend. And you—you won't meet any single girls at Takamatsu Sushi Bar. You should go to nightclubs."

Yuka's observation sounded accusatory, as if his pathetic loneliness could be attributed to his lack of effort. She looked at her husband searchingly.

"Yuka, it's not our business," said Ikeda. "You embarrass him."

"It *is* our business. Eri-kun is unhappy and that breaks my heart. Surely we must know someone suitable." She turned back to Eli in appraisal. "You're handsome and nice. You should shave, but clothes are neat. You have a car and a job. Have you tried a matchmaking service?"

A matchmaker? Mortified, Eli drained his cup and searched for a polite escape. "I haven't, Yuka, because I don't need to." Mind flailing wildly, he thought of Mary. "I've started seeing someone, as a matter of fact." Not a lie. He'd seen her that day, on the street, in the office, clever but vulnerable, cutting that ludicrous cake.

"Oh?" Yuka lunged at the information like a pit bull on a prime rib. "What's her name?"

"Mary."

"She sounds Japanese."

"Mary with a 'y', not an 'i'. I don't know her family background."

"You don't know?"

Eli shook his head.

"Is this girl real?"

"Yes. Definitely real." With long dark hair, wire-rimmed glasses, expressive gray eyes, milky skin, full lips, and a heart-melting smile.

"Okay. You must bring her here," Yuka demanded.

Ikeda looked pointedly at the clock and yawned, a conversational life preserver that Eli grabbed by remarking on the lateness of the hour and opening his phone to pay.

Outside Takamatsu, he paused on the sidewalk and double-checked the time. Ten-thirty. A bitter wind off the lake had blown away the urban miasma of vehicle exhaust and sewer fumes. He inhaled the fresh air to clear his sake-soaked head. Was it too late to text Mary tomorrow's plan? Nah. If she wanted sleep, she'd have her phone off and his text would find her in the morning.

Thumbs working as he walked, Eli messaged. — We'll start at Roaster's at 8. What's your pleasure.— *Holy shit. Your pleasure?* He sounded like a gigolo sexting a client. Better send a clarification. —I mean, what's your coffee order?—

—I could really dig a large tea. Earl Grey. No milk, no sugar. Thanks.—

He closed the exchange with a straight-forward, un-flirtatious yellow thumbs-up and walked home.

25

Chapter Three

Eli sat at a small table at a window facing onto Lakeshore. Eight-o-six. If Mary had to drink cold tea, it was her own fault. He sipped his espresso and watched a streetcar roll to a stop, that dreadful ad still stuck on its side. Mary exited by the rear door and hurried to the café in a baggy gray pantsuit—basically a frumpy office burqa, perfect for teaching Sunday school, wrong for real estate, and a travesty on a healthy, curvy young woman. Maybe Jonquil could take her aside, have a word. An image of Mary floating around the sales office in a shapeless boomer smock arose in his mind. He couldn't ask Jonquil. Someone else...

"Sorry I'm late." Mary took the chair opposite and pushed her foggy glasses up over her head.

Eli nudged her tea toward her.

"Thanks." She fished a small coin purse from her canvas rucksack.

"There's no need," he said. "The tea's a work expense."

"Really?"

"Really." As if he'd bother claiming a paltry eight-dollar expense, but it was better she not feel indebted. "You should start keeping your receipts so you can claim expenses yourself."

"I can do that?" Her face lit with delight as she put her coin purse away and hung her rucksack on the back of her chair.

Eli looked at his watch. "As of eight-o-seven."

Ignoring his rebuke, Mary tested her tea, frowned, and set the cup back on its saucer. "Thanks for yesterday, Eli. For being supportive. And paying for the cake."

"Another business expense," he murmured dismissively.

"I'm glad we're meeting here," she said. "The atmosphere in the office is intolerable. I feel as if Claudia is plotting to defenestrate me."

"She's pretty angry."

"I deserve it."

Mary did, but Eli shook his head anyway. "We can hide from Claudia here, and then visit the site. Synergy's hooking up a portable office for us and we'll be working out of there."

Mary nodded.

"Did Claudia tell you what your duties would be?" he asked.

"No. She just wanted to get rid of me. I think she chickened out of firing me and pawned me off on you."

As ever, Mary stated the unvarnished facts without batting an eyelash. "You're probably right," he agreed. He watched her face for signs that her banishment had upset her and saw none. Genuinely curious, he asked, "How do you feel about working with me?"

She returned his scrutiny with her beguiling gray eyes. "I'm fine with it." She paused and took a breath. "My concern, Eli, is time. After I left the temp agency, I stayed on at Hill because being a receptionist takes very little brainpower, pays adequately, and the hours suit me. I'm juggling grad school with work, and now that I'm in exile from reception, I don't know what to expect. I don't want to let you down, but I'm behind academically and I know how hard you work."

Very hard. He'd bootstrapped himself from a neglected child of a hyper-religious dirt farmer to a top-selling agent in a high-volume brokerage. Before he could think of anything reassuring to say, Mary asked, "How do you feel about working with me?"

"Uh, excited," he hedged. What a lie. He felt conflicted. After weeks of effort, he'd earned her friendship and hoped for more. Now, as his subordinate, she'd be his responsibility, and he was nervous as hell. He couldn't risk compromising the In-Spire contract with misunderstood teasing, with flirtatious innuendo gone awry, and he'd miss their banter. He had an intense crush on her, but she was off-limits now.

"Really?" Her face broke into a dazzling smile. That heart-melting smile he tried to coax from her daily. Those days were over.

"Really," he repeated hastily. "We can work around your schedule." He was promising the impossible. The sales office would be open on weekends and evenings. Late nights were inevitable.

"You're sure? Because I must prioritize my dissertation above all else."

"I'm sure," he declared gallantly.

"I'm so grateful. Working with you is going to be way more interesting than being stuck at the desk in reception."

Eli swallowed the last of his coffee to brace himself for the day—and the weeks—ahead.

\*\*\*\*

Mary stared through a plexiglass window into the third circle of hell, a deep, litter-strewn pit of slushy puddles reserved for the souls of gluttons in Dante's schema. An excavator shoveled scoops of mud into a dump truck. Three men in fluorescent vests and hardhats stood on the opposite bank, a high fence of chain link and plywood to their backs. Presumably shouting over the noise of machinery, one of the men amplified his words with sweeps of his arms, while the other two men huddled over a clipboard.

Eli spoke over the low rumble. "They'll start pouring the foundation in April. There'll be three underground parking levels and a floor for janitorial and maintenance equipment. Once the foundation is in, the rest of the project will go up fairly quickly. Some units will be ready for occupancy in late fall of next year."

"Three hundred and sixteen, you said?"

"That's right. Plus bike and stroller storage, a pool, sauna, and gym, and a common room with a fireplace and bar on the main floor. A rooftop garden, solarium, another party room and patio, and two penthouses at the top. There'll be three hundred fourteen regular units sandwiched in the twenty-five floors between. That's the meat in the middle."

"Laundry room?" Mary appreciated the coin-op in her building that saved her a weekly trip to the laundromat.

A shadow of bewilderment briefly passed over Eli's face, then he chuckled. "Each unit will have its own front-loading washer and dryer. Top of the line. No quarters."

"Oh."

"And a refrigerator with icemaker, a range, dishwasher, built-in microwave, and unit-controlled air conditioning and heating."

No need to block a draft with a rolled-up towel in winter, to angle a fan over the bed in summer. Mary murmured, "All the comforts of home."

"Because it *will* be home for our buyers," said Eli. "Well, most of them. And that's how we'll sell it, even to investors. Gives them a warm, fuzzy feeling to imagine themselves in their cozy investment before they flip it or rent it on Airbnb."

Mary looked up at Eli. "You said, 'we'll'. Who is 'we'?"

"You and I."

"But I'm not a sales agent, Eli. I'm not qualified. I have zero experience in convincing people to part with their money."

"You don't need a realtor's license to show people around a model unit or to hand out brochures. You just smile, be friendly and helpful, behave like the neighbor they hope to meet in the elevator, get their contact info, and I'll follow up."

"Be the perfect hostess?" Mary said sarcastically.

"With the mostest," Eli replied unironically. He looked away and gazed over the pit. "A hostess wearing a flattering blouse, nice shoes, make-up...."

"Pardon me?"

"What you'd wear to a social engagement. Dress like that. It'll help sales."

How dare he. How dare he dictate what she should wear to work. Her face burned with livid shame. "I wear jeans and band T-shirts to social engagements. Will that be all right, *papa*?" she said sharply.

Still facing the window, he shook his head. "No jeans. Go upscale. Think faculty wine and cheese, an evening at the theater." His voice was smooth. "You know—a nice dress. High heels."

"Like Claudia wears?"

"Exactly. And tasteful jewelry." Eli looked at her and swiftly looked away again, as if he'd glimpsed the shadow of Medusa.

Suppressing her outrage, she spoke in clipped tones. "My suits are modest and professional. They're a reflection of my personality and I'm comfortable in them."

He shrugged. "They're not you. They're bland. They're the oatmeal porridge of business attire. You're interesting, Mary, and we'll do better sales-wise if you up your spice level."

"Up my spice level? You mean, dress like a hooker? We could spin a Donna Summer platter. I could lip sync and strut around the model suite in a catsuit and, as you put it, make the buyers feel as if it's their home and it's sexy time."

"You're being absurd." He sighed.

"Am I? This portable is not a 'men's club'." She made angry air quotes around the words. "I'm an academic, not a sex worker. And besides, even if I agree to your demand—"

"Not a demand, Mary. Only a suggestion. I'd rather wear a sweater, jeans, and sneakers, yet here I am in my battle fatigues."

"I can't afford a whole bloody new wardrobe."

This time Eli turned directly toward her, his expression disarming, his arms open as if surrendering. "I'm sorry. You look fine, Mary Rose. Shipshape in all respects. However, we're working on commission."

"You are. I'm not."

"You could be."

"Oh?" she said slowly, brow arched with suspicion at his change of tack.

"I'll give you a cut of my commission if you pay attention to my counsel and follow my methods. You'll make way more money here than you would in reception."

So this was how it happened. How pimps talked girls into turning tricks, into writhing naked at a pole or in a male lap. Ten bucks for a peep, twenty for a grope, halfsies between the manager and the talent. An admixture of disappointment and nausea welled from the core of her being.

Eli read her like a book, or a tabloid headline, and his hand shot up like a stop sign. "Whoa. Slow down. We're selling condos, a residential lifestyle, not you, Mary. Every job has a uniform. Every buyer is drawn to an aesthetic, an image, a story. That's all I'm saying."

"Okay. I get what you're saying," she conceded. Her labor and time for her cut; her clothes and hairstyle akin to *The Illustrated Works of Molière* on the coffee table and the pre-drunk yet corked wine bottles in the rack under the kitchen counter in the model suite.

"Good," said Eli. "You deserve to be rewarded fairly for learning the theory and applying it."

Though he mocked in the language of scholarship, his statement had appeal. Gabriel could recommend her for an untenured professorship in an obscure college, help her publish in a pretentious journal with a tiny, nitpicking readership; Eli could solve her money problems. And furthermore, he wasn't asking her to abandon the ivory tower for the condo tower. He wasn't demanding an either/or.

"Money won't be a stressor in your life after we've made a few sales," he added. "In the meantime, you can borrow my credit card for your work-related expenses."

"I get paid tomorrow," she said. "I'll manage."

For an endless moment, neither spoke as they mentally moved their chess pieces. Mary peered up at Eli and blinked, as if seeing him for the first time. If there were a Klassen school of philosophy, it would center on the belief that penury and wealth were choices—as were misery and joy, meanness and generosity, lack and abundance, receiving and giving. Look into those dreamy dark eyes and there was the soul of a giver. She surrendered the board with a subtle nod. An acknowledgment that he'd closed the deal.

"First lesson?" Eli asked.

"Okay," she replied hesitantly.

He stepped forward, eased off her jacket, and set it over a folding chair. Next, he removed her glasses. A faint smell of soap, musky and masculine in the overheated room, lingered on his hands. "Two buttons. That's all," he said softly as he unfastened her shirt just below the collar. She felt his breath on her forehead and her heart fluttered with the unexpected, but not unwelcome, intimacy.

"There." He stepped back and admired her minor transformation as if he'd painted a masterpiece. "Now you look like a fun-loving, upwardly mobile, young professional. A typical resident of In-Spire at Forty Navy Street."

"Do I?"

"You do."

Eli cleared his throat and spoke in a Texas accent, "Ma'am, I'm relocatin' from Dallas, and I have scads of cash. More than I can spend, I'm 'fraid. So much, the bank has informed me that I oughta get rid of some of it, there bein' no room in the vault, and I'm huntin' for a hidey-hole for me and the missus."

"In Toronto?" Mary laughed.

He winked. "Anyway, I was wonderin' if you sell condos in this here mobeel home."

"We do...umm..."

"Name's Randy. Randy Dyck. With a 'y'."

"Randy? You're joking."

"Yes, ma'am. Course I am."

Mary tried to stifle her laugh and accidentally snorted. "We have a range of sizes from studio to our four thousand square foot penthouse suite."

"Ma'am, I'm from Texas."

"You wish to see our largest unit?"

"You betcha!" Eli broke into an appreciative laugh and became himself again. "Well done, Mary. You're a natural at sales."

"Am I?"

"You are." Eli opened his laptop case. "And you're also a student. Here's some information about In-Spire." He withdrew a file of paper documents and handed them to her. "I'll email you a link to the website and a username and password for the sales portal. There's more information there. We're not ready for showtime and won't be for a few days. You might as well go over everything at home and make some progress on your university stuff, too."

"But it's only eleven."

"It's the calm before the storm, Mary Rose." Eli's

voice trailed off ominously. "The calm before the storm."

****

Mary hadn't asked him what "a cut of the commission" meant. She was so trusting, so naive, so confident he wouldn't cheat her or treat her unfairly. And he wouldn't. *Au contraire.* He'd give her a reason to strive.

Now alone in the portable, Eli found his phone and sat on the folding chair. Jesus. It was as low as a toddler's seat at a Sunday school craft table. He was practically crouching. The sooner he could get some decent furniture and get the Wi-Fi hooked up, the sooner he could sell some condos. He stood, scrolled through his phone, and paced under the fluorescent lights.

Who was he kidding? The sooner he could call Mary into work and see her again.

He wasn't imagining their mutual attraction. It was real. Mary's face betrayed every emotion she felt. In a single morning, she'd run the gamut and taken him along for the ride. At 7:59, he vowed to maintain a professional, hands-off relationship with her. By 10:45, he was unbuttoning her blouse. It wasn't even noon on the first day of their collaboration and she was all he could think of. Mary tilting her head just so. Mary gazing into his eyes. Mary brushing a strand of hair from her face, cheeks blushing pink. Mary giggling. When she parted her full lips in a barely audible sigh as he fussed with her clothing, he could have kissed her. Instead, he retreated to his cool, hands-off default mode. Whether wise or cowardly, he was as frustrated as a priest at an orgy.

*Ping.* Phone. It was Jonquil Herrington, antidote to his sexual torment.

"Hello, Jonquil."

"Eli, hi. Thought I'd check in. We missed you at the office this morning," she gushed.

"I'll be by later."

"How's our Mary?"

"Fine."

"I'm soooo relieved. After everything that's happened, I've been quite worried about her. Young women are so sheltered at university, with safe spaces and trigger warnings. Emerging from the security of the classroom into the real world of frontline sales must be quite a shock for her."

"You could call Mary yourself, Jonquil. Express your support. Take her under your wing."

"I promise I will," Jonquil tittered. "You know, Eli, I'm here for you, too. The market's volatile. My offer still stands. If you need advice—"

"Thanks."

"From someone who's ridden the ups and downs. Someone who's been around the block and seen it all." Though she modulated her tone, he detected a plea. "What I'm saying is, I'm quite overscheduled, but I have some availability this week."

Eli's impatient footsteps echoed on the linoleum in the over-lit room. The first turn of a long rusty screw of a migraine pierced his right temple. If only he could swallow a handful of Advil and lie down on a couch— his fucking kingdom for a fucking couch—and read his email with a bag of frozen peas over his forehead. Whether rudely or kindly, he had to end the call.

"Actually, Jonquil, I could use your help with

setup," he said through gritted teeth. "You know what these portables are like."

"Quite unsuitable," she concurred. "Harsh lighting, ugly flooring, ghastly office furniture."

"You guessed it."

"I'll call Siobhan. We'll have a coat of paint on the walls and furniture and appliances in there within twenty-four hours. Mind you, not much we can do about the floor besides an area rug."

"Great! That's fine. Uh...the computer..." He was going down fast.

"Wi-Fi and phone?"

"Yes, please. If you have time." He flicked the light switch off. In cloud-shadowed, late February daylight, the room was marginally more tolerable, though still noisy with construction, still nowhere to sit.

Jonquil prattled, "I'm all about mentorship, Eli. Nurturing the next generation. For you, I'll make time."

Back against the wall, he slid to the floor in a heap of long limbs.

"Are you okay?" she asked.

"Yes. I'm fine. That all sounds great. Thank you."

"I should be able to organize something for around two o'clock."

"Great. That's great." Before she could ask after his health again, he blurted, "There's nothing here to steal, so I'll leave the office open, and I'll come back later when you and Siobhan get here. Just text me."

Eli ended the call in fetal position, his head cradled in his hands. Five minutes. He'd lie still for five minutes and then he'd rise like Lazarus, buy some painkillers and sunglasses, and carry on. He wouldn't call Mary, though. Not till he was strong again. She mustn't see him like this.

\*\*\*\*

With Dominic teaching social dance lessons at his studio and Gabriel at yet another conference, Mary had the apartment and the responsibility for Philosophy 307 to herself. She'd begin the Thursday evening Zoom class with a recap of last week's survey of Marxist theories of economic justice and then she'd introduce Rawls. Two minutes to seven, fifty-six hours since she'd left the sales office, and still no call or text from Eli. She wasn't concerned. She definitely wasn't hurt. He was busy; she was busy, and their relationship was purely professional, so big hairy deal if he hadn't communicated.

Mary put her phone on vibrate and turned it over to avoid any distractions, then removed the post-it notes from her screen. Camera on, her own face frowned back at her with the glow of streetlights reflected in her glasses. At this angle, she resembled a disapproving insect. She shifted the screen for a more flattering light and the background of Dominic's air-cleaning spider plants, and it was showtime.

"Good evening, everybody," she enthused. "Dr. Silverstein is away, so I'll be delivering tonight's lecture and facilitating the discussion. If everyone could wave a quick hello, cameras on for the first five minutes while we get started."

Zoom was an online *Romper Room* for undergrads, and she was Miss Betty, holding up the psychedelic magic mirror, like in the clip of the 80s children's show she'd seen on YouTube. "I see Skylar, and Finn, and Megan—like the princess—and Jaeden…and umm…you are? Oh. Brianna's mom…Kathy? I suppose you can take notes for her, but Brianna has the PowerPoints and the reading list already...well, okay...and Eve and Samantha...you're Samuel now?...That's fine, Samuel it is...and Joshua and Molly..."

*And you may all kill me now. Go on. Send me a stick of dynamite in a bouquet of carnations. The address is 613 St. Dunstan Avenue, Apartment 210. Only spare me the slow death of the next two and a half hours of Zoom.*

"Right. Any questions about last week's lecture? No?..Yes! Megan... Anti-American? Let's explore that briefly, shall we? I don't think Marx was attacking the former US President or the Republican Party, at least not directly... Yes, Joshua makes a sound point...Except insofar as our political class tends to buttress capitalist systems... However, if you'll recall, Marx was focused on Europe and the plight of workers in Britain and on the continent in the mid-nineteenth century. Jaeden? Ha, ha! No, I don't suppose any of us actually recall the 1850s. We weren't there. That's true. I meant 'recall from last week's lecture.'"

*Or a pizza topped with poisonous sliced toadstools.*

"Right, then. John Rawls, fairness versus equality, his critique of utilitarianism, and the mysterious 'veil of ignorance'...I agree, Jaeden. It isn't a mysterious facial garment at all. I was attempting to generate interest in his theory with some intrigue, but as you point out, his ideas need no embellishment. Okay—"

*Or a deadly hot, polonium curry. Anything.*

As Mary peered at the vacuous Megan, the literal-minded Jaeden, the eager Joshua, Brianna's mother clutching her pen, and the little squares of names standing in for the students who'd shut off their cameras, she realized she hated teaching on Zoom. She adored the world of ideas, the theories and tangents, and the labyrinthine debates. From the ancient Greek stoa to the post-modern, remotely attended seminar, teaching was the philosopher's bread and butter. It was what one *did,* and she couldn't do *it.* Not by Zoom. Not without contemplating the relief of seppuku executed with the sharpest pencil in her desk drawer. She was being histrionic, she knew that, but when she was honest with herself, when she had nowhere to hide, whenever she had to regurgitate the unpalatable contents of a dry lecture into a camera, she was forced to admit the truth to herself: she loathed teaching Gabriel's Zoom classes.

Mary split her screen, pulled up the notes, and with all the emotion of a lobotomized automaton, delivered the lesson. As nine p.m. approached, her phone rattled. The class was supposed to go for another half hour, but damn it, that could be Eli. She could peek. She sat on her hands.

"Umm...yes, Megan? Absolutely. Rawls' framework demands that we employ our imagination, that we strive to understand other people's hardships. Joshua? 'The poor will always be among us,' you say? Ha, ha! That's a depressing thought, though likely true. Let's discuss that for the remainder of the class. Is some level of poverty inevitable, and as a follow-up, must we sacrifice other expressions of justice if we prioritize the alleviation of poverty in the pursuit of a just society? Jaeden is asking, 'What do we mean by poverty? Relative or absolute?' Why don't you define it for our discussion, Jaeden?"

One by one, most of the class logged off as Megan, Jaeden, and Joshua held forth. Mary flipped her phone over. It was Eli!

—*Roasters. At 8. What are you wearing?*—

—*That's a personal question. A blouse and pajama pants.*—

—*Weird.*—

—*I'm dressed for Zoom.*—

—*I meant tomorrow. What are you wearing tomorrow?*—

—*Why do you ask?*—

—*So I can match my outfit with yours. Team colors.*—

—*Good night, Eli.*—

Mary turned her phone over, erased the smile that had infected her face, and looked at the screen. Brianna's mother was still scribbling notes while Joshua asked Megan if she'd like to continue their discussion offline and Jaeden grasped for re-entry to the conversation.

Perhaps she could end the class early without ruffling Jaeden's feathers too much. "Right, any final points?" Mary asked. "Nine-twenty is a round number. That leaves precisely ten minutes for individual preparation on our next topic, which is neo-utilitarianism." She watched Jaeden's grainy face for signs of discomfort, but he merely nodded his agreement. "I expect the ideas of Peter Singer will produce some lively debate. Good night and see you in a week, everyone!"

And cut.

And wine.

Mary stretched, padded to the kitchen, and filled a

wineglass from the spigot of a gallon-size box. She swallowed a finger-width draft of heavily tannic, tooth-staining liquid and, thus fortified, took the glass to her bedroom to consider her outfit for Friday.

Chapter Four

"Don't say anything," Mary warned as she sat down at the table.

"What do you mean?" Eli consulted his watch with a dramatic flourish. "You're on time today."

"You know what I mean."

He did. Mary's effort at fashion had paid off. Though unconventional, her outfit was highly successful. She'd swept her hair back in a loose knot, ditched her glasses, and applied eye makeup and pink lipstick. She wore a crisp, pale blue man's shirt cinched at the waist, a thick metallic watch on her wrist, and tight, black jeans. Audible only to her in the clatter of the café, he whistled appreciatively.

"I told you not to say anything."

"I didn't," he protested.

"If you must know, my roommate helped me. If they ever need a fashion guy for *Queer Eye*, Dominic should audition."

Eli leaned back in his chair and smiled to inform Mary that he understood her roommate was gay and, what's more, he understood that she hoped he, Eli Klassen, would understand she was imparting this information intentionally though not, perish the thought, aggressively. She blushed and hid behind her teacup.

"I'm sorry I didn't call you sooner," he said

casually. "To give you an update."

"You're busy and I'm busy. Thanks for the tea."

He wished she wouldn't thank him for an inconsequential cup of tea. He shrugged away her cool gratitude and asked, "How are your studies going?"

"Well, I think." She brightened. "I've learned a lot of interesting jargon—building envelope, certificate of possession, delineated space—"

"I meant your dissertation proposal, Mary."

"Oh, that. I didn't make much progress, unfortunately."

As he tried to think of something reassuring to say, she released her anxieties in a torrent of words. "Gabriel is an uncompromising taskmaster. He's left me to teach all his Zoom classes and do all his marking while he hobnobs at various symposia. And every time I float an idea for my dissertation, he either doesn't answer my email or he shoots it down." She mimicked her advisor, "The ancients are stale, the existentialists overdone, the utilitarians too pat, the post-modernists too trendy."

Amused, Eli doubted the man sounded anything like Mary's rendition. "What are *you* interested in?" he asked, ignoring the ping of his phone in his pocket.

"Everything."

"A grand meta-theory? A philosophy of philosophies?"

"Funny, Eli." She smiled. "Grand theories are the territory of religion, and Gabriel would think I was off my rocker if I went in that direction. I'm interested in everything, but I have to whittle that huge, shapeless mass of theory, that 'everything', into a singular idea that is unique and more or less defined. Something that

I can polish."

"Transform a hunk of marble into the statue of David."

"Pretty much."

Forehead knit in thought, Eli drank his coffee. He hadn't studied philosophy, but he also loved ideas, from the strange Biblical teachings of his boyhood to systems theory in the economics books he'd borrowed from the library. Although he didn't believe in "things happening for a reason" or a "master plan," he believed that making connections was a powerful way to find insight.

He set down his cup. "Are you interested in money? I mean, in a philosophical way?"

"Money? As in, 'filthy lucre?' Because that's how Gabriel sees it."

"Never mind Gabriel. How do *you* see it?"

"Well, not like that. I admit, I haven't really thought of it as a subject worthy of scrutiny."

"And here you are. Immersing yourself in the world of real estate and money. You're a fish who doesn't see water."

"That's not true. I think about money a lot," she countered defensively.

"When your Visa bill is due. Then money, or its lack, transforms into an existential crisis. While you struggle through a nonsensical Judith Butler essay, you ignore the very thing that motivates so many people."

Mary stiffened and crossed her arms.

"Forget what I said about Judith Butler," he said apologetically. "I shouldn't criticize what I'm not smart enough to understand."

"No, no." Mary shook her head. "You're not wrong about her. She buries her ideas in a quagmire of mumbo-jumbo. It's just, well, your accusation that I'm ignorant about money cuts to the quick because it's true."

"It doesn't have to be true. You're a fast learner. The things you're picking up in real estate—there are philosophical assumptions underlying it all. If you could combine the two worlds, work and school—"

"I could save myself a ton of time and effort. Maybe even think an original thought."

"Exactly."

She took another sip of tea, gazed pensively at her saucer, then raised her eyes to him. "What do *you* think of money?"

"Well, since you're asking, I've thought about it a lot. I don't believe that money's the root of all evil. Avarice, the love of money, is *a* root of evil among others. Money is a resource. I think the parable of the talents is a wise lesson. Money is actually a proxy for things like energy or the skillful application of ingenuity, and it should be put to use, to benefit others and yourself. It shouldn't be squandered or left to stagnate. That's wasteful. Also, financial wealth is better than poverty because it gives you the freedom to live your life on your own terms and contribute to the greater good."

"Aren't you the Biblical scholar," she remarked archly.

"Not really."

"Avarice? Evil?" she said with a smirk. "The parable of the talents?"

He'd taken a stupid risk and revealed too much of himself to this beautiful, intelligent woman whom he'd hoped to impress. Eli's face burned and he looked away. He should have realized that Mary Rose, PhD student at one of the world's top universities, would think his ideas were hokey and simple.

She reached across the table and squeezed his hand lightly. "You misunderstand me, Eli. I'm complimenting you. You're onto something."

He longed for the return of her hand, but she only smiled. "Maybe I could gain some traction in a conceptual exploration of real estate."

"A conceptual exploration?" he echoed.

"Do I sound insufferable?"

"No, you sound smart. I think you are smart. Smarter than me." *Than I.* Would she correct him? "I confess—you fascinate me," he added.

"I'm no smarter than you." She waved away his compliment.

For a moment, he regarded her in silence. She was perceptive enough to detect a single molecule of bullshit. Deciding he must always be truthful to her, even if she rejected him, even if he had to fight through self-doubt, he said, "I'm a humble real estate agent. In a couple of years, you'll be Dr. Rose, floating high in the rarefied air of the intelligentsia. I'm intimidated by that fact, but I'll teach you whatever I can about the world of money—if you want that from me."

To his chagrin, she laughed. "An open secret, Eli? The academy? The humanities? They run on hot gases. Fumes. Not air. Especially these days when even tenured professors appease their undergrads as if it's Mao's China and steer their grad students away from heterodox notions. In some ways, your mind is freer to run with ideas than mine is. You answer only to yourself, and you've let your natural curiosity be your guide. You have absolutely no reason to feel intimidated by me, okay?" Her gray eyes widened. "And yes, I want to learn from you."

Eli swallowed his bracingly bitter coffee and considered what she was saying. "Are you unhappy in grad school?"

"No, not exactly unhappy. Maybe disillusioned," she admitted. "I'll think hard on your suggestion of hammering what I learn from you into ideas for a proposal and dissertation."

"Cool. Then it's a deal. I'll help you in any way I can." He extended his hand over the table, and she placed her soft hand in his to shake on their pact.

"By the way, how do you know about Judith Butler?" she asked. "Have you read her work?"

If Mary imagined him wading through esoteric journals on gender theory, she was about to be disappointed. "Uh, I snooped," he confessed. "Last week you were reading something and scratching your head and frowning. When you left your desk to refill your mug, I was curious about what was upsetting you and I peeked at the journal on your desk."

"That's unconscionable," Mary said with a theatrical scowl.

"Hey—you said yourself that I'm curious."

"And you were appropriately punished for it with a dose of Butler-write."

His phone pinged again.

"Hadn't you better check that?" she asked.

"Yeah. Class is over. Back to the real world." Eli pulled his phone from his pocket and found twelve messages begging for his urgent attention.

\*\*\*\*

They walked up Lakeshore Boulevard in weak sunshine, Eli acting as tour guide, pointing out properties of note, and Mary asking what she hoped weren't stupid questions. As they neared Navy Street, they spotted a structure looming over the sidewalk beside the sales office.

"A new billboard?" she asked as the structure's street-facing surface came into view.

"I believe so," said Eli. "They must have installed that yesterday when I was—Jesus. It's all wrong."

"When you were what?"

"When I was…uh…nothing…just taking care of something," he said vaguely, eyes fixed upward.

Obviously the billboard concerned him, but his evasiveness was odd. Whatever the "something" was, he preferred not to share it with her.

Before she could ask a follow-up question, Eli put his hand on her shoulder. "Do you see the problem here, Mary?"

She nodded. "The ad shows a nuclear family. Mom, dad, a boy, a girl, and a golden retriever. They aren't our target buyers."

"Exactly. A silver-haired couple on a sailboat, a pair of gay thirty-somethings strolling on the waterfront with ice cream cones—anybody would be better than them. We're not selling split-levels in suburbia. Mr. Cleaver won't buy a studio starting in the 500s unless it's for his mistress." Thumbs flying over his phone screen, Eli texted someone and then took a photo of the billboard and sent that too.

"It's Tuesday all over again," he fumed as he unlocked the door. "I should buy us a cake. Make it all better with glucose."

Eli held the door and followed Mary into the office. "At least Jonquil didn't mess up," he said, looking around the office. "Acquaint yourself with our new digs, Mary. I have a call to make."

*So bossy.* Mary hung her coat in the closet, then peered into the kitchenette, now equipped with a coffee maker, bar fridge, kettle, microwave, and dishes, but lacking basic groceries. Maybe she'd make herself scarce. Slip out to buy the basics. Avoid Eli and his weird mood. Next, she checked the washroom. Someone, presumably Siobhan and Jonquil, had supplied it with toilet paper, lavender hand soap and lotion in ornate dispensers, plush hand towels, and an Impressionist print of the Champs Elysée. *"Ohlàlà,"* she whispered.

Mary walked over to the desk. In the opposite corner of the office, furniture had been arranged to look like a luxurious living room. There Eli was sprawled on a red leather sofa. Despite his relaxed position, he had a tense, angry energy. She'd never seen him in this mood. In the weeks she'd worked as a receptionist, he came and went from the Hill Realty office, ever quick with a compliment or a boundary-pushing joke, always cheerful, but never staying long. It dawned on her that she didn't really know this darkly handsome, charming man who, before the age of thirty, had become Hill Realty's top agent and was, therefore, likely worth millions. Now his current attitude made sense. He hadn't succeeded through wit alone; he had to be ruthless too.

She sat in a brand-new office chair, swiveled to face the desktop and door, and pretended to be busy. She lifted the phone receiver to her ear. Dial tone.

Flipped on the desktop computer. The Wi-Fi worked. Opened the drawers and found them filled with office supplies. And during her self-conducted orientation, she listened to Eli's barrage and vowed never to find herself the target of his fury.

His voice was gruff. "Brad Stefano, please. Yes, it's urgent. Thanks. Brad? Hi. Eli Klassen here. Yeah…the billboard. You've put a church family on the billboard advertising my goddam condos. I told you, millennials and boomers, enjoying their fucking lifestyle…Jesus Christ. A mistake? You don't say…My billboard's at Elmington Park?..What fun! No…Next week won't 'suffice'. Today. Change the fucking sign today or I'll come to your office and personally cut off your nuts and stuff them down your throat. Oh, and while you're at it? The Stephen Hill ads had better be off all the streetcars by the end of the day as well…I don't fucking care, Brad. This is your mess to fix."

Eli ended the call and tossed his phone on the sofa. For a moment, he closed his eyes and put his hands over his face. "Could you lock the door please, Mary? And switch the phone over to voicemail. Evidently, we're not ready to entertain yet," he said quietly.

Mary did as he bid, then sat in a cozy, pashmina-draped armchair. She crossed her legs and kept perfectly still. She didn't dare say a word.

"I'm sorry you heard that. I should have stepped outside to make that call." Eli opened his eyes and looked at her. "In fact, I should've dealt with Brad on Tuesday, because that way, today's disaster wouldn't have happened. He'd have learned his lesson."

"Do you think he'll remove the streetcar ads today, too?"

Eli gave her a funny look. "Yeah. Of course."

"Then why didn't you intervene on Tuesday?"

"Because I don't like Stephen Hill. The guy's a jerk."

"He has issues. Addiction is an illness."

"And I have compassion. I really do. But, you see, he cut me out of a deal last year, just before his latest hiatus, and I've lost patience. The cocaine sniffing and sloppiness I can forgive. Selfishness and deceit I cannot."

"So you left me to twist in the wind," Mary huffed. "Claudia nearly fired me over those signs."

"But she didn't. I would've pleaded your case if it were necessary. And here we are, Mary. In this gorgeous room, living the dream together." He smirked.

"Not cool."

"What's not cool? I'd say things are working out rather well."

Mary looked at her black leather boots that she'd shined especially for today and regretted having gone to the trouble. Not only had Eli spoken abusively to Brad at Out-of-the-Box, but he'd also revealed a Machiavellian tendency that she found off-putting, even scary.

"Are you sulking?" he asked.

"No." She wouldn't meet his eyes.

"Yes, you are."

"Holy shit, Eli. I can't figure you out. One minute you're threatening to castrate a graphic designer and force him into an act of auto-cannibalism, and the next minute you're teasing me."

"Am I speaking with Brad right now?"

"No."

"Correct. My conversation with him is over, to my satisfaction, and now I'm talking to you. I had to deal with Brad Stefano man to man because he performed poorly at his job and presented no credible excuse for why that happened. Now I'm sitting here with you, and I like you. I like you a lot. Your presence makes me happy and therefore my mood has shifted in a positive way. I'm not a mystery. I'm transparent."

"Okay, Mr. Transparent." She looked from her boots to his face. "What were you doing yesterday?"

"Recovering from a migraine."

"That's all?"

"Yes. That's all."

"Why did you ask me to lock the door?"

"Same reason the phone is going to voicemail. So we don't have to deal with anyone until we're ready to make a sale. We have brochures to collate, documents to review. We have to arrange cookies on a plate. Every single person who walks through that door must feel welcome and confident that we're competent or they'll take their shekels and run, and they'll tell other people to do the same."

"Okay." She focused on her boots again.

"Mary?" He spoke her name softly, and her fiery indignation cooled ever so slightly.

"What, Eli?"

"Is it bothering you that I asked you to lock the door?"

"No." Except it did.

"Okay, because on reflection, I can see how it might. I mean, the difficult phone call and everything. I assure you, I'm a gentleman and I'd never take advantage of a lady. You're safe with me."

"Take advantage? A lady?"

"It sounds old-fashioned, but where I'm from, a man and a woman who aren't married never work alone in close quarters together," Eli said bashfully.

"Where exactly do you come from?"

"That's a story for another time. My point is that people imagine all kinds of crazy things."

Crazy, wonderful things, thought Mary as her gaze inadvertently wandered over Eli's lean, muscular body. "By 'people' you're including the man and woman who are working alone?" she asked.

Eli shrugged and let her comment, which could mean anything to him, hang in the air.

What the hell was happening? Eli Klassen was now her boss. He wasn't even her type. She preferred cerebral, older men. She had to get that proposal approved and reactivate her dating app pronto before she did something daft, like swoon in Eli's arms.

Gathering her thoughts, she stood and went to the desk. "There's no food or drink in the kitchenette. I'll write a shopping list." Jeez. How easily she'd fallen into the role of a domestic helper as if under the spell of his conventional, unevolved masculinity.

"Okay," said Eli. "Rock, paper, scissors for the grocery run?"

Mary gave him an amused look. "You're on."

His playful nod to equality didn't fool her. He was in charge, and despite her feminism, she was submitting. Willingly.

\*\*\*\*

His rock beat her scissors and moments later Eli stepped into the sunshine, while Mary printed price schedules to collate with the brochures. They were nowhere near ready to launch an aggressive sales campaign, but he couldn't concentrate. Instead of following up with Synergy on the delay of their model units or calling investors, he'd blown off half the morning discussing philosophy with his "protégé." Conversing with Mary was like riding a spirited, poorly trained horse—exhilarating, unpredictable, demanding, and completely unproductive.

Working with Mary wasn't...working. On the other hand, after only three days, he couldn't imagine the alternative.

Eli walked through the sliding doors of Whole Foods and picked up a basket. They'd have to make up for lost time, push through lunch. He gathered the basics, then found the snack aisle. What would Mary like? Chocolate chip? Sandwich cookies? Coconut macadamia swirl? Damn it, Eli. What would *buyers* like? He grabbed some nut-free shortbread biscuits and social teas, cookies that never went stale, and added them to the basket.

And then to the prepared food section. A couple of salads, some chicken. Everyone liked chicken and Mary hadn't mentioned anything about being a vegetarian, which she would have if she were one because it was often the first thing people on special diets told you. Some fruit-flavored sparkling water—women seemed to like those—and done. A good thing too because the handle of the basket threatened to snap under the weight of it all.

Through the checkout and back to the office. From a ladder, a man was already removing Stefano's mistake.

He shouldn't have made that call in front of Mary.

He'd frightened her. Jonquil, Claudia, and Lori, all seasoned businesswomen, wouldn't have thought him out of line. Maybe Jonquil was right. Maybe Mary had been sheltered. She'd caught a glimpse of how sausages are made, in this case, not laws or actual meat in a tube, but money and she freaked out.

He'd have to protect her while she toughened up.

\*\*\*\*

After Eli left for the store, Mary opened the Word doc with the pricing schedule—basically a list of suites on offer, their prices plus or minus a few thousand depending on location in the building, and blurbs describing their features. Whoever put the document together had made several errors, and she set about correcting them.

When Eli returned, she was still editing. He put the groceries away and, without a word, hoisted a box of brochures onto the desk and ripped off the tape. He seemed annoyed that she hadn't printed anything yet.

Mary ignored his little hissy fit and frowned at the screen. "Eli, who put this document together?"

"Claudia...No, I think Claudia liaised with Synergy and then she had her niece, Felicity, type up everything."

"Oh, okay," Mary mumbled. "I'd have printed it, but there were so many typos. Some a bit funny. 'Walking closet, kitchen panty.' I'm almost finished fixing it."

"Felicity will be interning in your old job beginning in March."

She understood the implications of his statement immediately. An incompetent niece would be a loose cannon and immune to criticism.

Mary pushed away from the desk and vacated her chair for Eli. "Do you want to look this over before I print?"

He sat, peered at the screen, and with a few quick keystrokes, declared the document worthy of paper and ink.

After that, everything happened as if in a dream. Eli could've left her to collate the sales packages. He could've taken off to do whatever it was he did all day. Instead, he set up an assembly line in the fake living room while she made coffee, and a few minutes later they sat side by side on the sofa, stuffing papers into brochures. It was a mundane task made fun with conversation.

"So, Mary Rose," he began, "tell me about your childhood."

"I'm the only child of a textbook editor and a sculptor, and thus I grew up in penury. My parents divorced when I was in middle school. I lived with my mother in an apartment where I remain to this day. A few years ago, my mother met a painter online who 'understood her', went to BC to be with him and the ocean, and my friend Dominic replaced her in the apartment. Which is great because Dominic is fastidious and amusing. My father's second wife is his university sweetheart, who, fortunately, has not produced a second heir. And won't at her age."

"Why 'fortunately'? Wouldn't you want a sister or brother?"

"And compete for attention and resources?" She sneered. "Sorry. It sounds as if I'm bitter but I'm not. It's all fine. I'm happy. And you, Mr. Transparent, who said your past is a 'story for another time'. Here we are.

It's another time."

"Middle child of seven kids. Three sisters and three brothers. I grew up on a farm near Lake Huron. Dad earns extra money fixing tractors and things, Mom stays at home and works harder than anyone else I know. My family and kin fill half the local church and school, which are more or less the same place because the Klassen elders do not trust the government to educate their children. It's End Times, you understand, and only the righteous and repentant will have everlasting life in paradise after the horsemen lay waste to the earth. If the Klassen kids went to public school, we'd fall into sinful ways, so until about grade ten, I went to a private Christian school run by my uncle."

"And after that?"

"I relied on Mr. Andrew Carnegie's philanthropy in the form of the Eden Springs Public Library and the internet for my education. That and a little encouragement from my grandmother."

"Wow." Mary dropped a brochure onto the coffee table. She turned and regarded Eli with wonder. "That explains so much. So much that's unusual about you."

He said nothing. His expression begged her to tell him if what he'd shared was okay.

"They succeeded though," ventured Mary. "In spite of it all. You seem, um, well-adjusted."

"They fed me. I know where I come from. I'm under no illusions. My childhood was one very long, screwed-up bad hair day."

"Wow." She had to stop saying that. It was a word that shut people down. "I'm so impressed by you, Eli. Your knowledge of the world, of what makes people tick, and how things work. It's very broad and you learned everything yourself. That's remarkable. You're remarkable."

He shook his head. "I'm still figuring things out."

"Everyone is. It's the human condition. If we're lucky, we stay that way until the day we die. Believe me when I tell you, you're better at figuring things out than ninety-nine point nine percent of people. I teach philosophy to undergrads, so I'm able to judge."

"I don't know anything compared to you."

"That's not true. We know different things."

She had to touch him, to find out if he was still Eli—Eli, the suave. Eli, the secular, and not an alien being...a batshit nutty, religious fundamentalist in a normal man's clothing. She ran her fingertip over a pale crescent-shaped ridge on his wrist. "How did you get that scar?"

"Freeing a heifer from some baler twine."

"Oh."

He interpreted her lingering finger as an invitation and took her hand.

His hand was muscular, firm, and warm, a hand that could injure a foe or caress a lover. Sliding his thumb over hers, he looked into her eyes to confirm her permission and she licked her lips. She hadn't meant to behave seductively, yet the slide of her tongue couldn't mean anything else but "kiss me."

Eli released her hand, brought his fingers to her face, and brushed a lock of hair from her cheek. As he drew her face up, she closed her eyes, intensifying the effect of his mouth on hers. In the silence, Eli's kiss was everything. An exquisite everything.

She tasted coffee and man, and she longed to taste more. Slowly, tentatively, their tongues mingled. The kiss was unexpected, yet as natural as a dawning sun in the eastern sky.

After the kiss ended, Eli eased his arm around Mary's shoulders and held her. They leaned back on the sofa cushions as one, her curves tucked into his angles, and there she reveled in the rise and fall of his chest, listening to his heartbeat, steady and beautiful as a lullaby. Neither spoke until Mary's stomach grumbled.

"You're hungry," he said.

"Eli. What are we doing?"

"I don't know," he replied. "Let's have lunch and figure it out."

****

"I can't have sex with you until my proposal is approved."

Only seconds ago, that's exactly what Mary had said. The words circled like a cyclone in his brain. She'd blurted it out as if sex was a trivial pleasure. As if she were vowing not to eat chocolate until Easter Sunday or watch Netflix until she'd filed her taxes. Then she said, "This is delicious," and bit into her drumstick.

"I'm glad you like it," he said flatly.

"I wonder how they seasoned it." Mary closed her eyes and savored the food. "Mmm…I taste lime, chili pepper, some coriander…."

Eli set down his fork. Why should her declaration feel so offensive? Like a slap.

She opened her eyes and looked sideways at him. "Aren't you hungry?"

He shook his head. "Can we back up a little? To before your flavor analysis of the chicken?"

"You mean when I said I can't have sex with you

till my proposal's approved?"

"Yeah. That."

It still sounded awful in his head. They'd kissed for the first time less than an hour ago and now she was dictating the terms under which she'd sleep with him? He'd poured every ounce of his self-control into keeping his hands above her shoulders, into stopping with a single kiss, only to discover that if it weren't for her vow, she'd probably have given herself to him. He wanted her, desperately, but he knew right from wrong. How a man should behave with a woman and how a woman should behave in return. A lady did not tell a man when she would invite him into her bed. That was something two people discovered together.

He rubbed his chin. "That statement bugs me, Mary. I feel as if you're penciling me into your calendar. Like you're scheduling a fling as a reward for a job well done. And if I'm not willing, you'll find some random man to do the deed."

She chuckled. "Well, you are willing—and able— aren't you?" When he didn't laugh along, her face fell, and she stared at her plate. "Oh." She stopped eating and shifted to face him. "That was crass. What I said. I'm sorry, Eli. I shouldn't have presumed."

He took her hands in his and chose his words with care. "I want to be with you, Mary. I vowed not to go down this path with you because we work together, but it feels so right I don't want to stop. I also have certain conditions that must be met, and they depend on us, not on some external circumstance like whether I've met my sales targets."

"Okay."

She peered up at him, forehead furrowed, eyes

solemn and contrite. Her lower lip quivered. A pang of guilt stabbed his gut for scolding her, however necessary.

He laced his fingers in hers to reassure her. "The first condition is that we don't have sex. I'm not a boar servicing a sow. If we are to know each other intimately, unclothed, what we have together, what we do with each other, must be more than that. It must be sacred." He paused to check that she was with him, and she nodded. "My second condition is exclusivity. No other men. Only me."

Mary swallowed hard and nodded. Tears pooled in her eyes. He fumbled for his serviette and dabbed her tears with it. "I'm sorry," he said. "I spoke too harshly."

She shook her head and smiled through her tears. "No, Eli." She accepted the serviette from him, wiped her face, and blew her nose. "This is new for me. The way you're speaking, the way you treat me, from your heart. I've never met anyone like you, ever before. I feel so…seen. Valued. You're treating me as if I'm precious and I'm profoundly touched by that."

"But you are precious, Mary. Can't you see that?"

She shook her head. "Eli, what if I told you I wanted to, you know—'know' you today? What would you say?"

"I wouldn't believe you. Your education is everything to you and you made a promise to yourself with the intention of keeping it. I would never violate that."

"And if I hadn't told you about the vow?"

"I can't un-know it." He shrugged. "Maybe I'd push the table aside and take you into my arms and roll around on the rug with you."

"Can we still do that? With our clothes on?" asked Mary.

"Like fourteen-year-olds wrestling in the straw?"

"Yeah."

Eli nudged the table away with his foot and kissed her again.

Chapter Five

"What do you think, Mama Klassen?" Dominic held up an ankle-length skirt. "Denim is such a practical fabric for the homestead, and you can add a pretty floral waistband whenever you're with child."

"That's enough, Dominic," Mary said crossly.

"Okay, Mrs. Klassen."

"Stop calling me that! It is not, nor will it ever be, my name."

"Right-e-o!"

"We're wasting time. You told me you were going to help me, but all you do is make stupid jokes, and now the store's about to close."

"That's not my fault." Dominic mocked her in a goofy falsetto, "'Just one more paper, one more ungrammatical failure of logic to mark, and then I'll be ready, Dominic.' That's what you said, and that was at two o'clock! I put on my shopping shoes right after breakfast, girlfriend, so the blame for our tardiness is on you."

"Whatever." Mary shuffled through a discounted rack of blouses. "This one?"

"Salmon is not a power color," Dominic said, shaking his head.

"How about this one?"

"It has sequins and flounces. You have neither the time nor skill to iron it. Plus, it's ugly."

"Okay…um…this one."

"Yee-haw!" Dominic squealed. "A yoked shirt for line-dancin' and varmint shootin'. You can embroider roses on the collar. Mr. Klassen will love it."

Mary shifted hangers as if she were a panicked thief ransacking a closet. She'd left the laundry too long, and didn't have anything to wear for the evening ahead or for work the next day. Dominic would nix anything pink, frilly, or fancy, and rightly so. Ditto odd designs and patterns. There. A plain black cotton shirt. "Is this a 'yes'?"

"Mary. Please. You're not an undertaker or a waitress. You can't wear a black shirt with black trousers. Or navy or brown trousers, either."

The harder she tried, the quicker Dominic shook his head, taking obvious pleasure in doing so. Mary sighed. "Maybe we should forget it for today."

"This!" Dominic pulled a gunmetal blue satin shirt from the rack and held it up to her chest. "It flatters your skin tone, and you can wear it to work or après-work. Though not to the ladies' prayer circle, mind."

Mary ran her fingers over the fabric, so luxurious and silky in her hands, and checked the price tag. "Only twenty-three fifty. But I'd have to have it dry cleaned."

"My dear, even coin-op machines have a delicate cycle. Buy it. Really. You simply must."

Mary hesitated as twenty-three fifty transformed into *a whopping* twenty-three fifty in her mind.

Dominic turned her around and marched her to the fitting room. "Put it on, and then we'll pay for it and meet your dreamboat. Eli can be the arbiter on whether or not you've found a bargain."

\*\*\*\*

Eli had never been kissed on the hand before, let alone by a cologne-doused man in a pinstriped suit with a carnation stuck in his jacket lapel. Dominic had seized his extended hand, knelt on one knee, and pressed his lips to Eli's skin. Before Eli could react, Dominic performed a balletic maneuver, and was back on his feet again.

"*Enchanté*," murmured Dominic, bowing gracefully.

Disarmed by shock, Eli burst out laughing. "You must be Dominic. The man behind the invitation."

"Mary thought we should meet, and she graciously allowed me to borrow her phone."

A pink-faced Mary shook her head. "He stole my phone."

Dominic stood back on his heel and appraised Eli from head to toe. "He is everything you said and more, my dear."

At once, Eli understood viscerally the expression 'undressed with his eyes.' Helplessly turning to Mary for rescue, he kissed her cheek, still cold from outdoors. Mary squeezed his arm, as if to signal that they were in the same boat—that, yes, Dominic was outrageous but he, Eli, could hold her hand and enjoy the ride.

"You've nabbed a table most excellent in this over-peopled public house," Dominic pronounced as he hung his jacket on a hook.

Eli offered Mary the corner chair and seated himself. "I got here early and managed to grab it as the darts league was leaving."

Early enough to have polished off a pint of ale while he calculated his commission on the sale of two units and shifted funds into his ETFs and Bitcoin account. He'd had a profitable day, and he was in a celebratory mood. People chatted in congenial clusters, a blues song thumped low from the jukebox, and Mary was radiant. And Dominic? Eli decided he liked him.

A few moments later, Eli's tab included a martini for Dominic, a pint of cider for Mary, and another ale for himself. The evening commenced with a toast to the health of the trio assembled.

****

It was past two when Eli staggered through the door, and now he lay naked in bed, having woken abruptly with a prodromal hangover. He swept his hand over the bedside table to check the time, but his phone wasn't there. Probably in his jacket, which formed part of the boozy, sweaty heap of clothing by his bed. He turned his pillow over to cool his neck and waited for the bed to stop revolving.

As he lay still, his scattered memories coalesced into semi-coherence. A sense of dread washed up from his belly. He should've called it a night after the second drink. Instead, he'd have to face Mary knowing that he'd taken to the dance floor with all the finesse of a spastic giraffe and confessed to "comforting" Claudia when Stephen was in rehab. Dominic had ordered shots when they were already flying high and instigated a game of his own invention that he'd named "Inappropriate." But in the end, Eli was responsible for his own conduct and Mary might, very reasonably, reject him. *If* she remembered anything herself. Jesus. Fucking. Christ. Where was his phone? And his wallet?

He sat up, waited for his stomach to settle, then bent to locate the items. Thank God, they were there. Time: 4:37. At least he didn't have a headache—yet.

He stepped over his clothes and went to the kitchen for a couple of preemptive Advil tablets and a large glass of water. Sleep was hopeless now.

Eli gazed through the kitchen window over the urban expanse to the north of the building. Millions of lights twinkled under a starless hazy-ink sky. The view from the seventeenth floor was of a world upside-down, the mirror image of a rural night of black fields under a starry firmament. Skin cool with boozy perspiration, Eli shivered. In this very moment, in every neighborhood, some people were drunk, and other people were cleaning up after them. People were committing sins, and other people were weeping for them. Most people simply slept. As should he.

But he couldn't. Not yet.

He donned a sweatshirt and boxers and went to the living room to find something distracting to read that didn't require a screen. There was the pile of mail he'd left on the table several days earlier. Flyers, fast-food coupons, a mass-mailed offer from a competitor to appraise his condo *no strings attached!* And a letter addressed in even cursive from Mrs. Abraham Klassen of Eden Springs. Grandma.

He tore the flap from the envelope and withdrew the missive. A child's drawing of a fat, pink pig wearing a jeweled necklace and crown fluttered from its fold.

*Dear Eli,*

*In his infinite wisdom, The Lord has seen fit to bless us with sound health and we pray you are enjoying the same. Jacob's Ezra is only a month old and already eleven pounds and smiling.*

*The sap is running early this year. We burnt one*

*batch of syrup, but your mother will find a use for it, and we have plenty to sell. Today I started the tomatoes and pepper seeds and finished a blanket for Esther's hope chest so I'm not idle, though fine work is becoming harder with my eyes as they are.*

*Rebekah said she'd thank you herself, but in case she didn't, I'm happy to report that she loves the pastels you sent her. She's very good at animals, especially horses, and I have a fine chestnut pony on my bedroom wall—though perhaps its eyelashes, mane, and tail are longer and more colorful than one would see on a live horse. I've stuck in a picture she drew of a piglet. Becky's quite the little artist at age 8, isn't she?! She misses her Uncle Eli. We all do.*

*Now–My Big News!! The Holley Eye Clinic has given me a date for my cataract surgery. May 8th at 9:10 a.m. I'll arrive on the afternoon train on May 7th, and I don't wish to impose, but if you would please send me a key to your condominium, you don't have to find me at the station. Jacob will come with me–I can't lift anything heavy after the surgery –and he knows his way around Toronto, having attended the Ambassadors for Christ conference a few years ago. I have a check-up to make sure my eyes are good on the 9ᵗʰ and then home, but no bending or lifting. Your poor mother will find me quite useless in the garden!!!*

*Do you need anything, Eli? I'll bring your favorite elderberry jam and some gherkins and summer sausage. Don't be shy. We've plenty of surplus, and before long we'll be canning again so we can bring whatever you like.*

*My eyes are tired, so I'll sign off for now. I'll close by saying that it's a blessing you live in the city with my surgery and all, but I pray every day that the Lord will lead you back to us.*

 *Oceans of Love,*
 *Grandma*

 Eli refolded the letter and tucked it into its envelope. Becky's piglet would take place of pride on the fridge when he could muster the energy to tape it up. Though he'd mail a key so Grandma wouldn't worry over her plan, he'd drive her to Toronto himself. If she'd packed her suitcase, he needn't endure more than a meal in his childhood home. Jacob would be deprived of an excuse to escape from labor during the busiest month on the farm and it would spare Eli three days of Jacob's interminable prayer for the younger, prodigal brother who was lost in the temptations of Gomorrah.

 A sour brimstone of bile bubbled at the back of his throat and the first drumbeats of a headache thudded in his forehead. The poisons of the previous night coursed through his veins, leaving him as pathetic and limp as a grotty dishrag. His thoughts kept twisting back to the previous night.

 He'd have to do serious damage control followed by some uncomfortably honest soul-searching.

 The previous night he'd betrayed Claudia—and for what? To win Dominic's ridiculous drinking game that, in reality, turned the winner into the loser through sordid confession. Dominic was the declared victor for his shocking accounts of a men-only club he frequented, but even in his alcoholic daze, Eli hadn't missed the chill in Mary's attitude after his own "contribution" to the game. Her body went rigid, and she wouldn't meet his eye until she was too drunk to remember that she was disappointed in him.

He had to see her. Apologize. And do much, much better whether she accepted his apology or not.

The eastern sky glowed in an indigo light. In Eden Springs, birds—including the ancient, one-eyed rooster the girls named "Rufus"—would be waking and bragging to the world about it. Apart from a single, wayward pigeon that had flown onto the balcony, the condo was devoid of nonhuman life. Still, even here, dawn broke, a reminder that the earth had its own eternal rhythm, however colossal his screwup.

They were due to meet at In-Spire at nine—if Mary showed up. One more Advil to top up, a glass of water, and then, if possible, a shred of sleep.

****

Mary awoke in the same clothes she'd worn last night. Mouth furry, stomach somersaulting, head pounding. Even breathing hurt. Gradually her senses sharpened, and she was relieved to discover that she was alone in her bed. As she wiped the night from her eyes, her memories vacillated between crystal clarity and cloudy obscurity, as if she were peering through a windshield with its wipers swishing back and forth in sleet. Dominic snored in the next room and thank God for that, as she was in no shape to withstand a replay of her debauchery.

She was due at the sales office at nine. Sunlight spilled around the edges of the blinds. It was well and truly Sunday morning. Oh God! So late! According to the clock radio, 8:47, which meant it was only 8:42—a miniscule mercy of five minutes, but she'd take it.

Gingerly rising from a tangle of sheets, she located her phone on the desk where she always left it, thank the gods for habit. She tapped a message to Eli. —Hey. I'm running late. Be there in about 45 mins.—" For some reason, the sight of his name brought acid to her tongue.

She shed her clothes and showered away the toxic perspiration and stale odor of Saturday night, toweled off, and returned to her room to cobble together an outfit. As she rummaged through her drawer for a clean bra and underwear, the phrase "Dress like Claudia" popped into her head. A goddam push-up bra? Oh no.

Oh no, oh no, oh no. "Inappropriate." That'd been the game. Mary collapsed onto the bed and blocked her eyes with one arm. The evil genius, who claimed status of best friend, slept in placid contentment in the next room while her memories bounced like spiked bingo balls inside her skull. Dominic had ordered a round of tequila and they'd spilled their guts, depravities and all. After several go-arounds of mild revelation—lies on a resume, smoking weed at a funeral, soaping church windows—the final round went off the rails in spectacular fashion.

Dominic confessed to wearing a saddle and bridle get-up at the Peacock Club and being mounted by several men. Big hairy deal, though Eli looked as if he'd choked on a tequila worm. She admitted to having sex with the father of a child she babysat in her senior year of high school. But Eli's revelation— *that* took the cake. He'd mercy-fucked Claudia and bragged about it.

Nearly nine. Mary got up and put on her underwear, a vintage Pearl Jam T-shirt, and a pair of faded jeans. Today she wouldn't dress like Claudia. She'd defend her.

## Chapter Six

Eli brewed a pot of coffee, bracing, strong, and medicinal. Yesterday he'd accepted delivery of some display panels with images of the In-Spire concept as well as a scale model of the project in its future form. At the center of a broad plank stood a miniature condo tower topped with a garden of cotton-swab trees and surrounded by a neighborhood of matchboxes and ridged plaster streets, all to meticulous scale. The very thought of its maker bent in concentration over the mat-sized streetscape made his brain swell. He'd need Mary's help to install this masterpiece of commercially motivated sculpture on the unassembled table that accompanied it.

He poured himself a mug of coffee, held it under his nose like smelling salts, and slurped to cool the liquid before it reached his tongue. Still, it burnt like molten tar in his mouth. Through the front door window, he spotted Mary searching through her rucksack for her keys.

*Steady. Deep breath. Give nothing away and let her do the talking.* If he were lucky, she wouldn't remember anything. He opened the unlocked door for her.

A jean jacket and black T-shirt, ponytail, no makeup. Mary could pass for a teenager despite her twenty-six years and a rough night. She wasn't dressed for work. Was she about to quit? Please, God, no. If it came to that, he'd deal—an unearned cut of yesterday's sales to buy him a chance of apology and redemption. What the hell? Forgiveness couldn't be bought. He'd shut the fuck up and listen.

"Coffee?" Eli asked in greeting.

Mary nodded without looking at him. The silent treatment. Heart pounding in his sick chest, he went to the kitchenette and poured her a mug. Black, like his. They were alike, yet worlds apart. Worlds to explore and he'd wrecked it. Eli returned and handed the steaming mug to her. She blew on it and took a careful sip.

"Thanks," she said. A single word and then a tense nothing.

Okay. She probably wasn't resigning because she was drinking coffee with him, though her face and body were as stiff as a storefront mannequin.

"I'm sorry," Eli ventured as he sat on the sofa.

She sat too, though, in the armchair. "Sorry for what?" Mary finally met his eyes.

"For acting like a jerk. For *being* a jerk last night."

"*In vino veritas,*" she muttered.

Okay...spouting Latin. Was she trying to make him feel stupid?

"I don't suppose you know what that means?" she needled.

He did—the phrase described alcohol as a truth serum—but he shrugged to feign ignorance. Let her feel superior. "Dominic's game brought out the worst in us, especially me," he replied.

"You're blaming Dominic for you screwing your boss and blabbing?" Her voice was low yet dagger-sharp.

"No. Of course not. I'm responsible for my actions. I should never have been with Claudia. It was only once, but it was wrong."

"You think this is about fornication? Adultery?" She chose the words to mock him. "It's not. Not at all. It's about betraying a secret, about hurting Claudia by fucking her when she was under a ton of stress and then bragging about it."

Eli flinched. He didn't *fuck* women. The word was vulgar and disrespectful. A whisp of a memory wafted through his consciousness. Air fumy with the boozy breath of multitudes, neon Guinness sign blinking behind the bar, Mary on his right, laughing over music…what she said…he did remember!

"You kissed and told," said Eli. "A father and husband, wasn't it? A married man—"

"I was a nerdy, bespectacled loner itching to lose my virginity. He taught me what I wanted to know, and I don't regret it."

"His wife might take a different view."

"Yeah? Do you think so? Well, here's the thing, Eli. She didn't find out. And she didn't find out because even at seventeen I knew enough not to tell anyone who knew them. Not to name names."

She was right. His transgression was far worse than hers. He stared into his coffee mug. "I drank way too much last night, Mary, and I said things I shouldn't have. You and Dominic are the only people who know and I'm relying on you to keep it that way."

"You know we will."

"Yeah. I do. I'm fully aware that what I did with Claudia and my betrayal of her last night were wrong

75

and I'm very, very sorry about it."

With an enigmatic expression, Mary drank her coffee and set her mug on the table.

"If I could take everything back, I would," he added.

Mary sighed as if too tired to argue further. "I suppose everyone makes mistakes," she said vaguely.

"Where does that leave us?"

"I'm not sure." She was antsy. Shuffling her feet like a diner about to pull a runner. Before he could press her further, she said, "Look. I feel like crap. Okay if I take the day off to lie low and work on my proposal?"

There was only one answer to such a request. "Yeah. Go ahead. I can handle things here myself."

Pointedly ignoring his pain, she left her half-empty mug on the table, grabbed her rucksack, and hurried away.

This soul-crushing abandonment felt far worse than a slap on the face. Eli got up, wrenched the table box open, dumped the contents onto the carpet, and found the instructions. He'd rebuilt engines with his father and brothers, but he couldn't make sense of these simple line drawings. Nothing made sense.

His phone pinged with a text. Could it be? No. Claudia.

*—Eli. Lots of buzz about In-Spire. Have you set a date for the grand opening?—*

They—he—should've flung the doors open to all comers yesterday. He'd taken his eye off the ball and lost precious time, and she was calling him on it.

*—Thanks for asking, Claudia. This Sat. 2 p.m. Drinks, food, bunting–the whole 9 yds—*

*—Good. Email details and I'll send out invitations. If you need help, tell me.—*

*—OK. Sorry for delay. I'm sorted. How's Stephen?—*

*—Better. Is Mary there?—*

*—No. She has the day off.—*

A thumbs-up and *—Stephen may drop by later. Make him feel useful, OK?—*

Thumbs-up right back.

****

As Mary left the sales office, a cold drizzle claimed the street from all but the most stalwart exercisers and dog people. She was grateful to walk in solitude. On a Sunday morning, transit was infrequent, and she didn't relish a return to the apartment and Dominic, who'd regale her from the depths of his lungs with songs of their misdeeds, spatula in hand.

Her first steps energized with fierce indignation, Mary's moral certainty dissolved with each sodden block, and her pace slowed to an aimless stroll. She passed through the stone gates at the side of the small graveyard at St. Dunstan's and sat on a wrought-iron bench, cold and wet with rain. Through the barred fence, she watched parishioners, mostly elderly, shuffling in for the service. In a decade or two, they'd be buried also, their bodies feeding larvae, selves extinguished forever, their names engraved on headstones fuzzy with moss. Death was real; Eli was real.

In contrast, her righteous outrage was self-serving, contrived, and rapidly disintegrating.

What had she done?

Used Eli as a mirror and disliked what she saw,

that's what. With a spurious claim to the lofty construct of a feminist sisterhood, she accused Eli of the same transgressions she herself had committed. Her fury had nothing to do with naming names and everything to do with jealousy and shame. They were primal emotions that she intellectualized as quaintly outdated, yet they walloped her in the gut with the force of a fast fist.

Here, sitting in this rain-soaked memento mori, she remembered a night alive with music and joy. Dominic was flirting with an old friend, so she'd asked Eli to dance to an up-tempo blues song—Stevie Ray Vaughan? And though Eli shook his head, she didn't relent. She didn't take no for an answer. Shrugging with uncharacteristic shyness, he'd accepted her hand and danced with her. He was an awful dancer, stiff-limbed and self-conscious, tilting and shaking this way and that like an unbalanced washer on spin, and he made himself do it to please her.

She owed *him* the apology.

Mary marched straight back to the sales office. The door was unlocked. Eli hadn't turned the deadbolt after her, and that gave her hope.

She found him sitting on the carpet, his leg extended to brace a metal pole, left hand clutching a piece of paper, his right hand sifting through bolts. He looked up through a shock of brown hair that had fallen over his forehead. Her elaborate apology, rehearsed and refined during the return journey, escaped her when she saw him. He looked as innocent and wholesome as a boy building a rocket ship with Lego.

"I'm sorry," Mary said. "I'm such a bitch."

He nodded and rose to stand before her. "You're wet."

"No discussion?" she asked. "Don't you want me to account for myself?"

"Is it necessary?"

She shook her head, kicked her boots into the closet, and turned to him.

Eli took her into his arms and held her. She rested her head against the heat of his collar bone, and he nuzzled her forehead. He smelled of Eli—soap and salty sweat and an indescribable man smell that made her feel safe and horny at the same time. He forgave her.

"Do you want help with whatever it is you're building?"

"A table for that diorama." He broke away and grinned. "Yeah, I could use some help. But you're all wet."

"I'll towel off." She pulled the elastic from her ponytail to shake her hair loose and shivered.

"Wet and freezing cold." Eli went to the thermostat to adjust the temperature and the baseboard heaters hissed into action. "I keep a spare shirt for long days, in case I've got an evening appointment and I can't get home." He admitted to this minor vanity with bashful candor and Mary smiled. "What?" he asked.

"Nothing. Really. I'm charmed by your attention to detail. You're like a Boy Scout. Prepared."

He stood in front of the closet. "It's long enough to cover you. Just slip off your wet clothes and we can dry them over a chair in front of the heater." Holding a crisply pressed white shirt on a hanger, he turned to her.

"I accept your offer," Mary replied. "Why don't you help me undress."

"Your vow?"

"That still stands."

\*\*\*\*

It was the tease of the century. So consuming, Eli forgot his headache, his work, and his throbbing toe that he'd stubbed on a component as he crossed the room. His singular focus rested on Mary, the goddess before him.

This time, he didn't have to stop at a button or two, though he had to back off before they went too far.

"Umm...shouldn't we lock the door?" she asked coyly as she received his shirt and draped it over a chair.

"Oh, right." He was already hard, and when he turned to her again, he saw her eyes widen as her gaze fell to his tented fly.

Even bare of makeup, her cheeks and lips were red. He raked her thick, wavy hair off her shoulders, slid his hands under the denim fabric of her jacket, and eased it off. She lifted her chin, and he kissed her. As his lips made contact, she flicked her tongue over his mouth. The sensation was powerfully erotic, and he deepened the kiss, tasting toothpaste and coffee, caressing her softness with his lips. He slipped his hand over the hot, damp cotton of her T-shirt and cradled her breast, round and firm, nipple pressed against her clothing. He had to see, had to touch, and she understood this, for she raised her arms and allowed him to lift her shirt over her head and unclasp her bra.

Naked as Eve in the garden from the curve of her waist up, Mary gripped his shoulders and let him drink in her beauty. Her skin was smooth, her full breasts tipped like pink candy. He ran his finger around her areola, puckered from the cold, and bent to take her taut nipple into his mouth, sucking with such intensity that her breathing quickened. Left breast, then right. He was losing his mind in her flesh.

"We need some ground rules," he said, voice husky and deep.

"You can't enter me, but we can touch," she panted.

He nodded once and lowered her zipper, and she wiggled out of her jeans and panties. She moved like a confidant woman, and he was glad of that. He twined a slick curl on his finger, then pressed the heel of his hand over her mound. "I'm not inside you."

"No. But I'm at a disadvantage," Mary whispered hoarsely. She unbuttoned his shirt and unzipped his fly. "There. Better."

Eli's erection, long and hard, emerged from his gaping pants, and he longed for her to grip him, but she shook her head and ran her fingers through the hair around his nipple and across his chest. She tasted the flesh over his heart.

He guided her to the sofa, and she laid back, thighs separated just enough to drive him wild with lust. He knelt before his goddess, eased her legs apart, and tasted her. Drawing his tongue between her folds, he licked her, from her button-hard clit to her slippery opening, slow at first, then ever faster, ever more urgently, never going in, never breaching the gate. She was hot and smooth on his tongue, and she moaned as he adjusted his pressure to the shift of her pelvis, matched his tempo to her breath. As their rhythm crested, she cried his name. "Eli, oh my God. Eli!" Her body shook with a feminine power that thrilled him to his core.

Mary's eyes were on him as he moved over her and teased her nipple with his tongue. A final taste of ambrosia and he'd rest with her.

"Your turn," she whispered.

"You don't have to—"

She was already gripping his shaft, already lowering her face to him. Before she could take him into her mouth, he came, and she cupped her hand to receive his seed. She looked into his eyes and smiled, and he received her wordless message. Their communion was natural and beautiful and sacred.

Mary rolled to her side and reached for her underwear to clean her hand, and they rested, limbs entwined, breathing and being as one.

\*\*\*\*

Yet again, Eli surprised her.

They shared the sofa, his warm, sleeping body enveloping hers, chest rising and falling against her back, a lightly muscled arm draped over her with his hand tucked between her breasts. For a man who claimed to eschew dating apps and casual sex, he was fantastically skilled in the art of giving pleasure, equal and greater in tenderness to the older men she usually dated.

Cocooned in Eli's masculinity, Mary reveled in recollection of the previous hour. He was shy about his body, reluctant to reveal himself to her. She saw all right. He was lean and nicely muscled, sinewy, with a wildly unkempt chest and torso and an uncircumcised, eager cock. She wanted him and she wanted *it*. Every glorious inch of it. Deeply.

She had to write up that proposal and make damn sure it was good enough to pass muster. Perhaps an interrogation of theories of motivation...Socrates...Sartre? She'd read widely, indulged her wheel-spinning under the facade of intellectual exploration, and she could put together an extensive lit review on a range of topics. The sooner she could move ahead with her dissertation—and with Eli—the better.

A sudden knock on the door startled her. Knock? Hell no. A pounding.

"Eli. Someone's here."

"What?" he murmured.

"Wake up!"

Keys jangled on the other side of the door. Mary jolted free of Eli's embrace and pulled on her wet jeans.

Eli straightened as if hit by lightning, sat bolt upright, and jumped up to put on his trousers. "That'll be Stephen!" He fumbled with the buttons of his shirt. "Claudia mentioned he might drop by. I didn't think she meant today."

With a quick stride, Eli shielded Mary as she stuffed herself into her bra. The lock turned. She grabbed her T-shirt and ran to the washroom. As she shut the door, the office door swung open and Stephen Hill's voice rang through the pressboard.

"Klassen. My God, man. Why didn't you answer the door?"

\*\*\*\*

"Why didn't I answer the door?" Eli repeated. "Uh...because I was busy." The smell of sex hung in the damp, warm air. He slid open a window. "Do you want to see the site?" Maybe if Stephen took his nostrils to the bare screen, he wouldn't notice.

Stephen raised a bushy eyebrow at an offer better

suited to a four-year-old obsessed with heavy machinery, but he indulged him. "Definitely a hole. Deep. And mucky." He turned away from the window, took off his jacket, and threw it over the shirt Mary had hung from the office chair. "It's hotter than the Devil's asshole in here."

"Uh...heat helps the plaster dry on the model. That's what I'm working on. Putting together this table to display the model." Eli waved his hand toward the metal flotsam strewn across the carpet. Stephen made no comment on the heady scent that refused to dissipate. Thank God for a nose made insensate by cocaine.

"I'll turn down the heat." Stephen squinted at the thermostat. "Eighty-five! Jeez, Klassen!" He poked buttons and the baseboard elements clicked off.

Eli's headache returned with ferocity. He had to get Stephen to leave. *Let him feel useful,* Claudia said. If he took her advice, maybe Stephen would go without suspicion. "Do you want to help me?"

Stephen smirked. "Sure, Daddy. If you think I'm ready for big-boy tools." He bent to pick up the instructions.

Eli sank onto the sofa to rest his head. Perhaps Stephen would assemble the table himself.

"Ikea?" Stephen stroked his semi-matted beard and frowned. "That's a company you should'a bought stock in, but God help the bugger who can't find the Allen key."

"It's there."

Stephen knelt and dragged his sausage fingers through a pile of small parts. "Nope. Not here."

"I'm pretty sure I had it." As Eli scanned the

84

carpet, he caught sight of Mary's underwear, balled up and discarded by the very Allen key they sought. Unfortunately, Stephen's bulk blocked his path and made kicking the item under the sofa impossible. For an instant, he froze in panic, and then he dove for the key. Alas, Stephen had seen the direction of his gaze and beat him to the underwear.

"Well, well. Isn't this interesting," said Stephen. "A key and something frilly. Yours?" He set the tool on the instruction sheet and stretched out Mary's panties. "Ew. Gross. They're sticky."

Eli's face burned like a torch. He tried to speak, but only managed to choke out guttural sounds. "Urr...Ugh..."

"They're yours, aren't they." Stephen winked. "No worries. I get it. Some men enjoy that kind of thing. Ladies' intimate apparel. Even wear it under their regular clothes and no one's the wiser. They feel beautiful all day."

Eli gawped.

"Your secret's safe with me," Stephen added, "though I'd be more inclined to discretion if you gave me a generous cut on your sales. I'm open-minded, but Claudia, you know, everything's all about reputation with her. Optics."

Blackmail. The crime of roaches and rats. Eli wouldn't give Stephen a single red cent if hell froze over. "I'll think about it," he said coldly.

"You do that, Klassen, while I go wash my hands." Stephen's nostrils flared and his lip curled in an expression of disgust.

Mary. Oh no. If his betrayal of Claudia upset her, she'd be livid if he let Stephen discover the true owner of the cast-off underwear. "No!" Eli bobbed around him and blocked the bathroom door. "The plumbing doesn't work properly."

"Really? Jonquil told me you have all the comforts of home."

"I plugged up the toilet. No plunger. It's very embarrassing for me. My condition, that is. It's in my bowels. Uh...colonitis fecosis."

"Really? I've never heard of that. It sounds horrible."

"It is." Eli hung his head and shuffled his feet. "Even more horrible than my problem with underwear. You can't go in there."

"I don't need the toilet. I have to wash my fucking hands."

"It's not safe."

"That's fucking silly, Klassen. We both know what I touched. Get out of my way!"

Eli shook his head. "No. I won't."

Stephen went for a body check, but Eli ducked and shoved him with speed borne by years of fighting with older brothers. Stephen shoved him back and was eyeing his jaw and balling his hand into a fist when the bathroom door swung open as if pushed by a sudden draft. Visible from Eli's vantage, a toe disappeared into the vanity cabinet.

Stephen stayed his hand. "May I?" he asked sarcastically.

"If you insist." Eli gestured like a maître d. "Just remember what I said. Don't use the toilet."

Stephen took several minutes to wash his hands. Decontamination process complete, he grabbed his jacket.

"You're not going to help me with the table?" asked Eli.

"You can handle it. I've got stuff to do. Keep my suggestion in mind, Klassen. We can define the terms when you've had a chance to think." As he left, he stooped and hooked the waistband of the underwear with his pinky to take with him. "Evidence," he said.

Once Stephen left, Eli returned to the washroom to give the all-clear. Mary was already unfolding herself from the cabinet.

"Colonitis fecosis?" She giggled.

"It's a grave condition. Very rare." Eli grinned and offered her a hand up.

"You're full of shit."

"You could say that."

Chapter Seven

Eli dropped by the Hill Realty office on Monday morning. If Stephen had cranked up the rumor mill, he had to retaliate immediately. He climbed the stairs two at a time, passed through the corridor that Hill Realty shared with a law practice and a psychic therapist, and entered the office. He expected to find Mary's desk vacant. Instead, a blond girl greeted him. Eli pretended not to notice that she was gorgeous, an eleven out of ten, with a Dolly Parton bosom in a clingy sweater.

"You must be Eli?" she said in a little girl's voice.

"I am," Eli smiled.

"My Aunt Claudia told me all about you. I'm Felicity." She extended her hand over the desk.

"So that's why my ears were burning." Eli shook her hand. "Welcome, Felicity."

"Your ears?"

"It's an old expression. When people talk about you when you're not present, your ears burn. Or so they say."

"Cool."

"Is this your first day?"

"Yes. I was supposed to start next week, but Aunt Claudia mentioned a human resources emergency?"

Was that a question? If Felicity wanted the goods on Mary, she was fishing in the wrong pond. "It's good to have your help on such short notice," Eli said evenly.

She curled a strand of shiny yellow hair around her finger. "Aunt Claudia told me I should connect with you."

"Did she?" Eli scratched the back of his head, and to his dismay, Felicity mistook his stalling gesture as flirtation.

"To show me the ropes?" she added sweetly. "Train me in the art of sales?"

He dropped his hand and stepped back. "Your Uncle Stephen and Aunt Claudia have more experience than I do."

Felicity pouted. "Uncle Stephen isn't here today, and I'd rather learn from someone closer in age. You know...peer to peer?"

For Christ's sake. What had Claudia told this poor girl? What was she playing at? Saddling him with a spy? Scheming to replace Mary at In-Spire? Recruiting a harem for him? Even without Felicity as a tagalong, his performance at work was suffering, and he was damn sure Claudia would have something to say about that.

"Pretty please?" Felicity peered at him through caterpillar lashes and bit her cherry-red lip.

"You have a lot of responsibility here at reception," said Eli. "First you should learn this job."

"And then I can learn from you," Felicity squeaked.

Before he could temper her enthusiasm, she said, "I think my aunt mentioned she wanted to see you? In her office?"

"All right. Please let her know I'm here."

Felicity looked confused.

"With your phone. The big black one on your

desk."

She bestowed a patronizing smile on him. "Why would I do that, Eli?"

"In case she's busy now and she doesn't want to be interrupted."

Felicity rolled her eyes as if exasperated by a dull-witted child. "You work here, don't you? Can't you knock on her door and ask her yourself?"

"Yes, of course," he agreed. "You have enough on your plate as it is."

\*\*\*\*

Claudia had the drawn look of a mother who'd been up all night with a sick baby. The truth of the matter wasn't far off. Elbows on her desk, she cradled her chin on interwoven fingers and regarded Eli with droopy eyes, beige makeup unsuccessfully concealing the dark, pouched flesh beneath them.

"First things first," she said. "You've met our niece, Felicity?"

Eli nodded. "A pleasant girl. Perfect for reception."

"Do you think so?" Claudia forced a smile. "I think she might be helpful at In-Spire."

"And leave the front desk unstaffed?" He fidgeted. "I hope you won't consider this inappropriate—"

"Speak frankly, Eli."

He leaned forward and spoke in a confidential tone. "Your niece is a very beautiful girl, Claudia. And congenial. The ideal representative for Hill Realty—at the reception desk here. Much better than Mary in that client-facing role." Was he laying it on too thick?

"She's something else, isn't she? If we'd been blessed with a daughter, I'd have hoped for a girl like Felicity." Claudia settled back in her chair. "She's a psych major, catching up on a couple of courses she missed, but quite brilliant. It isn't business admin, but it's a practical degree in other ways. She's miles ahead of the pack in understanding people, and I don't have to remind you how crucial that is in our business."

Eli had no ready comment. Thankfully, Claudia filled the silence with a wink and a knowing smile. "If you promise to behave, I'll let Felicity shadow you."

"You don't have to do that," said Eli.

"Nonsense. I insist. She can get a feel for the business and help you entertain investors."

*If* said investors could tolerate her high-pitched voice and brainless questions. "I'll let you know when we're ready for an intern," he agreed noncommittally.

"That brings me to the second matter." Claudia's jaw clenched briefly and her lips formed a straight pencil line. "Mary Rose. Stephen says you're struggling to get the office up and running. How's her performance? Be honest."

Honestly? Spectacular. The grip on that soft hand. Eli coughed nervously. "Exceeding expectations. Mary's diligent, keen to learn. It's my fault we're behind schedule. I've—had a lot on my plate." Wincing, he averted his eyes as if in turmoil. He had to think of a fast excuse for his slow progress. Dead cousin? Car accident? Kitchen fire?

"I know. Stephen told me." Claudia put her hand across the desk, palm up. Eli swallowed hard and placed his hand over hers to accept her comfort. "It must be so hard for you," she soothed.

Eli nodded. He didn't dare look up.

She stroked his hand. "I can't imagine how awful it is. To suffer from such a serious condition and try to hide it. My sister had colitis. Went from a hundred forty down to ninety-five pounds. And the cramping." Claudia clutched her abdomen with her free hand. "The diarrhea! Stephen told me you're incontinent."

So Stephen hadn't told her about the underwear. Eli snatched his hand back and shook a virile fist in the air. "I'm feeling better now. Much stronger."

"That's my Eli. Putting on a brave face. If there's anything you ever need, anything I can do…"

"Thank you, Claudia," Eli said solemnly. "That means a lot."

"You're younger than I am, but you're so wise, like an old kindred soul."

Oh no. She was corralling him.

"Listen to me. I sound like Jonquil." Claudia sighed and gave her head a vigorous shake. "I realize you were feeling sick at the time, but how did you find Stephen yesterday?"

"Uh…normal?"

"Normal. Not wound up? Pupils like saucers and talking a mile a minute?"

"No, not that I noticed."

Claudia crossed her arms and sniffed away the threat of tears. "Okay. Maybe it was an isolated incident, but he came home late last night, hours after he said he'd return, and made the wild claim that he's going to earn seven figures this year—this with a gross income of precisely zero dollars for the first quarter."

"Maybe he will," said Eli. "It's not uncommon in real estate."

"Not for you and not for me. But Stephen? I'm worried, Eli. He's super confident. So grandiose. He bought himself a Rolex."

"I'll watch him and if I see any signs—"

"Thank you," Claudia whispered.

Eli reached for her tissue box and passed one to her. She dabbed away a tear, careful not to smear her perfectly applied mascara.

"I could use a hug," she said.

Claudia went to him, and Eli held her as requested. When her hand strayed down his back, he slid out of her embrace as kindly as he could. Not kindly enough, for Claudia turned to the window and didn't speak. Anything he said would hurt her more.

He'd resorted to a series of ridiculous lies to protect Mary's honor. If he didn't play his lousy hand with more skill, all three Hills would line up against him like a three-soldier firing squad. His job didn't matter—he could join a different agency—but In-Spire, his reputation, and his future with Mary mattered.

\*\*\*\*

Mary separated her wet laundry into two dryers, one for jeans and towels and the other for light items, pushed coins into the payment mechanisms, and set the temperatures. Despite a locked entrance, thievery was rampant in the building—even ratty, "theft-proof" garments sometimes vanished—and she preferred to camp out on a folding chair rather than leave the laundry room and risk the disappearance of her things. She'd brought a book, *Applied Epistemology,* but it bored her senseless, and soon she found herself mesmerized by the swirling colors of her clothing tumbling behind tempered glass.

As she stared into the drums, ideas mixed and folded in myriad variations in her brain. The sight of a striped stocking lodged between the glass and the rubber seal and flapping in the circular wind struck her like a Zen master's paddle. At once, the title for her dissertation blinked into her head as if its words lit a marquee in flashing bulbs.

*Territories of Desire and Greed: Marking the Border Between Amorality and Immorality*

She had a theme that was rich with potential. Mary couldn't wait to get started on her proposal. She pulled her phone out of the pouch of her hoodie and put together a rudimentary outline to send to Gabriel. This topic was right up his alley. Best of all, she was one step closer to investigating it from the real-world perspective of Eli's bed.

****

For three full days, Mary labored on her proposal. At last, as the streetlights flicked on outside the living room window, she clicked Send and her file landed in Gabriel's inbox. She received an immediate reply that he was away from his office until later in the week and checking email infrequently. Whatever.

Mary often felt hollow after completing important, difficult work. From grant applications to articles, a writer could always improve something, a fact that pestered her until she received feedback. This proposal had to clear a high bar.

She stretched, rose from her chair, and stretched again. "Sent!" she proclaimed.

Dominic emerged from the kitchen, drying his hands on a tea towel. "Well done!"

"Alas, that's not for you nor I to judge."

"Did you do your best?"

"Yes." Of this, she was certain.

"Then I say 'Huzzah, Mary Rose. Well done!' You

should celebrate."

"I think we have a little wine left in the box."

"Mary, Mary, Mary. That will not do." Dominic crossed his arms and slowly shook his head. "After you, the person who'll be most pleased by this momentous achievement is Eli. You must call him and share your glad tidings. He'll want to celebrate with you."

"Okay. Where should I tell him to meet us?"

"Not us. Just the two of you. And he knows the best places, so let him decide." Dominic picked up her phone and handed it to her.

"You sure? You've been bringing me tea and sandwiches for days."

"That, my dear, is another reason why I can't tag along. I've been stuck on the Mary Rose channel twenty-four seven, and I need some man time."

Mary smiled and hugged him. "Thank you, Dominic."

****

An hour later, she stood at the curb of the semicircular driveway in front of the building to save Eli the trouble of parking. He pulled up in his BMW and she hopped in.

"You didn't let me open the door for you." He laughed.

"Are we on a date or something?"

"Feels like it." Eli put the car in gear, and they drove onto St. Dunstan's Avenue.

He had to merge into the tail end of rush-hour traffic, and he kept his eyes on the road, which afforded Mary the liberty of an admiring stare. He wore a sweater and jeans—and he wore them well.

"Are you hungry?" Eli asked as he signaled and

changed lanes.

"Yes. Starving." She'd eaten her last peanut butter and jelly sandwich hours ago.

"Me too. Do you like sushi?"

"Yes." Like it? She loved it.

"Then we'll head down to my neighborhood. I know a good place. Friendly, and the fish is fresh."

Eli turned onto Main and risked a long look at an old, yellow brick building. "That's the Buttonville Lofts," he said. "It's a repurposed button factory. I think they did zippers and hook fasteners too."

The late Victorian edifice took up the entire block. Some of its tall windows were curtained, and others shone in a warm suppertime glow, but most of the windows were dark. "It's half empty," said Mary.

"Or half full and filling quickly. We're a stone's throw from the university and this old industrial district is gentrifying. They have fantastic promo material." He zipped round the corner to view the building's south flank. "You should invest."

"Me? I have student loans. Overdue bills. An empty wallet," argued Mary. "I don't even know where I'll be in five years."

"Details, details. The carrying costs for a Buttonville studio are less than your rent and you'd build some equity in an appreciating asset."

"Eli, even if I could scrape together a down payment, no bank would give me a mortgage. The only lender who would take me seriously is a guy named Guido who enforces his terms with a crowbar."

"You're wrong, Mary. You just have to think creatively."

"The lottery?"

"Co-investors. Or rent to own." Eli did a quick U-turn. "We'll come back another day."

"Will we?"

"We will." He glanced sideways at her and offered a heart-melting smile. "Now tell me all about the proposal you submitted."

It had to be bad luck to discuss her work before it was approved, but she couldn't help herself. Eli encouraged her with an occasional "Really?" and a "That's so fascinating!" as she held forth on the topic of desire and greed. A half-hour later, he parked the car, and Mary wondered if the gods of academia would overlook her temptation of fate.

Chapter Eight

Although it was only a dress rehearsal and not an introduction to the true Klassen family, Eli felt nervous as he walked hand in hand with Mary from the parking lot to the Takamatsu Sushi Bar. He wanted Yuka and Kenji Ikeda to like her and for her to like them.

He paused as they neared the restaurant and turned to Mary. "You're about to meet two special people. I told them about you, though I didn't tell them we were coming tonight, in case you didn't like sushi. Which you do. So here we are." Did he sound nervous?

"Like the movie, 'Meet the Parents'?" Mary joked.

Perceptive. "Uh, yeah…kind of… Listen—maybe it's too soon. If you'd rather go somewhere else—"

"Eli, I want to eat here. With you. You've met Dominic and we survived, barely, and I'd like to meet your friends."

She reached up and straightened his jacket collar, though it didn't need it, a small intimacy that touched him. Eli took Mary's hand again and they passed through the sliding doors and navy curtains.

"*Irashaimase!*" Ikeda's face lit in surprise, and he smiled and bowed deeply to Mary. "Welcome to Takamatsu." Before Mary could respond, he called, "Yuka! Eri-kun is here."

"Ask him if he wants *inarizushi* with his soba," Yuka called back.

"He says he does," replied Ikeda. He put a finger to his lips, then gestured to the stools at the corner of the bar.

Thusly perched, they waited in silent smiles. A minute later, Yuka appeared with a large bowl. "What? Two of you! Eri-kun! You should have told me we have a special guest," she scolded, then set the bowl in front of Mary.

"I thought I'd surprise you," said Eli. "This is Mary."

"So you *are* real girl! I thought Eri-kun was lying to make me stop asking why he's single. And you're so pretty, too. I'll get tea. Or sake is better? Do you know how to use chopsticks? Oh—I forgot." She bowed. "Welcome to Takamatsu. I'm Yuka."

"Thank you, Yuka," said Mary. "I'm not very skilled with chopsticks."

A half-truth to appeal to Yuka's maternal impulses and draw her in? It worked, for Yuka sat on the stool next to Mary and smiled in a nurturing way. "I show you. First, you break them apart." When Eli asked about his food, Yuka pretended to be cross. "You must wait. Ladies first."

Ikeda grunted. "*Douzo.* For you." He pushed a plate of nigiri across the counter to Eli and whispered behind his hand, "*Unagi*, for male stamina."

Blushing, Eli nodded. "*Arigato.*"

The sake came next, then more food, and then more sake, though Eli switched to green tea. After the last diners settled their bill and left, Ikeda, Yuka, and Mary became very merry indeed. The introduction was a success. As Mary and Yuka laughed over Ikeda's lewd paper napkin origami, Eli sipped his tea and wondered what the Klassen family would make of the progressive, atheist intellectual who'd stormed into his heart and set up camp.

****

"Let's pretend I'm a teenage girl in Eden Springs," suggested Mary as they walked from Takamatsu to the car. "It's a pleasant evening for March, and we're on our first date."

"Do we go to the same church?" asked Eli.

"Sure," shrugged Mary.

"In that case, I'd have to take you home and apologize to your father for allowing you to drink alcohol."

"No way. And if I weren't tipsy?"

"I'd still take you home. It's eleven and past your curfew."

Strange. Eli was born in the same country in the same decade and spoke the same language as she, yet Mary felt as if she were comparing cultures with an exchange student from a distant nation.

"Let's begin again since we're in imagination land," said Mary. "I'm sixteen and it's only eight o'clock. I drank lemonade at the sock hop, and we had a swell time, but the gym was stuffy, and Betty Sue was mean to me, so we left. Then what?"

"Your scenario is not only anachronistic, it's impossible," said Eli. "The Brethren Church forbids dancing. We wouldn't attend a school dance."

"God. That's weird."

"Uh-uh...careful, Mary. You're taking the Lord's name in vain." Eli threw a bill into the overturned, faux fur hat of a bag lady and acknowledged her with a friendly nod. "She's new on this block," he murmured.

Mary shook her head in confusion. "Eli, I feel as if you grew up on another planet. Okay, let's cancel the dancing because it's against the eleventh commandment or whatever. What would we do instead?"

"That's easy." Eli grinned. "I'd take you for a drive and we'd wind up in a quiet, hidden-away spot at the lakeshore."

"And would you kiss me?"

"Well, you're awfully pretty. I'd definitely try."

Laughing, Mary punched his shoulder. He asked, "What would Miss Mary Rose, age sixteen, do on a first date? I mean here, in the city?"

"Sixteen-year-old Mary didn't date. She hid in her room and read angsty vampire novels."

Eli regarded her with sympathy. She stared at the sidewalk to rebuff his pity.

"What would she have wanted to do?" he asked gently.

"She'd have wanted to go for a drive with a good-looking boy and wind up at the lakeshore and be kissed."

He unlocked the passenger door with his key fob and opened it. "Then let's go."

"Okay, but I might play hard to get," Mary joked as she got into the car.

"I hope you do." Eli carefully closed the door.

As he strode round the front of the car, she realized he was only half joking. His chivalry wasn't an act. Unexamined patriarchal beliefs were baked into the very marrow of his bones. He might don the persona of a worldly man, but underneath, Eli was happier when their interaction conformed to narrow, mid-twentieth-century gender roles. He was generous and protective toward women and fiercely competitive with men. He liked being in the driver's seat, both literally and figuratively, and she had to figure out if this presented a problem. If she let herself fall in love with him, she didn't want to become his potted ornamental flower, lovingly tended but rootbound, weak, and stunted.

They drove for several blocks in silence. Mary opened her window an inch, and a refreshing wind lifted her hair. "Music?" she asked.

"Sure. Whatever you want."

She played with the dashboard gadgetry and found a singable Chili Peppers song. Eli didn't know the lyrics. "Let me guess. The Brethren weren't into music?" she goaded.

"Only hymns," said Eli. "To my profound regret."

"The soundtrack of my childhood was rock music, everything from bluesy stuff to grunge and death metal. Music was the one thing Mother and I had in common," said Mary. "If you want an introduction, I can make a playlist for you."

"Sure. I'd like that." Eli checked over his shoulder and geared up to merge onto the expressway.

"Where are we going?"

"East side. Five minutes on the highway, then down to Sugar Point."

"I think I've only been there once when I was about twelve. We didn't have a car, and it's not convenient by transit."

Eli looked across at her, smiling with incredulity. "You don't know how to drive, do you?" he guessed, regaining his masterly footing after his confession of musical ignorance.

"Affirmative," Mary admitted. "I didn't have

access to a car to practice and it wasn't a priority."

"I'll teach you."

"What if I don't want to learn?"

"You do, don't you? I mean, it's a basic life skill, like frying an egg or knowing how to swim." Though the traffic was fast, he chanced a glance from the road to her.

"Are you calling my competence into question, Eli?"

"Yes." He redirected his eyes to the road and accelerated around a van. "Everyone who's capable should know how to operate a motor vehicle."

*And that's that,* Mary mentally finished. She pushed aside her prickly defensiveness. She *did* want to learn to drive. "Okay, teacher. Teach me. Not tonight, though. I'm disgracefully sodden, and I'd cause an accident."

"Next Friday morning in a mall parking lot. It's a holiday—Good Friday for the faithful—and the mall is the safest place for the first lesson."

As they exited from the expressway and drove through empty streets, they fell into silence again. He parked under a willow, its bare fronds hanging in graceful arcs under a nearly full moon, high in the sky.

Eli tossed the key fob onto the dash. "Play something slower please, DJ," he said. "Set the mood."

She chose a Blue Rodeo song and the lead's mournful tenor filled the car. Maybe it was too much. Too sentimental. She reached to change the song, but Eli grasped her wrist.

"No, Mary. Leave it. I like this."

Eli took her into his arms and his mouth commanded hers in a deep, sensual kiss, and there he lingered. Her body cried for the succor of his touch. She slid her hand up his thigh to find him, but he trapped her hand with his own and blocked her advance.

He nuzzled the margin of hair and skin at her temple and spoke gently to soothe the sting. "You made a vow and when you touch me in that way, I find it hard to stop."

"You'd use force?" she teased. Her lips brushed against the sinew of his neck. They'd fooled around so many times before. Why should tonight be different?

"One night, I might go too far," he whispered into her hair.

What a strange thing to say. Mary withdrew her hand. Obviously, he hadn't received the standard, public school, sex-ed instruction that insisted 'no meant no' and that permission could be revoked in an instant. She turned to put some distance between their bodies. "I have to know: have you ever forced a woman to have sex with you?"

"You mean raped someone?"

She nodded, afraid of the answer.

"No." His brows knit, and his jaw tightened as if he were offended by the question.

"Have you ever had rough sex?"

He hesitated. "Yes, because it was what she wanted. I didn't hurt her."

"How do you know that?"

"I asked her, and she answered me."

"By 'her', do you mean Claudia?"

"Come on, Mary. Do you think I'd play rough with my boss? Anyway, you shouldn't ask me that question."

"Do you think I want it? Rough sex?"

"What is this? An inquisition?"

"No, Eli. Not at all. I'm wondering what's going on in your head."

"Okay then, no. You probably don't." He exhaled and looked directly into her eyes, leaving no room for dishonesty."Actually, yes. I think you might want that."

She felt sick.

Eli continued. "You're not a naïve, innocent girl and yet you toy with me as if you have no freaking clue how men are. You do risky things and withdraw, and that sends a signal to me that you're out of control and you want me to take over. So I am."

"That's not true. I made a vow with a clear boundary. I'm in control."

Eli shook his head. "You have the ultimate veto. That's true. But your vow doesn't give you control when we're alone in a car on a desolate beach. If I wasn't a gentleman, or if you were with some random jerk you met on Tinder, your game could get you into trouble."

She wanted to cover her ears, but she sat as still as a rock and listened as he plowed on. "As for your vow, I see that as a tool. It increases the value of a precious thing that you were giving away for free. So yes, Mary. A good hard ride with a man you care about, after you've earned it, might be what you want."

"Wow. Umm, okay." She gazed through the windshield at the reflection of the moon in the black water without really seeing it.

He asked, "Am I wrong?"

"I don't know." She forced herself not to cry. Her beliefs about herself and womanhood and power were collapsing under the shifting weight of a century of feminist dogma. Eli pushed against a pillar, and everything was falling. She didn't ever want to submit to a man, yet she wanted to submit to him. Her silence spoke for her.

Eli slipped his arm around her shoulders and hugged her. "I won't hurt you. You can trust me."

"A minute ago, you told me I couldn't trust you."

"That's not true. I made you stop and I kept you safe. Anyway, you shouldn't be ashamed of wanting what you want."

"Driving lessons?" Mary smiled, though her eyes glistened.

"Sure." Eli kissed her on the cheek and started the car. "That and more."

As they sped down the highway, he asked, "Would you send me your proposal?"

"Okay. But have a pillow handy. It's soporific."

"That, Miss Mary Rose, is for me to judge."

Chapter Nine

"Easy! Nice and slow!" said Eli. "Good, good. A little more gas—"

Thunk. Mary let the clutch out too quickly, for what...the twentieth time? He wouldn't draw her attention to the small audience she'd attracted at the edge of the parking lot. Or the spotty prodigy who'd taken his dad's VW up to second within the first ten minutes of their lesson. Maybe the dad would agree to swap students before Eli lost his cool.

He took a deep breath. Patience. "Okay, Mary. Make sure you're in first. The first to the left of that first."

"You don't have to patronize me," Mary hissed. "I knew that was third."

"But you were in first already, so there was no reason to—"

Her eyes hurled daggers.

"Never mind. You've found first gear. Now, press the clutch right down and turn the key in the ignition...and very, very slowly, let out the clutch and give a little gas with your right foot."

This time the engine roared, and the car lurched forward with a pained squeal. Mary screamed as if she'd discovered Mrs. Bates in the fruit cellar.

"Easy on the gas! Just give'r a little bit!"

Mary looked at her feet.

"Steer, steer! Away from the light post!" Eli grabbed the steering wheel and corrected course.

"I'm steering," Mary shouted.

"Yes, you are." Eli sighed.

With knuckles like snow-capped mountains, she gripped the wheel, turning it this way and that. Thank God the VW duo were now practicing three-point turns well out of harm's way.

"Try driving in a big circle to the right."

She went left. It didn't matter. They'd wind up in the same place.

"Well done, Mary. A full three hundred sixty degrees. Now the other way."

"Left?"

"Whatever. Just keep your foot steady on the gas and watch where you're going."

Fuck. A police car.

With divided attention, Eli coached Mary and watched the officer park, lumber out of the cruiser, and lean against the hood, coffee in hand, to watch the lessons. Time and a half on Good Friday and free entertainment. Not a bad life.

"Do you have your license with you?" Eli asked nonchalantly.

Mary caught sight of the cruiser. "License?" she choked.

"Your learner's permit."

"I never got one." Eyes wide with panic, she slammed on the brake with her left foot and the car thudded to a halt in a toxic cloud of burnt rubber.

Eli engaged the parking brake and turned the key in the ignition. "I think that's enough for the first lesson."

Mary released her hands from the wheel and flexed

fingers, then looked across at Eli, gray eyes ıdlike behind her glasses. "How did I do?"

"It was your first lesson," Eli evaded. He'd taught younger siblings and cousins to drive all manner of vehicles—cars, trucks, tractors, snowmobiles, dirt bikes—and Mary, bar none, was his worst student by a country mile.

An ominous pressure rose in his forehead. He needed caffeine and Advil.

"You didn't answer my question," Mary cajoled.

"Rome wasn't built in a day," said Eli. "Driving's a skill like any other. It takes practice."

"And?"

"I commend your enthusiasm."

Mary's shoulders sagged under her denim jacket. "I was awful, wasn't I."

"You did your best and that's most the important thing." Along with a professional instructor in a well-insured car with an automatic transmission, a sign on its roof, and an extra brake.

"Thank you," said Mary.

He tipped his head toward the cop. "I think we should switch places before Toronto's finest takes more interest in your novel driving style."

\*\*\*\*

It was a relief to sit in the passenger seat. Mary disliked feeling incompetent, and Eli was so jumpy about his precious car. When she could afford them, she'd take formal driving lessons.

Back on the expressway, he drove aggressively, darting around other vehicles and switching lanes for the gain of a few yards. Was he disappointed by her ineptitude?

It was he who suggested they go back to his place and order pizza. Was she meant to decline? Too late now. She fiddled with the radio and found a classic rock station to cover the silence. Good old nihilistic Nirvana. Perfect after a disastrous driving lesson on the day that marked the Savior's death. A joke was too much of a risk, so she watched Eli drive.

She should've paid more attention to what drivers actually do before trying it herself. Eli didn't look at his hands and feet. He looked through the windshield, glanced in a mirror or over his shoulder occasionally, and left his limbs under their own command. Face relaxed and breath even, he controlled the car as if it were an extension of himself. Which it kind of was, since they were buckled into it.

"Do you think I'll ever drive as well as you?" Mary asked.

"Me?" He glanced at her with his striking dark eyes, his mouth in the sensual curve of a sneer. "No. Of course not."

"No? Elaborate please."

"You're twenty-six, right? You're making a late start. I'm twenty-nine and I've been driving since I was twelve. That's a head start of seventeen years. If skill is a function of practice, which it is, you'll never catch up."

*You'll never catch up.* A gauntlet thrown to her feet. She might not catch up as a driver, but she would in other ways.

When she didn't reply—because what would be the point—he said, "That doesn't mean you can't become a safe driver, Mary."

They were back on narrow downtown streets. Eli's

building stood among a canyon wall of towers. As they approached a closed garage door, he slipped his card key from the visor.

"Nice building," she said.

"It's a good investment."

The door rolled back, and they drove into the building's dank, underground maw.

Investment. Not *home*. Not *place to live*. Mary's envy of Eli's swanky address vanished.

****

Mary stared straight forward as if riding the elevator with a stranger. He should've driven her home so he could take some painkillers and go to bed, but he'd been looking forward to this day all week. And a profitable week it was. While she wrapped up the semester, he'd bagged the sale of the south penthouse to a pack of horny Saudis *without* having to procure local female talent to close the deal, and he got the office ready for its official Saturday opening while managing to avoid all three Hills. A hat trick worthy of celebration—if he could only loosen the screws in his temples.

The elevator doors slid open and Eli followed Mary into the corridor, guided her to his unit, and opened the door.

"No key?" she asked.

"Nothing to steal."

"You're right," she muttered, kicking off her sneakers and looking around. "You live like a monk."

Not true. He had a decent sofa and a queen-size bed.

"Or an inmate." She took off her jacket and dropped it onto her sneakers. "What is that color, Eli?

On your walls."

"Whatever was in style three years ago. Builders' gray?"

"What a view!" She went to the living room window. "I can see all the way to Sugar Point!"

"Better than TV," Eli called from the kitchen. God. The pain. A rivulet of cold sweat cut a line between his shoulder blades. He washed down three Advil with some flat Coke, leftover from a takeout meal. Right—pizza. He should ask her about toppings.

Mary stood by the window, goddess-like, shimmering...because his bloody eyes couldn't focus. "What do you like on your pizza?" he asked.

"Eli, it's only eleven. Can't it wait a bit?"

"No. I mean yes. Yes, it can wait." Each syllable etched a groove on the interior of his skull.

She turned and cocked her head to the side. "Is everything okay?"

"Yes. We'll have pizza later." Jesus. He sounded autistic. Or angry.

"Maybe I shouldn't be here. I can go—"

"No. Please stay, Mary." It came out like a plea. Gingerly, he lowered himself onto the couch and propped his feet on a wooden crate. "Sit with me."

"Eli, you don't want me here."

Too loud. "Shh, Mary. I do. If you won't sit, can you run the cold water..."

"What?"

"Headache. If I get an ice-cold cloth over my forehead, it helps."

"Oh."

Eli closed his eyes. He'd ask Mary to close the blinds. Grandma used to rub an oily salve on his neck and forehead when he got this way. Yet it wasn't the salve that soothed him. It was her abiding presence. It was not suffering alone.

Mary returned and pressed a cold terrycloth to his head.

He closed his eyes and said, "In a minute, I'm going to lie down in bed. It will help me, more than I can say right now, if you would stay with me. Nearby."

"I'm here, Eli."

"Thank you. There's not much to do here, but you can use my laptop. The password is 'Maryrose'."

\*\*\*\*

Mary opened the bedroom door a few inches and peered in. Stripped down to his T-shirt and boxers, Eli slept with a pillow over his head, curled on his side like a baby, chest rising and falling in a slow rhythm. Later, if he felt better, she could snuggle in beside him. She padded over to the bedside table and replaced the half-empty glass of lukewarm water with a full, icy-cold one, then left the room, closing the door behind her.

Back to Eli's laptop. She'd snooped only enough to discover that he wasn't into porn, and that he'd actually downloaded her proposal. Now she had to get some work done. No more procrastinating on Substack. She reached into the recesses of her memory to retrieve her password and managed to log into the university portal on the second try. Still nothing from Gabriel—it was a holiday—but there were more essay submissions from the Thursday evening class for her reading delight. Ready, set, mouse click.

*How Nietzsche's Philosophy Helps Performance*
*Philosophy 307 Theories on Justice*
*By Megan M. Morris*

*Friedrich Nietzsche was born in Germany in 1844 except it wasn't called Germany then because it was still called Prussia and he was named after the King who had the same name and birthday as him. Nietzsche is the famous philosopher who stated, "What doesn't kill me makes me stronger." This essay will argue that Nietzsche's quote is a useful idea to keep in mind when life is hard or difficult or when you have a goal that seems impossible to achieve and—*

Weary with boredom, Mary rubbed her eyes. Her stomach growled. She went to the kitchen to find something snackable.

As she opened the fridge door, she made a closer examination of the child's drawing of a pink pig in a princess getup that Eli had taped to the freezer door. The picture was dedicated to 'Uncle Eli' and the artist was 'Rebekah, age 8', as credited in an old-fashioned, childish cursive. Eli had a family who cared enough to send him this.

The contents of the fridge were dispiriting. If condiments in various states of decay and an inch of cola in the bottom of a plastic bottle were a meal, she was all set. In the cupboard stood a row of mason jars filled with jewel-colored liquids and jellies, all sealed. She wouldn't touch those sacred objects.

Plan A, ordering pizza, was the most sensible option. A large pizza, because Eli might be hungry when he woke. It would be expensive. She'd seen a stack of flyers on the table. Perhaps he had a coupon.

Mary shuffled through the brightly inked cardstock and newsprint. Pizza-Pizza, Dominoes, Little Caesar's, Papa Gino's—the last one sounded authentic. Maybe there was a real Gino tossing dough in the air while belting out Puccini instead of a sullen adolescent with ears buds shoveling frozen discs into an oven. Papa Gino offered two dollars off a large pepperoni. And what was this? A letter.

From Mrs. Abraham Klassen of RR #2, Eden Springs. The edge of the envelope was torn. Eli was fast asleep. He wouldn't mind, would he? If she read it? Since it was already open? And so, she did read it, three times through, the letter's poignancy intensifying a vicarious pang of loss in her jaded urbanite's heart with each reading.

Today was Good Friday. Eli's family would attend church. Kids would dye eggs and women would bake sweet breads for Easter. Men, well, who knew what they did. Eli, that's who. Whatever his reasons for leaving Eden Springs and the Brethren community, Eli would miss celebrating Easter with his family. Maybe not every Klassen, but some of them. Mary tucked the letter into its envelope and slipped it under the flyers, where she found it. When Eli awoke, she'd have a hard time unknowing what she knew.

****

A beam of light at the edge of a crooked blind cast the room in hazy shapes and shadows. The door was closed, the room quiet apart from the low hum of distant traffic and the downtown airport. She was still here. Though Mary didn't make a sound, he sensed her presence.

His head ached, though nothing like before. Water. He rolled over, reached for the glass, coughed when it hit his dry throat. Like a downpour on a parched field, rainwater spilling into ditches.

The door opened slowly. She was checking on him.

"I'm awake," he said.

"Do you need anything, Eli?"

"You."

"There's pizza."

"In a bit."

Mary snuggled next to him, and they lay together in a damp cloud of linen. The room was stuffy, probably smelled of sick body odor, but he didn't feel like getting up to crack a window open.

"How are you feeling?" she asked.

"Better. Weak. After a bad headache, I feel kind of limp and wrung out."

"Have you seen a doctor?"

"No, not recently. Doctors are pill-pushers. I don't want to get addicted to anything."

Mary's muscles tensed. He kissed her forehead to forestall a concerned scolding. "I've had these headaches for years. My grandma used to make a salve and an herbal tea that helped."

"Maybe your family could send you some."

"Nah. I have Advil. And you."

Mary wiggled in closer and rested her head in the hollow below his shoulder. He liked it when women did this. He wrapped his arms around her body and held her. This wasn't the way he imagined welcoming Mary into his bed. This was better. She'd stayed by his side when he needed her. He could trust her.

"What kind of pizza is it?"

"Pepperoni with onion, green pepper, mushroom, and tomato so you get your vegetables. There's a Caesar salad, too."

"Thank you, Mary."

"Hey, it's a business expense."

Chapter Ten

Mary dressed with care on Saturday morning. Blouse and blazer, fitted trousers, and boots with enough heel to satisfy Eli and Claudia. Hair swept up in a silver clasp, dangly earrings, mascara, and lipstick, and she was ready. It was only 10:30. Enough time to go to her desk, check her bank balance, and answer a couple of emails.

April's rent was coming due. If she only made the minimum payment on her Mastercard she could just cover it. What? Holy shit! There was over ten thousand dollars in her checking account! Mary laughed in disbelief and Dominic, a human moth drawn to any sound of joy, poked his head through the doorway of the kitchen where he was repotting plants.

"I'm rich." Mary stared at the number. $10,450.45.

"How rich?" Dominic stuck his trowel in a soil-filled pot and wiped his hands on his apron.

"About ten thousand dollars richer than I expected." She clicked on the balance. Eli. It had to be. "Problem is I didn't earn it. Eli just gave it to me."

"Quite right. You must return the money," Dominic sniffed with a sanctimonious air. "Ten thousand dollars is pocket change for Monsieur Klassen, but you're not a charity case. I mean, the nerve of the man."

"But I haven't been contributing, Dominic. In the

last month, all I've done of real value is edit a document that Felicity Hill screwed up. When I show up at the office, I just get in Eli's way."

"Ten thousand dollars. You must feel so dirty."

Mary swiveled her chair to face Dominic, who stood in the doorway with his nose in the air and an offended scowl on his face. "Never mind that he's paying you from the tens of thousands of dollars in commission he earned this week alone. You have principles!"

"It's the power dynamic. I'm self-reliant. Independent. Equal. If he gives me money, it makes me beholden to him."

"What's so bad about that? I'd gladly let a stud like Eli behold me."

"I'm a feminist."

Dominic rolled his eyes. "A feminist with overdue bills."

"There'll be strings attached."

"Strings," panted Dominic. "Grab my bridle!"

"Expectations. Unstated but ever present."

"Lucky you."

"I'll have to talk to him." Mary turned back to the screen. The money was kind of nice. Actually, it was super nice.

Back in the kitchen, Dominic sang to his plants. "Mary, Mary, quite contrary, won't let her garden grow."

"Because I *do* have principles," called Mary.

"And overdue bills in a row," sang Dominic.

****

Mary entered the sales office as Claudia pirouetted with a can of Febreze spraying from her raised hand like a citrus-scented liberty torch. Dressed in matching smock dresses and sequined scarves, Jonquil and Siobhan lined up wine glasses next to a fan of cocktail napkins on the cloth-draped reception desk. An air of nervous anticipation filled the room.

Mary greeted the trio, hung her coat, and found Eli in the kitchenette. He wasn't alone. While he knelt in front of the fridge and crammed platters of sushi next to bottles of white wine, a blond girl bent over him. Her breasts hovered over his head like twin dirigibles buzzing a field.

"That's it, Eli." The girl spoke in a breathy, effervescent voice. "If you set the bottles sixty-nine style, everything will fit."

"From Takamatsu?" Mary asked to make her presence known.

"Yup. Ikeda-san's best," Eli said without looking up.

The girl turned and thrust her chest forward aggressively, or so it seemed. Mary extended her hand. "I'm Mary Rose."

The girl waved away her hand and substituted an elbow bump. "Felicity Hill. Stephen and Claudia's niece?"

"Yes, of course," said Mary. "You're working at the reception desk in the main office."

"For now." The girl turned and batted her absurdly thick lashes at Eli. "Aunt Claudia wants me to learn from the best, so I might be working here soon."

Now Eli was standing, too, and Mary saw his gaze drift briefly to Felicity's cashmere covered boobs. Unbelievable. The girl spoke like a cartoon character but apparently, that didn't bother him, given her other assets. Mary had read about this phenomenon in a dog-eared *Cosmopolitan* at a walk-in hair salon. The article stated there were two kinds of males, ass guys and breast guys, with a quiz to inform the reader which type she was dating. Eli was definitely the latter, utterly distracted by the presence of hypertrophic female breast tissue.

"Well, I'm sure Eli has given you a warm welcome," said Mary.

"Oh, he has." Giggle. "Haven't you, Eli?"

Eli smiled vacantly, cleared his throat, and checked his watch. "A half-hour to show time. Claudia and I like to hold a quick team meeting before events like this."

Mary was already backing out of the kitchenette.

They gathered in a circle, she and Felicity on either side of Eli, Jonquil and Siobhan opposite. Claudia took the floor and nodded to each of them.

"First, I regret to inform everyone that Stephen won't be with us today." She stared wistfully at the floor. "He's developed a sniffle, and with our enlightened knowledge of viruses and infection control, he has opted to do the responsible thing and remain at home today." She looked pointedly at Mary and sighed. "It's probably for the best."

"That's why I'm elbow bumping," squeaked Felicity.

Brittle as an ice sculpture, Claudia smiled. "You're so considerate of the health of others, Felicity. However, if a guest offers you their hand, I urge you to shake it. You may keep a small bottle of sanitizer on your person, to be used discreetly." She looked to Jonquil and Siobhan. "Refreshments?"

Jonquil stepped forward. "Siobhan and I have

several bottles of red wine at the desk, white chilling in the fridge, freshly pressed juices, mineral water, coffee, and tea. Eli?"

"Sushi, cheese and fruit platters, and a plate of cookies," he replied.

"Well done, Eli," Claudia purred, as if he'd been up all night baking. "And the sales packages?"

Felicity rocked forward on her toes. "Written, formatted, and ready, Aunt Claudia."

Mary broke in. "I had to edit—" Eli's elbow connected with her ribcage, though only hard enough to bruise her ego.

"Mary printed the document," he interrupted. "Thank you, Felicity. It's very well done." Yuck. Eli flashed a smile at the feather-brained girl, then looked to Claudia. "Mary and I collated the packages and I've put them on the table beside the scale model, along with the guest book and our business cards."

"Then we're ready. Agents from one to two p.m., and the general public from two to four. We unlock the doors in ten minutes. Stations?"

"Jonquil and I are tending the bar," said Siobhan.

"I'm on meet and greet at the door. First impressions!" Felicity smirked at Mary.

"And Eli and I are handling sales," said Claudia. She also turned to Mary. "That leaves you on clean up. Crumpled napkins, shrimp tails, dirty glasses. You know the routine."

Mary nodded. Ten thousand bucks for maid duty. Later she'd even throw in a hand job if Eli behaved and unglued his eyes from the two elephants in the room.

"Remember our motto," said Claudia.

"Future focused?" squeaked Felicity.

*"Eyes on the prize!"* corrected Claudia.

\*\*\*\*

Mary wiped the counter in the kitchenette and rinsed and wrung the sponge, then tied up a garbage bag and deposited it by the front door. Done. Solo. Because Eli told the others they'd handle clean-up, and after everyone left, he yacked on the phone, "doing deals."

"That went well." Eli stuck his shoeless feet on the coffee table and took a belt of red wine.

Mary poured herself a glass and sat in the armchair. "Cheers." She raised her glass in the air. The wine, from a bottle with a real cork, washed over her tongue in rich flavors of spice, but she was in no mood to enjoy it.

"Cheers, way over there." Eli raised his glass in return and drank again. "We did it, Mary. A holiday Saturday was a risk, but it paid off. We even ran out of brochures."

"It was busy," she agreed sourly. Eli and Claudia had been in fine form—establishing rapport, flattering and jollying, easing visitors into an idealized vision of their clients or themselves in a luxury suite. She'd witnessed two real estate pros operating at the top of their game as she scurried around their ankles in domestic drudgery.

"We'll have to print more packages on Monday," said Eli. "And add the guestbook entries to the mailing list. I'll be tied up in follow-up calls."

"I'll do it. Unless Felicity replaces me."

"What? No. Why would you think that?"

"Oh, I don't know. I can think of a couple of enormous reasons."

"I'll pretend I don't know what you mean."

"How P.C. of you."

"Anyway, Felicity won't be working here."

"Really, Eli? She seemed pretty gung-ho on the idea, and she really likes you." Mary raised her voice to pre-schooler register. "Aunt Claudia wants me to learn the ropes from the best."

"You're jealous." Eli laughed.

"I am not. I just don't think it's appropriate for men—" Mary pointed her finger at Eli— "to stare at her breasts."

"Number one: I didn't do that."

"Did so."

"Did *not*."

"Did *so*."

"And number two," Eli continued, "she shouldn't wear tight sweaters if she doesn't want to attract attention, but since she does wear them, she draws eyes. Not mine though."

"Eli, you are so wrong about that. Your eyes were bulging out of their sockets."

"Let's drop it."

"Them."

"Now you're being childish. An accidental glance means nothing, and you know it." Eli shifted on the sofa and crossed his ankles the other way. Away from her. Creating distance. Maybe she was reading too much into his body language. Those damned *Cosmo* articles gave women a complex.

They drank in a silence so tense, Mary could burst it with a fruit-kebab skewer. Or with a humble admission.

"Hey," she said softly. "You're right. I'm jealous.

And I stared, too."

He looked back at her, half smiled, and patted the sofa cushion. "I hate arguing. Come on—"

"Me?" Mary batted her lashes in imitation of the fake ingénue who'd so unnerved her.

"Yeah. You and only you," said Eli.

Mary joined him, and after they'd arranged themselves in a warm snuggle, she said, "Thank you."

"For what?"

"For ten thousand dollars."

"Oh. Yeah. That," he said. "You earned it."

"But I didn't."

"Trust me. You did. My life is infinitely better since we started working together."

"Infinitely?"

"Well, maybe not infinitely. Now if you wore a little French maid outfit while you cleaned the place…something low-cut…no underwear."

"That, Mr. Eli Klassen, is exactly the problem. I'm turning into a lousy feminist in your company. Your simpering help meet."

"You know how to simper?"

Mary lightly batted his chest, and he bear-hugged her, pinning her arms to stop her mock assault.

They settled back in the sofa cushions together. Eli lazily twined her hair in his fingers. "Mary, you need money. You're in grad school. That's your priority. As long as you handle the routine secretarial stuff, I can run the show here. And you don't have to worry about money."

Mary sank further into his arms. Eli made everything sound simple and easy.

He said, "I told Dino I'd deliver leftovers to

Belgrave Park around six-thirty. Want to come with me?"

"Sure." Mary had never brought food to homeless people before. Despite his conventional social attitudes, Eli was opening doors and pulling her into unfamiliar worlds. He was old-fashioned yet radically open-minded, ruthless yet generous, wild yet self-disciplined. With Eli, a "yes" meant adventure.

****

After he dropped Mary off, Eli drove through late evening traffic, with music she'd chosen thumping low from the speakers. Spring weather meant more cyclists and skateboarders on the roads. He envied their freedom to dart around vehicles and bullet through alleys. Tomorrow he'd haul his bike out of the storage locker, pump up the tires, oil the chain, and go for an Easter Sunday ride. He'd buy a bike for Mary if she didn't have one.

Mary. So naïve, though she didn't see herself that way. University types were like that. They took themselves very seriously. When he bagged the wine for Belgrave Park, she looked horrified. He pretended not to understand her objection and jokingly accused her of wanting to keep a good vintage for herself.

How had it gone? "You can't take wine to people who are addicted," she'd protested. "You're harming them."

He pushed her buttons. "No harm in a fine Bordeaux."

What was the word she used? "Enabler."

"It's healthier than the cheap vodka they usually drink and it's a treat," he argued back. And so it was. Dino appreciated a fine wine as much as a sommelier in a Michelin-starred restaurant. Perhaps more. Wine, sushi, and cookies were a strange combo but the look of delight on Dino and his friends' faces made the errand worth it. To Mary's credit, she saw that. She was open-hearted and changed her mind when confronted with real people and real problems.

The feminism thing was frustrating. It was an ideology that shamed women for being women. For being nurturing, life-giving, kind, and sensual. Feminist women unconvincingly imitated men while dishonoring their natural qualities. Mary had far more power than she knew, a feminine power, but she didn't see it in herself. No one had taught her this.

Eli drove into the garage, parked, and went to the storage locker. Tomorrow. He'd ride up to St. Dunstan's Avenue and celebrate Easter with the woman he loved. It was too soon to tell her he loved her, yet it was what he felt.

Chapter Eleven

On Easter morning, Mary gathered her awakening senses by trying to focus on her textured ceiling, a plaster moonscape of mountains and dry lakes lit by a rising sun. It was a pointless endeavor without glasses or contacts. She'd fallen asleep while reading *Applied Epistemology* and hadn't closed her blinds.

Gabriel couldn't delay forever. She reached for her phone and glasses to check if he'd passed judgement on her proposal. Penny Wong, his closest collaborator on the faculty, had read it and praised her ideas as refreshing and original. "All it needs is Gabriel's rubber stamp for review by the committee," she'd said. Gabriel's "yes," however begrudgingly given and tempered with criticism, meant Mary could proceed, academically and with Eli.

Jeez. Finally. An email from one Gabriel A. Silverstein in her university account.

*Hi, Mary. This isn't well-developed. Lit review passably extensive. However, over-reaching in historical span. Was Jesus a philosopher or a cult leader?? Incoherent in key places. Will need major rewrite. See margin comments. I'll be in my office on Tuesday. BTW, have you finished marking the 202 papers?*

She couldn't breathe. Tears flooded her eyes. This was so fucking wrong. Gabriel might as well have grabbed his pretentious brass letter opener off his desk and stabbed her in the guts.

****

Three miles away, Eli woke early as well. Today, the Brethren would permit themselves the extravagance of potted lilies in church and enough ham and chocolate to put themselves into comas. He wouldn't mind missing the ecstatic "The Lord has Risen!" stuff, but he'd miss hiding eggs for his nieces and nephews. At least he had the distraction of brunch with Mary and Dominic. As he stretched at the east window and admired the rising sun, his phone rang. It was Mary.

"Hey."

She was crying. So choked up, she couldn't talk.

"Mary. Easy. What's wrong?"

"My…my proposal. Gabriel. He rejected it."

"That's awful."

"I got the email this morning." A tortured sob filled his ear.

"You worked so hard on it. Did he say why?"

"Does it matter? Too many themes. Incoherence. He wrote a bloody diatribe in the margin. All total bullshit. Or maybe he's right and my work is garbage. I don't know…"

"What he said *is* bullshit. I read your proposal last night. It's coherent. Hard reading for a mental midget like me but I followed it."

She blew her nose without setting down her phone.

"I thought your ideas were really cool," added Eli. "You even threw in the New Testament."

"I'm so frustrated. I gave it to another member of the committee, and she thought it would sail through the process, but, as my advisor, Gabriel holds all the cards. He won't allow it before the committee until I rewrite it and there's no guarantee he'll okay it then either. This is a massive setback." She started crying again.

"Hold tight. I'll be there in fifteen minutes."

"Thanks, Eli." She sobbed. "Apartment 210. Text and I'll buzz you in."

He dressed quickly, grabbed the gift bag of chocolate bunnies and wine he'd left by the door, and drove up to St. Dunstan Avenue.

\*\*\*\*

Eli nabbed the last of five spots in visitor parking, helped an elderly lady leading three unruly pugs into the drab foyer, and ran up the stairwell to the second floor. He knocked softly in case Dominic was still sleeping, and Mary opened the door. She looked worse than she sounded on the phone—eyes puffy, nose red, hair tied back in a bird's nest of a ponytail. He stepped into her narrow hallway, set the gift bag on a cluttered table, and hugged her.

Mary's body shook with the pain of a cruel betrayal, and she wept. There was nothing he could say to make it better. He could only hold her. When she ran out of tears, they went to the living room couch and sat together.

Dominic emerged from his room, saw them, and read the situation in an instant. "I'm going for a run," he said to Eli, and after giving Mary a long hug, he left in a flash of fluorescent Lycra.

Mary's voice was husky from crying. "This wasn't supposed to happen."

"No, it wasn't."

"It was my best work. Penny said so too. I poured

all I had into it. Now I'm stuck in this fucking Kafkaesque nightmare. I don't know what Gabriel wants. His criticism is contradictory. If I rewrite it the way he says to, it'll be incoherent nonsense and the committee will reject it. Also, he was deliberately nasty."

"What did he say?"

"Well, he made a lame attempt to deliver a shit sandwich. You know—praise, criticism, praise. He said the lit review was okay, the proposal itself sucked, and he asked if I'd finished the marking for his intro to ethics course." Mary picked up her phone from the coffee table. "You might as well read his email yourself." She thumbed her screen. "Here."

Eli frowned at the phone. *Gabriel A. Silverstein.* A memorable name followed by a terse, nasty message. He passed the phone back to Mary. "He's a prick. He even picks on Jesus."

"This wasn't supposed to happen. I figured he'd want me to tweak it a bit, but he'd give me the thumbs-up."

"What are you going to do now?"

Mary shrugged. "Talk to him on Tuesday, I guess. And quietly look for another advisor, though I don't think anyone will take me on. He has a lot of power in the department. They'll all be afraid of stepping on his toes or embarrassing him."

"He's a bully. Someone has to stand up to him."

"Not me."

"No, not you. A colleague with power. Is there anyone you could reach out to?"

She shook her head. "I have to work with him. Mark all his fucking papers. Teach his classes off his boring PowerPoints. I even sent roses to his wife on Valentine's Day, 'Love, Gabriel.' I should've added, 'and his slave' on the card."

Eli sat back and watched Mary take off her glasses and wipe her eyes with a balled-up tissue. She was paying good money to ass-kiss an abusive man, and for what? To prove she was intelligent by getting a PhD? It wasn't a route to wealth or power. Appeasing an asshole like Gabriel for a smart badge wasn't worth it, but the assholes of the world couldn't be allowed to win. He scratched his chin and thought.

She met his eyes. "What?"

"Just curious. Why did you choose Gabriel to be your advisor?"

"I didn't. He chose me. When he offered to mentor me, I was thrilled because his publication list is long and he's heavily cited. He's a giant in the world of applied ethics. I didn't know I'd be his Sherpa on his climb up the last leg of Everest."

"The Sherpas get paid."

"I do too."

"As a TA you get peanuts. Anyway, I think your situation is more like some of the wives in the Brethren Church. They cower in their husbands' shadow. Living a small life—supper ready before he's home, asking permission to use the car, agreeing with everything in case he gets mad and yells, or worse." This wasn't the time to reveal that he thought of his father, his Uncle Gideon, and his brother Jacob when he said this.

"No, no. It's not like that at all. Gabriel occasionally lectures in the gender studies department. He's a feminist."

"You think he'd bully a male student?"

131

"Yes." She looked away as if confused. "I don't know."

"Those Brethren husbands who hurt their wives? They love their wives. They're damaged men and they get away with bad behavior because no one stops them and makes them learn to do better."

"Eli, I don't think the analogy is apt. Gabriel teaches philosophy at a university. It isn't like that."

He'd pushed her to defend an indefensible man. He had to back off.

Mary sighed and took his hand. "I really wanted to be with you. You know...this weekend. My proposal would advance and so would we."

He wanted the same thing, desperately, but she didn't need the pressure. "I'll wait for as long as it takes."

"You will? Because this morning I was tempted to drop my vow, but you're really strong motivation for me to pick up the pieces and persevere."

"I guess I should be flattered."

Mary smiled. She was a beautiful, mysterious mess. Hair a frizzled halo, eyes steaming her glasses, braless under a frayed Rush T-shirt, lips parted and begging to be kissed. She took off her glasses and set them by her phone.

Eli leaned over her, and she nipped his lower lip. He backed off and returned, pressed his open mouth to hers, explored her softness with his tongue. Her mouth was slightly sour under lingering mint toothpaste. He tasted more, and she tasted back and moaned. She was incredible. He was rock hard. Need ripped through his body, but this kiss was all they could have. Dominic would return.

Their lips sealed and moved in erotic communion. Mary's hands gripped his thighs. She wanted to be touched. He slid his hand from her waist, under her T-shirt, slowly up, over smooth skin to a firm, round breast, and she tilted her head back. They came apart, panting, needing breath. He moved over her, and her legs were around him, drawing him close. He pushed up her T-shirt and sucked her nipple. If he was crazy with lust, he'd make her crazy, too.

What if Dominic…never mind. Mary knew how long he usually ran.

Even through her jeans, she was hot against him, tilting her pelvis for contact, moving under him. God. If he could unzip those jeans. No. Off limits. She moaned his name, throaty, urgent and he sucked harder and caressed—

The door opened, and before they were apart, Dominic strode in with his hand in the gift bag. "Eli, you sinful devil. Chocolate!"

Mary took the intrusion in stride. With a sigh, she fixed her T-shirt and sat up.

A mischievous gleam sparked in Dominic's eyes as he feigned ignorance to what they were up to. He plopped into a chair and smiled slyly. "Do you know what carbs do to a man's figure?"

It was shameful to be caught.

"I could use some of that," said Mary.

Dominic passed her the bag. She unwrapped a bunny, pronounced it "cute" and bit off an ear, Mike Tyson-style.

Sexually frustrated in the extreme, Eli needed a cold shower, not chocolate, but the roommates were happy. For the time being, Mary had forgotten her troubles and Dominic, as conveyed through a mouthful of chocolate, needed energy to whip up "a divine eggs Benedict for a blessed Easter morn."

\*\*\*\*

Mary was too long on Skype with her mother, who was now asking if she was in love. "You have that distracted look, Shipsy. A mother knows her daughter."

"Yeah, well, I'm not," lied Mary. "And if you knew me so well, Mother, you'd know that I hate that nickname."

"Your nickname and your real name are just so *you*."

"'Mary Rose' is a ridiculous thing to call a girl."

"It's romantic," she drawled. "Your father was editing a history text on the British Navy when you were born."

"Ugh. I've heard this story too many times."

"Anyway, we put 'Mary' with your father's surname and voilà! *Mary Rose*, flagship of the Tudor fleet and our precious daughter. Namesakes."

"Mother. The ship sank and all the sailors drowned."

"If you dislike your name so much, you could go by your middle name."

"Hortensia?"

"It means 'of the garden'. So romantic." She smiled dreamily. A man's voice rumbled indistinctly in the background, a dog growled, and her mother craned her neck to see something off-screen. "Listen, I've got to go, Shipsy. Jean-Claude is stressed to the max with puppy training. Our healer has diagnosed the poor man with a variation of postpartum depression that she says is common among new fur parents."

"It's not easy being a father," said Mary. "Happy Easter, Mother."

"Happy Easter. Luv ya!" And she was gone.

Mary closed her laptop and went to the kitchen to tackle the dishes. Dominic swept in behind her and took a tea towel from the drawer.

"I can do them myself." She ran hot water over a squirt of detergent. "You made brunch and supper. Fair's fair."

"And miss a chance to hear news of your flamboyantly crazy mama? Not a chance."

"Well, let's see…they've adopted a psychopathic Labradoodle and that's pretty much it." She picked up a potato-encrusted pan. "I think this needs to soak. That was amazing food, Dominic."

"Do you think Eli liked it?"

"He said he did and he ate a lot."

"But he wolfs down his food and doesn't taste it. That silky, pistachio mousse flew over his tongue without contacting a single tastebud."

"He grew up on a farm. Probably food was fuel in his family."

"We must civilize him." Dominic dried a glass.

"I don't think we can do that. He's just…different," said Mary. "When we're alone, he says things you're not supposed to say."

"Honey, with me, ain't nothing off limits."

"You'll laugh. He's like a time traveler from the fifties." Mary transferred a stack of plates into sudsy water.

"Try me."

"Um, okay. Felicity Hill wears tight sweaters because she wants men to look at her boobs. Oh, here's another: women shouldn't tempt men sexually because some men can't control themselves."

"Uh-huh. Retrograde notions to be sure," Dominic snickered.

She set a crystal bowl to drain and turned. "You agree with him!"

"Yes. It's what most people think but won't say in case an SJW is lurking, ready to pounce. I'm all Felicity Hill when I go out of an evening, leather-panted for the male gaze. And the more provocatively I dress, the rougher the manhandling I get in the clubs. Everything he says is true for gay men, too. Times ten."

"I'll take you at your word. How about this: men value women more highly when women play hard to get and restrict access."

"That's straightforward, Mary. Supply and demand."

"So a woman who partakes in a casual lay is of less value than a prissy leg-crosser?"

"To some men, yes. Chaps like Eli who are shopping for a wife."

"I doubt Eli wants a wife."

Dominic held a wine glass up to the light, checking for spots.

"All right. Here's a topper," said Mary. "Gabriel is a misogynist—not the word Eli used, but it's what he meant. He thinks Gabriel is engaging in a proxy of spousal abuse. He actually equated Gabriel's rejection of my proposal with wife beating."

"Hmm." Dominic put the glass in the cupboard. "Let me see. You mark *all* the papers, perform menial tasks unrelated to school, write a decent proposal only to have it torn up. Gabriel *is* like an angry man throwing his plate against the wall because the pot roast is tough."

"So you agree with Eli."

"Yup."

Mary shook her head. "Sure, Gabriel is difficult, maybe even sociopathic, but an abuser needs a victim to close the circle and that isn't me."

"You'd better send a memo to Gabriel informing him of the same."

Mary dropped her dishcloth. "What?"

Dominic turned to face her eye to eye. "Once again, I agree with Eli. Your relationship with Gabriel is toxic. You've done everything in your power with that proposal—put months into the lit review, vetted your document with another prof, assumed the lion's share of Gabriel's workload thus coloring your nose a deep shade of brown, and for what? A cruel email on Easter morning. And now, if I remember correctly from supper, you plan to visit him on Tuesday so he can criticize you while you massage his feet and tell him he's the bestest advisor ever."

"I have to communicate with my advisor, Dominic. In person is better."

"You also have to fight back. Not directly, though. Strategically."

"Hmm. You might be right. Think before I act." Mary returned to her task. Hands deep in dishwater, she reflected. "'The opportunity for defeating the enemy is provided by the enemy himself.' That's from *The Art of War*. The ancient Chinese general, Sun Tzu."

"Finally! Now we're getting somewhere, darling. Elaborate, please."

"I wonder…there must be other students who've

run afoul of Gabriel. Grad students who've dropped out or transferred due to frustrated ambition. If I start with reconnaissance, put out feelers in the department..."

"Connect with the prof who pre-read your proposal?"

"Penny?" Mary shook her head. "No. She collaborates with Gabriel. Though there might be someone in gender studies who's seen Gabriel's dark side and would step up with me."

"Step up to what?"

Mary stared into the murky, lukewarm dishwater. "I don't know yet. For now, I'm going to play it cool, meet with him on Tuesday, and quietly investigate."

"Now you're talking. Take decisive action!"

"You think I'm a wimp." She pulled the plug to change the water.

"No, though I'd say you're cautious."

"I *will* get that proposal approved, Dominic, but the situation is delicate. The department is a Balkan powder keg of explosive egos and I can't be a match thrower. If I'm perceived to be a troublemaker, I might as well kiss the prospect of a doctorate goodbye."

\*\*\*\*

Eli sat in his car and typed "Gabriel A. Silverstein" into his phone. A cursory search revealed that Silverstein lived at 64 Briarmont Court, a cul-de-sac of brick Victorians and mature trees near the university. Jonquil had sold a house on that street three or four years back. If Silverstein bought before the pandemic, he had a sweet investment. The photo in his LinkedIn and faculty profiles showed a pasty middle-aged man in front of shelves of leather-bound books. He wore an open-necked shirt and a smug goatee—high-maintenance facial hair that required him to shave and still wipe food off his mustache and beard. No need to check if the stoop-shouldered Silverstein was into martial arts. The shape of his body told all. Eli tossed his phone onto the passenger seat and started the car.

Sixty-four Briarmont was a ten-minute drive from Mary's place. It looked like Silverstein was home. There was light shining through stained glass panels at the front door as well as a Prius and a Jetta, both about a decade old, in the driveway. Unless he'd married an heiress, a prof couldn't afford more car and house than that. A paved path ran from the cul-de-sac to the next street. Silverstein would walk or cycle to work by this shortcut. It was way quicker than driving, and campus parking was notorious.

Tuesday morning. Silverstein told Mary he'd be in his office all day. Unbeknownst to him, he'd have an impromptu, remedial session on how to treat a lady first thing in the morning. Ambushing the professor would be easy if Eli rode his bike.

Chapter Twelve

Easter Monday was a holiday for government employees, but not for Hill Realty. In the morning, Mary updated the database and compiled a list of serious prospects for individual follow-up. Eli came and went, his phone pressed to his ear the whole time. Only a few passersby ventured into the office, mostly window shoppers who wanted to view the model unit, yet unbuilt. By noon, she'd completed everything Eli had asked of her.

Coffee mug refreshed, it was time to gather intel on Dr. Gabriel A. Silverstein.

He had the usual love-hate ratings on "Rate my Prof," though a recent entry caught her eye. "Never saw the prof. Bored grad student taught all the classes. Yawn." Guilty as charged. Next, she searched Gabriel's name with the keywords "bully, professional misconduct." Nothing. Even "gaslight," favored term of disgruntled undergrads for "we didn't agree", didn't score. She had to dig with a sharper spade on social media.

Gabriel was absent from Facebook and Instagram but rambunctiously snarky on Twitter, correcting minor errors in other people's tweets and wielding his sword of rhetoric with condescension. No one had made any allegations against him. Wait—here was something. A tweet on the paper Gabriel presented at the conference.

"Silverstein spoke on neo-Utilitarianism. His paper, "Whither the Common Good?" was passably adequate, but his talk was overreaching in theoretical span and weak in key places. Could use a major rewrite. I feel sorry for Gabe's grad student." #ToxicProf

Holy shit! It was uncanny. The tweeter must've received similar feedback to what she'd received from Gabriel. Rubbing salt in the wound, the tweeter called him "Gabe." He detested diminutives. Gabriel's tweet followed. "Replying to @candace_kaine- Hegel is hard. Don't feel bad. Not everyone is capable of understanding complexity, Candy. BTW, how's hairdressing school?"

Mary investigated and found that Candace Kaine was a kindred spirit who was very active on social media and working at Laurentian University. So excited she bounced in her chair, Mary sent her a Facebook message. With a little more digging, she would surely unearth other Candaces.

Thirty minutes later and no further ahead, Mary was hungry. She texted Eli, —You coming for lunch?—

—I wish. Dealing with a cranky mortgage broker. Save me something?—

He was so busy that she didn't see him for the rest of the day, which was too bad because she wanted to tell him all about the Twitter skirmish.

****

On Tuesday morning, Eli cycled over to Briarmont Court, past number sixty-four, to the path at the end of the cul-de-sac. He parked his bike against a fence and watched Silverstein's house from a gap in a juniper hedge. People were leaving for work or school from other homes and both cars were parked in sixty-four's driveway. With luck, Silverstein would depart soon.

After a five-minute stakeout, Eli shuffled impatiently. How did cops do it? He had stuff to do and hiding felt silly. He could google the location of the man's office, though if he went there, he'd risk being caught by Mary. On the other hand, skulking in bushes was a creepy waste of time. He drew his phone from his pocket.

Absorbed in the labyrinthine puzzle of the university directory and map on his screen, he sensed a presence at his foot and looked down. A hairy toaster was sniffing his ankle, and on the end of its leash, a refrigerator of a woman was checking him out with narrow-eyed suspicion. The dog growled, then yapped.

The woman spoke like the late Queen. "Bingley is perturbed because your bicycle is parked in his water closet."

So that explained the stench of dogshit in the fragrant juniper. "Oh, sorry." Eli shoved his phone back into his pocket. "I'll move it."

"What is your purpose in hiding amidst the shrubbery?"

"Uh...I'm waiting for a friend." The woman looked dissatisfied with his answer. "He lives on this street."

"I know everyone on Briarmont. We're quite the merry little village. If you tell me his name, perhaps I may be of help? You've forgot his house number, haven't you? After all, if you knew it, you wouldn't be here, would you?"

"No, ma'am, I wouldn't. He'll be along shortly," Eli replied sheepishly. "I'll move my bike for Bingley."

As he stepped away, he flashed his most charming smile. "Bingley's a handsome fellow. Lhasa Apso?"

"Yes, a champion—and obedient too." She looked fondly at the toaster. "Small breeds tend to rule their masters, but I won't stand for it. I trained Bingley from a pup to respect my rules."

"Dogs are happier for it," said Eli, grasping for common ground. He bent to let the dog sniff his hand, then scratched him behind the ear.

"Much happier indeed." She smiled.

Now he was a harmless dog lover. She wouldn't call the police.

As Eli rolled down the path, he heard the woman say, "Good morning, Gabriel."

And the reply, "Good morning, Hilda. How was your Easter?" The man walked right past her, footsteps thudding on the sidewalk.

Eli dismounted at the other end of the path, stuck his bike behind a pine, and leaned against a signpost. Hopefully, he'd complete his mission before a bike thief noticed it. Silverstein waddled up the path, briefcase in his gloved hand, felt cap perched at an affected angle. A regular Toad of Toad Hall.

Eli waited till he'd passed, then strode alongside. "Mr. Silverstein?"

"*Doctor* Silverstein. That's my proper honorific."

"Right. *Doctor*. Of philosophy. I always forget that it isn't just for real doctors." Let him underestimate his foe.

"Do I know you?" asked Silverstein.

"Probably not. I'm only an undergrad, though I know your TA, Mary Rose."

"Aw, yes. The talented Ms. Rose." Under the

shadow of his cap, Gabriel's face lit up.

"She's so smart," encouraged Eli. "The philosophy department is lucky to have her."

"I concur. I'll pass on your praise."

"Please do."

Now what? This was freaking awkward. Usually, Eli could wing it. Overconfident, he'd walked on stage without a script. Silverstein huffed along at a jog-walk, trying to outpace him, briefcase swinging like a frantic pendulum. In another block, they'd be on campus and Eli would lose his chance.

"I hope Mary is a professor like you someday," he said.

"In all likelihood, she will be." Silverstein frowned at the nuisance who stuck to his elbow like discarded gum.

"Do you think so? I heard she feels discouraged because her proposal was rejected."

Silverstein shrugged a round shoulder and smirked.

"Others have read it, and thought it was great," added Eli.

Panting and pale, Silverstein slowed to a walk. "I'm sorry. We really must part. You're straying beyond the bounds of confidentiality."

"I read it myself, Gabe. If I were you, I'd approve it. As is. Today."

"Oh? And who in the dickens are you to advise me?"

"That doesn't matter."

They were nearly at the iron gates of the university's western flank. Silverstein stopped, turned, and peered closely at him for the first time. "Hmm. You're not really a student here, are you? You're too old and too uncouth to play the part."

"Approve it today or I'll make your life hell."

"I'll do what is warranted." Silverstein started walking again. When Eli kept pace, Silverstein said, "I imagine you're fucking her, and you think she loves you."

"Approve her proposal and you won't see me again."

"She's fucked half the profs in the department, has our Mary Rose. I'm quite certain you're finding her well-practised. Over-adept, if you will…with a seadog's steady hand on the old tiller."

Silverstein saw him flinch. He'd revealed the chink in his armor. He hadn't wanted to escalate to physical enforcement, but Silverstein was so blinded by his lofty self-regard that he was reckless.

"I'm a monogamous, married man, yet she—"

Rage engulfing him, Eli seized Silverstein's tie, twisted it around his fist, and hissed, "You're a fucking liar and a creep." The man was the weight of a market-ready hog, but Eli lifted him onto his toes without strain. "Approve her proposal today or I'll chop you into pieces and feed you to Bingley. And Mary must never know that we met. Is that clear, *Mister* Silverstein?"

"Yes," gasped Silverstein. Panic in his bulging eyes, he flutter-kicked his legs. "I'll do as you say." A booted toe connected with Eli's shin and Eli dropped him. Silverstein toppled over, hat and briefcase strewn in the woodchip mulch of a dormant garden. "Help! Help!" he howled. Eli offered his hand, but he waved it away. "I've been assaulted!"

Eli looked around. A few passersby might have

witnessed the altercation, but they were either too absorbed in conversation to intervene or wearing earbuds, oblivious and uncomprehending. All the same, Eli got the hell out of Dodge.

His bike was where he'd left it and minutes later he was home, unwelcome drumbeats of pain thumping in his head and shin.

\*\*\*\*

Exhausted from a late night of marking and fruitless investigating, Mary climbed the stairs to Gabriel's office. The philosophy department was housed in one of the oldest buildings on campus. Candace Kaine had fled from this ivy-covered temple of reason for a modern box of glass and concrete in the hinterland. Whatever it took, Mary refused to do the same. She loved it here.

The third-floor hallway carried a vanilla aroma of old woodwork and smoke from tobacco pipes long extinguished. Jeez, she was nervous. Mouth dry, hands sweaty, guts churning, she took a deep breath through her nose. The smell of the place settled her nerves just enough to proceed.

Gabriel had left his door open. Mary took another deep breath to fuel courage and knocked on the jamb.

"Yes?" He maintained focus on his desktop monitor.

She cleared her throat. "Good morning, Gabriel. Umm...Do you have a minute? I've finished marking the 212s and I've printed the grades for your files."

He swiveled in his chair and waved her in. "Sit, sit, Mary." He looked like hell. Sweat beaded his forehead and his skin was the color of dried glue. He always buttoned his shirt to the top and wore a tie, but today he'd discarded it and opened his collar, freeing his neck to wobble with rubrous abandon beneath his jowls.

She took the wooden chair he reserved for students. "Are you all right?"

"Yes, quite. The grades if you please." His voice was hoarse. A virus?

She rummaged in her rucksack and withdrew a leaf of paper from a folder. "The average is seventy-two, the mean is seventy-three, and there were eleven As and ten Fs with the bulk of the marks Bs and Cs. That's for the term paper. The final exam is next week. I've emailed this document to you as well."

Gabriel put the paper on his desk without looking at it. "Thank you. I appreciate your hard work on that."

Gratitude. Weird.

"Now, your proposal."

"Yes. I've carefully reviewed your feedback and I'll tackle each suggestion systematically beginning with—"

"That won't be necessary."

Fuck. He'd thanked her, hadn't mentioned the proctoring schedule for the finals, and now a discussion on her proposal *wasn't necessary?* He was about to pull a Candace on her. There was no remedy other than to beg. "Please give me another chance, Gabriel. I've poured my soul into that proposal and I can fix it."

He shifted a jowl to rub his neck and shook his head. "I've considered the matter further, Mary, and I've decided to approve it without major changes."

"Pardon?"

"You may contact the committee members to arrange a meeting. Penny, Priya, and Stuart should suffice at this juncture. Do confirm each citation, proofread for overuse of the word 'nevertheless', and strengthen your conclusion. Not in substance, but in language."

"You mean I don't have to rewrite the whole thing?"

"No, you do not."

"And I'm not being asked to leave the program."

"Whyever would you think that? You're aware of my high standards, Mary, and you exceed them. I believe you're quite capable of writing a robust dissertation. I wouldn't have taken you on otherwise."

"Thank you." Had she squealed with relief? She hoped not.

Despite his obvious state of ill health, he managed to crack a smile. "You may hug me now."

"I admire your sense of humor, Gabriel," said Mary as she accepted his flabby handshake.

Two minutes later, she texted Eli and Dominic from the foyer. "Gabriel changed his mind. He approved it!"

Dominic replied with a champagne glass and a row of heart emojis and Eli texted, —Well done! Congratulations! I'm still at home. Want to celebrate?—

—On my way".—

—Want a ride?—"

—Subway's faster.—

**\*\*\*\***

Eli always left his door unlocked, so Mary opened it to find Eli speaking on the phone. He stood on the balcony like a post-modern king, his hair spiked by the blowing wind as he surveyed his dominion. Despite the chill, he remained barefoot, clad in a T-shirt and jeans.

She joined him outside.

"All right. I'll touch base with you later," he said into space, and flicked the screen off, putting the phone in his pocket.

Then Eli looked at her with his deep, dark brown eyes, grinned, and pulled her close. Head against his shoulder, she felt his heat and inhaled the musky smell of him.

She stepped back and peered up, drinking in his handsome face. "I haven't showered yet."

"Neither have I."

"And I forgot to brush my teeth."

"Smile," he commanded, and she did. "They look clean to me."

"And I'm very willing, but I was up all night marking essays, so…"

"I have a headache, but I'm good to go." He shrugged.

"I don't have a condom."

"Neither do I. You're on birth control, aren't you?"

"Yes. The pill. But—"

Eli touched his finger to her lips. "We made a promise to each other. We're exclusive."

She nodded.

"We trust each other?"

She nodded again and surrendered to the pull of his body, and he kissed her. It was a self-conscious, under-the-mistletoe, office-party kind of kiss. And then he led her indoors, lifted her into his arms, and carried her through the doorway of his bedroom. She landed with a bounce on his unmade bed, and he dove in beside her in a long-limbed sprawl.

"Careful! My glasses," Mary scolded.

Eli lifted them off her face and set them on his bedside table. "There. Safe and sound."

They lay with their foreheads pressed together, need rising between them, lost in the wonder of the moment. Her heart raced, and she ached with desire for this man. She combed her fingers through his unwashed hair, then tracked her fingertips through his whiskers.

He exhaled. "Ready?"

"Yes."

He laid her back and they kissed, his mouth familiar and reassuring as they headed for new territory.

Mary slid her hand under his T-shirt, from his flank through the hair of his belly and chest, lifting it. He reached round his shoulder and pulled it off. In the cool air, two male nipples hardened into tiny, brown nubs, and she teased one with her tongue. His skin was rough there, in that tiny patch, and he tasted of dried sweat. Eli pulled off her shirt and sports bra, and they were together again, skin on skin, chest to chest, exploring with caresses.

She had to have what was in his jeans.

Before she could unzip him, his hand was on her fly, fumbling, releasing the button. He eased her jeans and underwear off together. She lay back and, letting him look where he pleased, she followed his gaze. Breasts first, of course, then everywhere else.

"Your turn," said Mary as she ran her palm over his bulge and undid his fly.

He took off his jeans and threw them on the floor. Eli was shy, positioning his body near her so she couldn't see him. He let her push him back. His cock was exquisitely ready. She gripped him and watched his face. As his breath deepened, he closed his eyes and clenched his jaw. He was fighting for control.

So was she. Breath rising to a pant, she only managed a guttural, "No more teasing."

Eli didn't listen. He drew his finger through her curls, over her clit, and through her folds. She was falling into madness. She had to have him. And since it was Eli, strange and wonderful Eli, she had to have him over her to feel the weight and strength of him.

He nuzzled her cheek, and whispered, "You sure you're ready, Mary Rose?"

She could barely breathe. She kissed his lips and nodded.

They rolled together, Eli on top, pushing her thighs apart with his. At first, he teased at her opening, thrusting gently, gaining entry little by little. Her pussy yielded, and she gripped his shoulders. He glided deeper, ever deeper, slowly and tenderly.

"More," she groaned.

Eli responded with a strong thrust, and another, his body setting the rhythm, tempo fast and urgent. He led and she followed him, submitting to his power, surrendering to instinct. He pulled her knees up to gain depth and took her hard, watching her face all the while, confirming her pleasure. She was falling, and it was ecstasy.

The first ripple caught her low in her belly and hitched her breath. He clasped her hands in his and pressed his face against her cheek, beard scraping, breath tickling her skin. Wave upon wave of pleasure welled from her core. She couldn't even call his name. Her universe was this joyous meld of flesh, Eli inside and around her, consuming her yet making her whole. Then, he pushed his hands under her hips, forcing her body up against him, and he buried himself inside her. His entire body trembled.

Afterward, they lay together, and everything had changed. *I love you,* she thought, but she didn't say it.

\*\*\*\*

Eli woke alone, next to an imprint in the rumpled sheets, and no Mary. Gone? No, she was near. She was humming a repetitive tune over the cascade of the shower and her glasses lay on the bedside table.

He rolled over and took stock. Already midafternoon by the angle of the sun. He smiled. She'd folded their clothes and left them on the foot of the bed. The air smelled of sex, and also fresh coffee. That could wait.

He didn't want to wash away her essence, but he needed a shower too.

Mary's form was hazy behind the misty glass. He stepped in and she reached for him.

"You're finally awake." She smiled. He'd never tire of that smile.

Her hair was pasted in tendrils on her shoulders, and water ran in streams over her curves.

"I'm clean now, Eli. And you're not." She turned away from him to lather her hands and he stepped forward, drew her close, and pressed his cock against the pillowy softness of her ass. If she bent just so, he could seek her heat, but she turned and lathered his shoulders, arms, and chest, rubbing and circling ever lower over his abdomen, then balls and cock.

Brow furrowed in concentration, she knelt before him. He wanted this, but did she? "You don't have to, Mary. We can—"

"I want to." She didn't look up.

Her tongue was on him first, over the head of his cock, then licking along the veins of his shaft as she gripped him. If she stood up, they could both enjoy—oh god. Her lips encircled him, taking him into her mouth. Every muscle in his body shivered with the pleasure of it. He came fast. She stayed with him till he started to soften, and then she stood before him and kissed his shoulder. Her mouth released his seed there, and it trickled down his skin.

He could barely breathe. "That was...thank you..."

This time, she pressed her finger to his lips. "No need to thank me. I liked it too."

Later, they stood together watching the sunset from the balcony, mugs of coffee in hand. Mary wore her jeans and an old, faded hoodie she'd found at the back of his closet. Her wild hair blew in the lake breeze. He loved her and he didn't want this day to end.

"You want to go to Takamatsu?" he asked.

"I'd better not," she replied. "I still have the third-year essays to mark and work tomorrow. With you."

"With me."

Chapter Thirteen

When Mary got home, a message with a phone number from Candace Kaine awaited her on Messenger. Though Gabriel had changed his mind, he could change it back at any step on the road to her dissertation defence. It was only seven o'clock and it would be rude not to follow up. Besides, she was curious.

"I've been expecting your call." Candace's voice was a rich, radio announcer's alto. "How are you, Mary?" she asked in a tone of concern.

"I'm actually okay. This morning, Gabriel approved my proposal."

"Oh? You must be so relieved. What changed his mind?"

"I have no idea. I vetted the proposal with Penny Wong, so she may have had a word with him."

"I must say, congratulations!"

"Thank you. He wasn't himself when he told me. He looked unwell, and he was polite instead of brusque. I'll stay on my guard with him."

"That's wise."

"I'm still interested in your story, Candace. What happened at U of T, and about your journey to Laurentian." Phone clutched to her ear, Mary left her desk for the comfort of the couch.

"I'll give you the Coles Notes, or we'll be up all

night." Candace chuckled. "Three years ago, I was Gabriel's 'specially selected doctoral student and I was flattered. This towering intellectual chose little old me. However, it soon became clear that he only works with one student at a time because A—he's lazy, B—the rest of the department lets him get away with it, and C—he can control you better because you're isolated and working like a dog with scant peer support."

"You're telling my story," said Mary. "So there you are, doing his bidding, teaching all his classes, doing research, and marking papers—"

"Exactly. And I figured, as long as I got a PhD out of it, we had a fair bargain. However, the harder I tried, the more he demanded. In a matter of months, I was picking up his dry cleaning, and returning his library books. I'd transformed into his dutiful office wife."

"Sounds familiar. Except I see myself more as a servant," said Mary.

"For me, it was wife, and that was the last straw. He panned my proposal and then told me he wanted what he euphemistically called 'a closer working relationship' to fix it. Hugs and kisses leading God knows where. That was the key to my success in the program."

"Like Harvey Weinstein."

"Yes, but more subtle, less greedy, and brilliant."

"What do you mean, Candace? Spell it out for me because my head is spinning." Mary stood and started pacing.

"Well, brilliant because he is. Gabriel's a leading scholar in the field of justice and ethics. Less greedy because, as far as I can tell, there are very few victims."

Mary bristled at the word victim.

Candace continued. "I know of only you, me, and a woman from before my time who now teaches in Abu Dhabi. We've lost contact. Anyway, he has a pattern of alternating female and male students, and the men sail through his hoops. When he mentors a woman, she does not."

"And subtle?"

"He ensnares you in his trap. You invest so much of yourself in time, money, and sweat. It's too much to throw away, so you keep working with him. If you put out feelers for a new advisor, he makes your life miserable. But he doesn't just pull down his pants and ask for a blow job like creepy old Weinstein. Gabriel gets handsy. And then, when his moves are rebuffed, he blackmails you with your proposal."

"And this time his fatal mistake was using the same criticism for both of us, which you then tweeted. Three years on."

"Some words can never be forgotten."

"How did you resolve your dilemma?"

"My PhD?"

"Yeah."

"I'm from northern Ontario and never liked living in Toronto, anyway. I did some soul-searching, contacted my undergrad profs at Laurentian, and transferred. It wasn't easy, but it was worth it. Now I harass Gabriel on Twitter. I know it's petty, and I also know he hates it."

"Do you think he has targeted others? I mean, besides you, me, and the woman in Abu Dhabi?"

"There are only rumors. It's hard to say. By the old photos on his wall, he wasn't a bad-looking fellow when he was younger. Charismatic. Attractive to young women who go for older, intellectual types. The rules were different once upon a time. He may have flirted, had consensual affairs, and found he missed the fun as he aged out of contention so he resorted to manipulation."

"But he's married."

Candace snickered. "She's an anthropology prof. They probably experiment with non-traditional, uncolonized forms of conjugal relationship."

"Maybe Gabriel's a neglected cuckold."

"No, no, no, Mary. That's unscientific, value-laden terminology. He'd be a male-identifying partner within a polyandrous contract."

Mary laughed. Speculating with this funny woman on Gabriel's marriage was minor revenge.

Tone serious again, Candace said, "I'm so glad you reached out. After three years, I'm still angry with him. Our conversation tonight has been therapeutic."

"For me, too," said Mary.

"What are you going to do now that we've talked?"

"Well, I'll be vigilant. There may be other women he's hurt. I'll look for allies in the department and over in gender studies."

"Will you lodge a complaint?"

"No. I haven't grounds. Other than his personal errands, Gabriel assigns me work that is within the scope of a doctoral student's duties, albeit in supertanker volume. I can't complain about harsh criticism. The administration would view it as my problem, not his."

"Sadly, that's true," said Candace. "Anyway, let's stay in touch. If you need to talk, call me. Anytime."

"Thank you, Candace. I will."

Conversation over, Mary returned to her desk and ruminated. If she were a grad student a decade or two ago, Gabriel might have been her type. Before Eli, she'd occasionally hooked up with men, including profs outside the philosophy department, whose ring fingers featured a band of suspiciously pale skin. She wasn't an innocent party on the battlefield of sexual politics, nor was she a victim. If Gabriel messed with her again, he'd get his just desserts.

Mary yawned. It was getting late. After a head-clearing stretch, she returned to the task of grading papers.

****

The next morning, Eli gave her a funny look when she told him about Candace Kaine. A patronizing look. As if women linking arms against an exploitive man was a feeble strategy. When she told him so, he delivered a hasty apology, kissed her on the cheek, and breezed off to a meeting at Synergy Developments with a silly smirk on his face. He might as well have said, "You're cute when you're angry."

He hadn't left the sales office more than ten minutes when Claudia marched through the door like a drill sergeant on snap inspection of the barracks. "I was in the neighborhood and decided to drop in while Eli is over at Synergy," she said ominously. "Now we can have a chat, just the two of us."

Mary swallowed hard. "Here, Claudia?"

"Where else? You can't simply lock up and leave. A buyer might happen by anytime."

If only one would, and stay long enough for Eli to return, but the chance of that was remote so early in the day.

Claudia sat on the sofa, crossed her thin, stockinged legs, and bounced a stiletto-shod foot. "Sit, Mary. Please."

"Would you like coffee?" asked Mary, hoping to score points by remembering to welcome *all* visitors per Hill Realty protocol.

"I think not, thank you."

Mary sank into the armchair and crossed her legs as well. Like Claudia.

"Yesterday, Eli texted in the morning that he was working from home. A courtesy in case myself or another member of the team needed him. I sent a client here, oh, let's see—" She frowned at her gold watch. "About three. Imagine my horror when the gentleman phoned to inform me that the In-Spire office was closed. Curtains drawn, doors locked, nary a soul on site."

"Eli gave me the day off for school," said Mary.

"Did he? How very generous of him."

"Well, now that you know why—"

"Oh, I know why," said Claudia.

Fuck. Were they that obvious?

"You're taking advantage of his kind nature. I keep statistics, Mary. Hill Realty is a future-focused organization. Eli and I developed sales targets with Synergy that were specific, measurable, achievable, relevant, and time-based, and he's not meeting them. His performance is suffering."

"Well, umm, interest rates have risen."

"Good try. I don't buy it." Claudia tapped a manicured finger against her vermillion lips and stared into middle space. "I know Eli and I know when he's troubled. He and I go way back. He started at Hill as a birddog, hunting down deals and bringing them to me for my clients. Only nineteen and instincts sharp as a tack. Within months, he had his real estate license, and two years later, he was matching me in sales." Her eyes darted to Mary. "Do you understand who Eli Klassen is, Mary?"

"Yes. Your top seller."

"Indeed. My top seller and *my dear friend*. Since you started working together, he's distracted. Off his game. Something has happened to Eli."

"Um, he seemed fine this morning. But I'll watch him, Claudia, in case he's in some sort of trouble."

Claudia gave a delicate snort. "Eli plays by the rules. The question is, *do you?*"

"Me?" Mary straightened like a prim A plus pupil. "Today I arrived early, made coffee, and checked voice mail as outlined on the receptionist's duty list you gave me, and the office is clean and neat. You can see so yourself, Claudia. If the environment shapes one's experience, as the philosopher John Locke—"

"I'm not here for an educational seminar, Mary. I'm here to warn you. Lately, I've noticed that Eli has the look of the hunted. Wary and tired. As if someone is chasing him, mercilessly, and he's too kind to extricate himself…too afraid to draw clear boundaries and risk hurting her."

"I assure you, Claudia, I'm not chasing Eli."

"Deny it if you will, but it's a story as old as time itself. A frustrated female pursuing a man who's out of her league. He's forced to avoid the office, he's stressed, his productivity falls…"

Mary felt nauseous. To be thought a predator was humiliating.

Claudia's voice cut like a steel blade. "Hill Realty has a bullet-proof anti-harassment policy. No member of the team should ever feel unsafe."

"Un...unsafe?" Mary stuttered. "But...but Eli has the power here. I'm his subordinate."

"Puh-lease. I shouldn't have to tell a philosophy major that power is dynamic and there's such a thing as manipulation." She shook her platinum helmet head and made a strange face, as if trying to fix her forehead in a frown. She gave up and briefly pursed her lips instead. "I have *zero tolerance* for sexual shenanigans. If the policy is violated, I shall be forced to terminate you."

"By terminate, you mean fire?"

"Yes, Mary. Fire." Claudia bared her teeth in a menacing grin. "Do you think I'd waste money on a contract killer?"

"Umm...no, you wouldn't."

"That was a joke, Mary. Really, where is your sense of humor?"

Mary giggled weakly.

Claudia rose. "I feel our conversation has been productive. We have clarity on expectations, and *consequences*, don't you think?"

"Yes, we do," agreed Mary, standing with her. "Is there anything else I can do for you, Claudia?"

"Well done, Mary. I'm not a client, but that *is* how we close a meeting." She smiled. "Only one teeny tiny little thing. I plan to send Felicity here for extra training with Eli so we have coverage when you're absent. Please be welcoming."

"Of course," said Mary, though she made a face and mocked Claudia's words under her breath as Claudia left the office.

Later, Mary searched for Hill Realty's anti-harassment policy on the employee and agent portal. Among policies ranging from dress code to disaster preparedness, she found nothing. For an oft-cited policy, it was funny, genuinely funny, that Claudia hadn't bothered to post it. Maybe the policy had never been written.

She and Eli weren't breaking any rules, Mary thought indignantly. Falling in love on the job wasn't a criminal offence.

****

No one had bothered to turn the calendar page in the reception room at Synergy Developments, so Eli did it. There. Over its numbered grid, the month of April featured a clump of daffodils by a brook and a ruined castle. First Wednesday of the month already. He hated waiting, but he had to nail down a plan for the installation of the model suite with the project manager and communication was more efficient in person.

A ceiling-mounted TV was set to an all-news channel, weather and traffic on a side panel, a ribbon of market updates along the bottom of the screen. In the middle, the mayor announced funding for a new community center...a rash of burglaries terrorized residents in the east end...an old man was accosted at the gates of the University of Toronto. What? Crap. It couldn't be! The news advanced to the next item in the morning's loop.

Gripped with dread, Eli sat in a vinyl armchair and found the news site on his phone. A grainy image captured from CCTV footage showed a young man bent over an older man who appeared to be defending himself with pudgy fists. The caption read, "U of T campus police have turned over security images to Toronto Police in the hope of identifying an elderly victim and his assailant. In a press release, spokesperson Sandra O'Hara stated investigators are concerned for the victim's safety. Anyone who was near U of T's western entrance at approximately 8:30 a.m. yesterday and may have witnessed the attack is asked to call Crimestoppers."

Eli enlarged the photo. Silverstein's porcine body lay supine on a bed of mulch, fat legs bent into inverted Vs, arms extended like cricket bats. The younger man's hand, *his own* hand, was extended in aid but anyone examining the still image would mistake the gesture for a blow. On the other hand, both faces were obscured by position and motion. Silverstein and he would recognize themselves, but would anyone else? And why hadn't the police released video footage? CCTV cameras were notoriously unreliable. Had there been a glitch?

He wouldn't panic. Surely the story would blow over? Unlikely. Not when the police used words like "assailant, victim, safety, and attack." The buzz on campus, on Briarmont Court—hell, in the whole city— would be deafening. You'd have to live under a landscaping rock in Bingley's pissing grounds to miss this kind of news. He'd have to turn himself in. Mary would be livid.

His phone pinged. Mary? No. A nuisance text from Stephen under a link to the Victoria's Secret catalogue. "Don't forget, Klassen. My cut before you go shopping." Stephen's relentless pestering was a zit on a butt cheek compared to the volcano of pus infecting the day's news and threatening to smother his life.

Eli deleted Stephen's message as the project manager's assistant summoned him for the meeting.

\*\*\*\*

Eli looked like death warmed over when he returned to the sales office at eleven.

"How did it go?" asked Mary, forgetting she was still cross with him.

"Well." Eli kissed her and slumped into the armchair. "The model suite will go in by mid-month. We'll work off-site for a few days and have Jonquil and Siobhan stage it. There's only space for the one bedroom plus den, but that's fine. Sales are brisk without a model anyway."

She wanted to tell him that Claudia begged to differ and to commiserate over their awful conversation, but Eli wasn't well. Face drawn, skin sallow, tone weak, he looked as if he was on the verge of tears. She sat on the edge of the sofa so their knees were touching and peered into his eyes.

"You okay, Eli?"

"Yeah. Just a headache."

"That's not just a headache. You can barely hold yourself up."

"I took some Advil. I'll be fine, Mary." His voice and hands trembled. When he saw she'd noticed, he tucked them under his thighs.

"You need a doctor. St. Joe's is only a few blocks away."

"No way. I'll feel better after a nap. I think I'll head home. You okay here? On your own?"

She took his hand. Clammy as a wrung-out rag. "I'm getting an Uber to take us to the hospital."

"Don't, Mary. I know you're worried, but I'm

okay. I'm going home." Before she could object, he clambered to his feet and headed for the door. "Come by my place after work?"

He left without an answer, and without kissing her goodbye.

By Mary's count, this was his third headache in a week, one blending into the next. Advil and coffee weren't cutting it. There had to be something she could do for him. He'd mentioned his grandmother's salve and tea. If Mary wrote to Mrs. Klassen and asked her to send some, she would. By the old woman's letter, she loved Eli dearly and would help him. Mary remembered her distinctive name and address. A few mouse clicks and presto, she'd have her postal code too.

She took a leaf of letterhead from the drawer and dashed off a note.

*Dear Mrs. Klassen,*

*My name is Mary and I work with your grandson, Eli. He doesn't know that I'm writing to you.*

*I have a favor to ask. Eli gets terrible headaches and he mentioned that you make a salve and a tea that helps to relieve them. Could you mail some to him? I'm enclosing ten dollars to cover postage.*

*Apart from the headaches, Eli is well. He's a hard worker. He must have learned to be industrious by growing up on a farm.*

*Thank you for your help.*

*Sincerely,*

*Mary Rose*

\*\*\*\*

What a coward. He went back to the office to confess and he couldn't do it. Now he lay on crumpled sheets that smelled of Mary. Every breath through his stupid nostrils reinforced his terror that he would lose her if he couldn't work a miracle.

He'd tricked her into believing that Silverstein approved her proposal of his own accord and then he'd bedded her under false pretense. If the deception weren't bad enough, he'd threatened Silverstein and accidentally upended him in front of a goddam camera. *Full story at eleven.*

Eli cringed at his own smug attitude that very morning. Mary was capable of handling a bully in her ladylike way. She'd freaked out when he had to deal with Brian at Out-of-the-Box and he hadn't even laid a finger on the guy. Wait till she found out he'd physically confronted Silverstein and didn't have the courage to tell her. Or the police.

Damage control. That's what he had to do.

Eli shifted the wet facecloth covering his eyes and forehead, reached for the phone, and checked the news. Every media outlet in town carried the story of the dangerous criminal, still at large, who'd beaten a poor, defenseless old man. By the reporter's accounts, the police could have located the victim by following the trail of blood dribbling from his ravaged body as he crawled away, unaided and uncomforted in his anonymity. Eli searched for more images, but there was only that one.

He scrolled to the comments.

*We should of never outlawed spanking...Cops too busy taking sensitivity training to catch criminals...Why didn't anyone help that poor, elderly gentleman...Prayers...It's called bystander syndrome...I don't feel safe in this city...Wish I could see there faces so I could find the a\*\*hole and teach* *him a lesson...Pathetic...*

Pathetic. Both he and Silverstein *did* look pathetic. As Eli repeated the word over and over, a grain of sand grew into a pearl of inspiration deep in his subconscious and surfaced. Silverstein was a bully and this story was his kryptonite. No one would kowtow to a pathetic victim. If Silverstein's identity was revealed, the cloak concealing his weakness would be yanked away and he could kiss his power good-bye.

Eli found Silverstein's number in the U of T directory. Damage control demanded immediate action.

"Yes?" The professor's voice was high-pitched for a man, yet gruff. Old-sounding compared to yesterday.

"Mr. Silverstein?"

"Doctor Silverstein. Please identify yourself."

"It's Eli Klassen, your unknown assailant." Might as well give his name, establish the illusion of an equal footing.

Eli heard breathing, then a slow chortle. "Calling for a proverbial chess match."

"Pawn to E4," said Eli. "Listen, first off, I'm sorry about yesterday."

"No, you aren't. What did you say your name is?"

"Klassen. You're right. I'm not. We don't like each other, but that doesn't mean we don't have certain interests in common."

"I can predict where you're going, but please, continue."

"You've seen the news with the CCTV image."

"I have."

"It's grainy and our faces are blurry. No one can identify the men in the photo except us. And it strikes me, Silverstein, that neither of us comes off in a flattering light. I look like a bully and you look like a fucking pansy."

"And if we don't tell anyone, we can go off to our own corners, live our lives in peace, with no one the wiser," finished Silverstein. "A mutually beneficial stalemate."

"Yeah, that's how I see it."

"What about Ms. Rose?" asked Silverstein. "Won't she recognize lover boy in the photo?"

"I have an alibi. That guy looks like me, but I was nowhere near U of T yesterday morning."

"And what of me?"

"Are you the only portly prof on campus who dresses like an undertaker?"

"No. They abound," Silverstein conceded. "Though you may find it expedient to spare me your observation of my weighty corporeal habitus during our negotiations."

"Are we agreeing to silence?"

"Yes. Mum's the word, Mr. Klassen. It would be remiss of me not to wish you a good day, but I'd rather tell you to fuck off."

Eli laughed. "Good day, Mr. Silverstein."

Call concluded to his satisfaction, Eli went to the kitchen to take a couple more Advil, though he felt better already. He had enough time to change the sheets and order food before Mary got off work.

That evening, maybe they'd laugh at the bizarre resemblance between the men in the viral news photo and him and Gabriel.

Chapter Fourteen

Fridays, the most optimistic day of the week, brought more people to the sales office than other weekdays, so Mary made a full pot of coffee, filled the carafe, and set up a self-serve area with cream and sugar. By late morning, she had names and contact info for two retired couples, a newly divorced woman and her son, a nurse who'd finally passed his board exam, and a thirty-something lesbian couple pushing a cat in a stroller, though she doubted the women's names were really Clee Torres and Connie Lingus. She was washing mugs when Eli and Felicity arrived.

Felicity hung her trench coat in the closet and said to Mary, "Aunt Claudia and Eli thought I should begin my orientation at In-Spire today." Then, tossing her hair over her shoulder she giggled, "Didn't you, Eli?"

Eli cleared his throat. "Claudia strongly suggested it."

"Lovely," Mary said tightly.

"We've been all over town in Eli's racy little car, along the lake, through the old garment district, even up to the Buttonville Lofts! He's so knowledgeable," Felicity gushed. "I learned more from Eli in one morning than in two weeks with Aunt Claudia and Uncle Stephen."

"He certainly knows his business," said Mary.

Eli blushed. "I'll let Mary take over from here,

Felicity. She knows her way around the sales office better than anyone."

"No need to rush off," said Mary. "Claudia told me Felicity would be 'learning the ropes' from you."

Eli took a step back. "Uh, I'm taking a client to lunch. A businessman from Shanghai whose daughter will be starting college here. I have to secure a table. You know how Fridays are." He tapped his watch. "And you can't keep a client waiting."

"Silly Eli," said Mary. "I'll make a reservation for you. What restaurant?"

"Roasters."

"The coffee shop? Really?"

"Mr. Fung said he likes their sandwiches."

"If you leave now, you'll be forty-five minutes early," said Mary, "by racy little car or on foot."

"I'm going by the bank first." Eli stepped back again and vanished.

She was alone with Felicity, whose heavy sigh betrayed a lack of enthusiasm for being trained by anyone other than Eli. However, Felicity was Claudia's niece and Mary's margin for error was narrow. She had to be nice.

"Coffee?" offered Mary.

Felicity flashed her too-gorgeous smile. "Yes, thank you. Cream and sugar."

Mary poured mugs for each of them and gestured to the faux living room. "We might as well be comfortable. I'll show you the administrative stuff after lunch."

After they were seated, Felicity said, "It's a pleasant surprise to be here. The main office is so boring."

Mary smiled. "Why don't you tell me about your morning so far, Felicity?"

"Well, first thing this morning, Aunt Claudia and Eli had a meeting. I couldn't hear everything, but it sounded to me like Aunt Claudia thinks Uncle Stephen and Eli would make a strong team here, at In-Spire. Sooo, Uncle Stephen and I would work here, and if you pull up your socks, you'll be allowed to go back to Hill Realty."

"What did Eli say to that?"

Felicity twirled a lock of hair around her finger, scanned the ceiling for an answer, then looked at Mary. "Nothing. Well, nothing I could hear. His voice didn't carry like Aunt Claudia's, but I think he'd be pleased, don't you?"

Mary nodded. "And then? Off you went to see the city?"

"Yes, though Eli yacked on his phone half the time. We drove by condos that he thought Mr. Fung and his daughter might like while I picked his brain on how to get my real estate license. I've heard the exams are hard, but Eli said he passed on his first try and he thought I could too."

So there really was a Mr. Fung. She shouldn't have doubted him. Eli wasn't a liar, but he'd acted so cagey. "What about psychology, Felicity? I thought you only had a term left in your program."

"I do, but Eli is succeeding without a degree and now I'm rethinking my goals."

"Your Aunt Claudia has a BA in economics. Maybe you should discuss your plan with her."

Felicity shrugged and sipped her coffee.

"What did you think of the Buttonville Lofts?"

171

asked Mary.

"They were cool. A bit far from the college, so Mr. Fung won't buy there, but Eli wanted to see them for a friend. Eli doesn't trust pictures. He says photographers play with the light and shoot from a wide angle. He took their sales material. For reconnaissance, he said."

"A clever word."

"He's so smart. And good looking." Felicity leaned forward and lowered her voice, no mean feat for someone who spoke at a pitch verging on ultrasonic. "I'll tell you a little secret."

Mary drank her coffee and nodded. Here it was—

"I think I have a crush on Eli Klassen. Every time we're near each other, I get this powerful feeling." She slid her hands up and down her trunk. "Jonquil calls it 'tantric energy.' And you know what else?"

"No," said Mary.

"I think Eli likes me, too."

Jesus. "You know what I think?" said Mary. "I think you've had a long morning and you should take your lunch break early. Relax. Process all the new information you've had to stuff into your little head. That way, you'll come back fresh and ready to learn more."

As Felicity was about to reply, a battleship of a woman entered the office with two younger women in tow.

"Be back by one o'clock?" Mary said as she stood to greet them.

Felicity nodded, abandoned her mug, and flounced away.

\*\*\*\*

After viewing three condos, Mr. Fung resolved to

sleep on his decision, so Eli dropped him off at the Sheraton, then drove back to Hill Realty to confront Claudia without Felicity or Stephen eavesdropping on their conversation. Claudia's niece was a sweet girl, but her voice bore into his skull like a dentist's drill. Claudia knew that he and Stephen didn't get along. She'd repeated the word "dream team" like a motivational mantra, but to Eli, Claudia's plan was a nightmare. The real dream team was Mary and him. Mary was a whiz with paperwork, which freed him to sell.

As he walked up to the front doors, Claudia was leaving the building, so he held the door for her and joined her on the sidewalk.

"We discussed everything this morning," she said crisply.

"Within earshot of Felicity," he countered. "We couldn't speak frankly."

Claudia marched like a Russian soldier and oncoming pedestrians gave her a wide berth. Despite his long legs, he had to hustle to keep up. "I only need a few minutes of your time," he added.

"You may walk me to yoga. This conversation must be over by the time we get to the Bodhi Tree." Claudia looped her arm under his, an unwelcome intimacy, but at least she slowed down.

"I think you should reconsider placing Felicity and Stephen at In-Spire," he said in a measured tone. "Mary works well independently, and I need someone there who can troubleshoot. And Felicity, well, she's very young."

"She's twenty-three."

"And untrained."

"The job isn't neurosurgery and she'll have Stephen to help her."

"Claudia, you know that Stephen doesn't like me."

"Ah-ha! You're finally catching on. I'm not asking you to like each other. Stephen needs tough love, Eli. A role model who can stand up to him and rein in his impulses. Our therapist says it shouldn't be me because I feed his mommy complex."

"What about Jonquil?"

"Didn't I mention his mommy complex?"

"Okay. Lori or Alex or Bill."

"They're ecstatic if they make a single sale each quarter. They're low volume."

"Stephen's fifty years old. I can't 'rein in' Stephen. I feel like you're setting me up to fail."

"Fine. Forget working with Stephen. But you're keeping Felicity. You need someone bubbly, someone cheerful and outgoing. Studious, serious Mary is like a bloody sea anchor. A drag on your sales."

"That isn't true, Claudia. She's changed. She works hard and she's competent."

"Eli, you and I have always understood each other." Claudia tightened her grip and drew closer, pressing an unnaturally firm breast against his arm. "Felicity has her heart set on working with you and she's more than capable."

He shuffled for space. "I'll only work with Mary."

"Oh. Oh, no." Claudia stopped. Her voice quivered. "You've violated my rule, haven't you? With her. She has you wrapped around her teeny-tiny pinky."

"Mary and I spend time together."

Claudia pushed his arm away. "Spend time together? What does that even mean? Share a table at bingo? You're screwing her, aren't you."

Such a vulgar word. He answered with silence.

"You are." Claudia started hyperventilating, then pressed her hand to her forehead and took a long breath through her nose. "You leave me no choice, Eli. I have to fire Mary."

"Don't, Claudia. We can keep the status quo. Felicity and Stephen stay with you, and Mary stays with me. If you prefer, I can explain the situation to Felicity."

"So you can play house with Mary in the sales office? Fool around in the bed of the model suite you've been too distracted to have installed?" Claudia stamped her foot. "Eli, do *not* forget who butters your bread. I gave you your start. I gave you a golden goose on a golden platter. I have the power to take everything back. Do not make this worse than necessary. Mary Rose no longer works for Hill Realty, effective immediately. Please have her come to my office tomorrow morning. I don't want her turning up and making a scene at In-Spire."

Eli stood speechless on the sidewalk as Claudia stalked to a double door with a stylized tree stenciled on it.

When she glared over her shoulder, he said, "I'll tell Mary myself."

Eli walked back to his car, blind to the stacks of colorful fruit the greengrocer displayed outside his shop, deaf to the shouting of kids playing basketball after school. He kicked an empty plastic bottle, too dispirited to even consider picking it up for the trash can.

"Hey, Sunshine." The gravelly greeting came from

Dino, crouched on a step in front of a padlocked, graffiti-covered door.

Eli stopped and smiled weakly. "Dino. How are you?"

"Better than you. You look like you've lost your best friend." He held up a mickey of gin and smiled like a jack o' lantern. "Want a swig?"

"No thanks. I have to drive."

"Never stopped me."

"And look where that got you," Eli joked.

"A bed in any park in the city, fine dining for life at the Sally Ann Bistro, and not a care in the goddam world. Free as a fucking pigeon."

"Your lifestyle has its merits." Eli turned to face the sun. "It's a pleasant afternoon."

"Bit of advice?"

"Sure."

"Slow down and smell the fucking daisies. Whatever problem you got is ten times worse when you rush at it like a goddam linebacker."

"Thanks, Dino. I'll try to remember that. You need anything?"

"Nah. I'm good."

"Truly you are," said Eli.

By the time he got back to the sales office, Felicity had left and Mary was arranging brochures on the rack in preparation for a busy April Saturday. His heart ached and his eyes stung at the sight of her. She was so precious. Tendrils of hair had come loose from her ponytail and her glasses had slipped down her nose. He had an inkling of how Abraham must've felt when he took Isaac up the mountain. Except Claudia wouldn't stay his knife.

"You okay?" Mary asked, arms open to him.

"Yeah. Just stressed." He hugged her long and close. "Let's go down to Sugar Point."

She peered up at him and smiled. "It's a date."

\*\*\*\*

Something was wrong. They drove with the windows down, wind blowing his wavy hair, the Beaches belting out a happy tune from the playlist she'd made for him, sunshine energizing the city after a long winter, and Eli was morose. Nothing she said would shake him from his foul mood. He parked between two SUVs and they strolled along the boardwalk to a bank of boulders, a bulwark against erosion. She sat on a bench-like rock and watched Eli pick up a flat, gray stone and skip it across the water.

"Five. Not bad," said Mary.

"Not good either," he grumbled.

Gulls circled overhead as he threw stones until he achieved a dozen skips three times in a row, and only then did he sit and take her hand in his.

"You going to tell me what's wrong?" she asked.

"Remember how I told you I'd make sure you stayed with me in the sales office?"

"I remember. I know Claudia can be difficult. Some promises are impossible to keep." Jeez, was that all it was? A minor broken promise? "Is Felicity taking my place at In-Spire?"

"Yes."

"Stop worrying, Eli. Felicity is flighty and she'll get bored and want to switch back."

He gazed over the lake. He wouldn't meet her eyes. At last, Mary understood. Claudia had gone nuclear.

"I'm fired, aren't I?" Mary asked softly.

177

Eli finally turned to her. "Claudia asked me directly if you and I are together. It doesn't make sense to lie, especially when we've got nothing to be ashamed of and she'd find out eventually."

"You did the right thing." Mary had never been fired before. It felt like an assault. As if someone had punched her in the gut and kicked her legs from under her.

"Don't worry about money, Mary. I'll make sure you're okay."

"I won't be a 'kept woman', Eli." A warm, salty tear rolled down her cheek. "I'll get another job."

"You don't have to."

Yes, she did have to, but he wouldn't understand that. "What are you going to do?" she asked.

"Wear earplugs to the office." He loosened a stone from their rock bench and pitched it into the lake. "I don't know. I've worked with Claudia for ten years, but it might be time to move on."

"Not on my account, Eli. You enjoy your job and you're making good money."

"Hill Realty is a cash cow that steps on its agents' toes," he said wistfully. "Mary, I'm so sorry. If I had more courage, I'd have quit today on principle."

"When you're ready, I'll type up your resume."

Eli wrapped his arm around her shoulders and nuzzled the top of her head. He'd fired her, then comforted her, and now all she wanted was to be naked with him. To forget the awfulness of the situation and lose herself with him. Mary slid off the rock and hugged him and he suckled her earlobe, hot breath raising the fine hair behind her ear.

"Dominic is out tonight," she whispered.

"In that case, I'd best see you to home port, Miss Rose," he replied.

## Chapter Fifteen

Eli left at dawn. Mary rolled to the still-warm place where he'd slept. A rush of conflicting emotions made further sleep impossible. Just for today, she'd let herself wallow in them, root through the gamut and examine each item, and tomorrow she'd update her résumé.

First off, she was angry. Angry with Claudia for being a ruthless bitch and getting away with it, and angry with Eli for not defending her, which made her feel guilty because he felt terrible too and her dismissal wasn't his fault. And she felt jealous. Felicity would now be the lady of the manor, thrusting her chest at Eli. Also, she was hurt and ashamed. Being fired was rejection at an elemental level. It meant you were neither needed nor wanted. And of course, there was fear, albeit mild. Thanks to Eli, she now had twelve thousand dollars in her checking account and a paid-up tuition bill and she could coast for several weeks. And finally, there was liberation. Office clothes felt like a costume. If tights didn't combust into toxic smoke, she'd burn every pair in her drawer. As of today, she was a full-time scholar in comfortable shoes and her time was her own.

All in all, she felt okay. Better than okay. She rolled out of bed and did some push-ups against the window frame. The sky glowed in cheery pink and a pigeon landed on the sill. Though she couldn't fly, she felt as free as the pigeon staring at her through the glass. Mary Hortensia Rose would begin the day with a run!

****

If ever a person tried Eli's patience, it was Felicity Hill. She arrived late, prioritized the viewing of TikTok over all other activity, and generally made herself useless.

Eli was checking his messages by the window when a heavily tattooed and pierced couple dressed in leather entered the office. With a sigh, Felicity unglued her eyes from her screen, seemed to make an appraisal, and after a lukewarm nod of greeting, returned to a video on beauty tips. The couple looked around the office and then at each other. As they turned to leave, Eli stepped forward.

"Great weather for April, isn't it?" He smiled.

"It is," said the woman. "Got the Harley out for the first time yesterday. Thought we'd come down before the traffic got bad."

"Aw, nothing like that first ride. I'm jealous."

"You gotta watch the potholes this time of year," said the man. "The QEW's the worst."

"You're brave. Where'd you ride from?"

"Hamilton," they replied in unison.

"Nice. Great waterfront, the escarpment…"

"We like it," said the woman.

"But Sonia has a new job at Queen's Park, so we're thinking of buying a place for her to crash if she misses her train," added the man.

"Well, Queen's Park is a quick ride on the subway and only a fifteen-minute walk from here. I'm Eli, by the way." He extended his hand. "Eli Klassen."

Sonia and Mike had warm, firm, business-like handshakes. As Eli befriended them, he watched Felicity from the corner of his eye. Her butt was crazy-glued to her swivel chair.

After ten minutes of easy conversation, and a refusal of coffee but contact info willingly provided, Sonia and Mike accepted a sales package to share with their cousin, an agent based in the west end.

"The model suite opens later this month, and I think it matches what you're looking for," Eli said in closing. "May I contact you when it's ready for viewing?"

"Sure," said Mike. "Shoot us an email."

And off they went.

Felicity rummaged through her purse, a leather sack large enough to transport Christmas presents to every household in the Great Lakes basin. Eli addressed the top of her head. "Uh, may I ask if you intended to greet that couple who just left?"

Felicity put a tiny bottle of nail polish on the desk and looked up. "Yeah, you can ask. I did greet them."

"You tore your eyes away from the screen for three seconds and nodded to them."

"They're tire kickers, Eli. They wasted, like, fifteen minutes of your time."

"She's a lawyer. They have need of a one-bedroom condo and the means to pay for it."

"You bought that story?"

"Yes. It's credible. Until we get to know people, we have no idea who is walking through that door. Everyone who comes into this office is our guest. At a minimum, I'd like you to get up from the desk, smile, ask how their day's going, and offer them a hot drink and information. And try to get their contact info."

"Like Connie Lingus at 555-1234?"

"Especially if it's Connie Lingus. I need all the laughs I can get."

Felicity shrugged. "Okee-dokee. You're the boss."

"Do you want to rehearse your spiel? So you feel more comfortable interacting with people?"

She shook the tiny bottle. "It's just 'good morning' and yada yada yada."

"All right. I'm stepping out for a bit. I'll be back in a couple of hours." Eli grabbed his jacket, then paused at the door. "Text me if anything comes up that you're not sure about, okay?"

Felicity rolled her eyes. "This job isn't rocket science, Eli."

So true. And yet, however simple her duties, Felicity was capable of failing through lack of effort. Eli stepped into the sunshine. Until noon, he had no place he had to be except out of that claustrophobia-inducing sales office. He strolled over to the plywood wall surrounding the construction site and peered through a window guarded with chain link fencing. Though Saturday, workers were taking advantage of the fine weather to prepare the site for concrete. *Concrete.* A tangible thing. A foundation for a building that would shelter real human beings.

For the first time in over a decade, Eli wondered what he was doing with his life. He was good at real estate, but was he proud of his work? Sure, he had money, but he was trapped in a game-show world. He was a male Vanna White showing off fabulous properties. When Claudia had cornered him, he'd obeyed her command like a submissive, neutered lapdog and he'd failed to protect Mary. Even Bingley had tougher nuts. Eli envied the men who set the forms in the pit below him. In the evening, they'd go home to their wives and children, having accomplished something real. They had less money but more self-respect.

In contrast, he was an emasculated refugee from his own sales office. If only Mary were behind the desk, greeting visitors with her shy, disarming charm and organizing files with breezy efficiency. He wanted to call her, hear her voice, and share a laugh, but he didn't deserve her.

\*\*\*\*

Apart from several tender exchanges by text, Mary didn't communicate with Eli for the remainder of the weekend and she used the time to fix her proposal according to Gabriel's instructions. On Monday morning, she awoke rested and ready for a week devoted entirely to philosophy. As she filled her water bottle for a long day on campus, Dominic sidled into the kitchen with a sneery grin and a twinkle in his eye. Without a word, he passed his phone to her, then leaned against the counter and crossed his arms to control his unconcealed mirth.

"Must be a funny one." She peered at the screen. "Breaking story in the Toronto *Meteor*."

"Oh, it's a doozy."

"Identity of victim revealed," she read aloud. Then she read in silence.

*Meteor* reader, *Hilda Bainbridge, resident of Briarmont Court, has identified the elderly man who was assaulted at the western gate of the university last Tuesday as Dr. Gabriel Silverstein, a renowned professor of philosophy. Although Mrs. Bainbridge initially contacted the police, progress on the case appears stalled and the assailant remains at large. Dr. Silverstein has declined to speak with the media.*

*In an exclusive interview with the* Meteor, *Mrs. Bainbridge stated that while walking her dog on Tuesday morning, she witnessed a young man lurking in the parkette between Briarmont Court and the university. She also alleged that the same man accosted Dr. Silverstein as he walked to work. Mrs. Bainbridge has provided a photo taken at her annual garden party of Dr. Silverstein reclining on a chaise longue. Expert analysis suggests with high probability that the victim in the CCTV image released by police is Dr. Silverstein. However, Dr. Silverstein denied Mrs. Bainbridge's assertion stating, "appearances deceive" before slamming the door of his tony Briarmont home on* Meteor *staff.*

*Mrs. Bainbridge told the* Meteor, *"I shan't feel safe in my own neighborhood until that dangerous miscreant is arrested and brought to justice. Unfortunately, the police have proved ineffectual in solving this crime and have left the citizenry to perform the legwork for them. Obviously, Gabriel is too traumatized to cooperate with their investigation, and who could possibly blame him?"*

Mary stopped reading and looked closely at side-by-side photos, the first of Gabriel lounging with a martini glass and the second of a fat man who looked uncannily like him lying in a garden as a tall man who looked just like Eli loomed with an outstretched arm. She'd seen the CCTV image in her news feed, but her brain hadn't made the connection.

Mary looked to Dominic, whose shoulders shook with a stifled giggle. "You think this is funny?" she asked.

"It is." Dominic descended into a tailspin of belly laughter. "I mean, they are Eli and Gabriel. It's as obvious as that pimple on your chin."

Mary felt her chin. It was smooth. "I've read enough," she said crossly as she returned the phone to Dominic.

"But you're missing the part where Hilda Bainbridge says her impeccably pedigreed dog Bingley detected the odor of pure evil on the miscreant's lower leg. You have to read below the photos."

"I've read enough. I've got an exam to proctor."

"Not until ten. Come on, Mary. You've got to admit it's funny." Dominic rubbed his hands together with relish. "I can't wait to hear the real story."

"I'll buy popcorn on my way home." Mary turned on her heel, snatched her jean jacket and rucksack from the table, crammed her feet into sneakers, and left in a huff.

With each step down the hallway and stairwell, her confusion grew. Tuesday was the day Gabriel had approved her proposal and she'd played hooky with Eli in his bed. Eli had been home with a migraine that morning. Gabriel had been in his office. Unless.

The lobby's vinyl upholstered bench, customarily occupied by people waiting for rides, was vacant and Mary sat down. She pulled her phone from her rucksack, reread the article, and examined the photos again. The CCTV image was timestamped at 8:34. She'd gone to Gabriel's office...when? 9:00? 9:15? That was ample time for Eli to strong-arm Gabriel into approving her proposal and to return to his condo to wait for her call. They'd both acted peculiarly, Gabriel the model advisor, warm and supportive yet pale and disheveled. Eli, pleased with himself, like a cat who'd eaten the goldfish. She'd seen how he dealt with male adversaries. Why not add Gabriel to his hit list?

Her phone pinged a message. It was Eli.

—*Good morning, Mary Rose.*—

Mary turned the ringtone off and tossed the phone into her rucksack without responding. She'd deal with Gabriel first.

\*\*\*\*

Her first stop was the place where detectives traditionally began an investigation, the scene of the crime, though she had no clue what she was looking for. A talking squirrel who'd witnessed Eli and Gabriel's altercation? In only six days, the drab garden in the CCTV image had come alive with crocus and daffodil shoots and a fountain-like bush blooming in golden yellow. So pretty. What was the name of it? Eli would know. She probably wouldn't ask him.

Mary crossed the northern sector of the campus, tranquil in the hour before students would arrive to take final exams. Over several weeks, she'd learned a few tricks by observing Eli in action as Claudia had suggested. One lesson he'd unwittingly imparted was the strategy of silence. When he wanted an advantage, he'd ask a question or two, look empathetic, and wait for his counterpart to talk. And talk. Today she would ask the questions and Eli and Gabriel would do the talking.

Gabriel was in his office. She pushed the door open without knocking and he looked up as if expecting her.

"Miss Mary Rose." A close-lipped smile nested in his goatee. He dropped his pen, nodded to her usual chair, and leaned back in his own.

"Good morning, Gabriel." She sat down and took inordinate time to arrange her rucksack on her lap. "Interesting news in today's *Meteor*."

"I don't read tabloids. Well, aside from an occasional perusal of page three." His lips shifted into a leer.

Few people read print media anymore—she didn't—but she recalled that page three featured a new pin-up girl every day. She said, "You should make an exception for today's edition. You don't have to read past the front page."

"Ah, yes." Gabriel tented his fat fingers. "I believe I scanned it at the newsstand. Irresponsible of their cub reporter to dredge up muck and call it pudding. The police won't be amused by the *Meteor's* antics. Media interference is bound to be a nuisance during an investigation, though one also questions the competence of the detectives."

"Gabriel, it's you in the paper."

"An unflattering photo to be sure. I'm afraid Mrs. Bainbridge egged me on rather aggressively. I was imbibing my third cocktail and somewhat worse for wear when the picture was snapped on that glorious July afternoon."

"I'm referring to the image from the security camera."

"That overturned tortoise is not Dr. Gabriel A. Silverstein."

"It is though."

"Your claim is preposterous, Mary. As I'm certain

you'll recall, last Tuesday I was here, reviewing a submission for *Intersections of Meaning.*"

"And you looked awful. As if someone had mugged you that very morning."

Gabriel waved his hand, then patted his abdomen. "*That very morning*, I had dyspepsia from an indulgent breakfast. Ham and Swiss croissants tend to disagree."

Exasperating. His denials were walling off the truth. Mary needed a Trojan horse to breach his defences. She fidgeted with the drawstring of her bag and sighed meekly. "Now I'll never know if my proposal met your standard. Am I good enough or am I just another Olympic skater whose boyfriend knocks down obstacles in her path with a hammer or a fist?"

Gabriel puffed his chest and spoke in a superior tone. "I'm afraid I'm in no position to reassure you."

"So, it *is* you."

He shrugged and put his index finger to his lips.

"I should do my duty as a citizen and go to the police," said Mary, managing to sound both threatening and sanctimonious.

"And risk your academic future?" Gabriel shook his head. Unlike last week, the wattles of his neck were braced with a tight collar and tie. "You wouldn't dare."

She'd achieved her objective, confirmation that Eli had forced Gabriel to accept her proposal, but there were bothersome gaps in the narrative forming in her mind. "I'm puzzled. You must've been terrified. And furious. Most people would've gone to the police. Why didn't you?"

Gabriel's smug smile returned. "First, I accept that I was somewhat 'furious', but I deny being 'terrified' in the least and I'm as rational as ever. I'm a master, not a victim, and neither is your brutish lover. Nor are you, Mary. All three of us have a metaphorical bomb in our possession and we travel in the same boat. If the truth of last Tuesday's incident were exposed, we'd all lose. Our self-identities, our social currency, our reputations, everything we hold dear would explode into smithereens. Wouldn't it be a pity to lose what we've each endeavored to gain by blabbing like babes? To be thought weak or violent or stupid by our peers?"

"Yes, it would be a pity, Gabriel, but I think I have the least to lose," she replied, hoping to unbalance him, even if only a little. "You're the only one of us with a Wikipedia page and it's updated regularly."

Gabriel didn't flinch.

Through the window, Mary glimpsed the time on the tower clock. Fifteen minutes till the doors opened to the gym in which hundreds of science students would take their compulsory stats exam.

She stood and said, "I have one last question and I want an honest answer. I know you were giving me the run-around and I know that you were bullied into changing your mind last Tuesday. However, I have to know: is my proposal truly good enough? Not according to a committee of your sycophants, but in your opinion. As my advisor."

Gabriel pulled on his beard as if pondering a thorny philosophical question. After a lengthy silence, he met her eye. "I can't say."

Damn him! "Right. I have to go."

"Could you double-check the references in this paper?" He thumped his hand on a thick manila envelope.

"If you say 'please'," she said icily.

Gabriel didn't say 'please'. He pursed his lips and handed her the envelope.

Swallowing her bitter rage, Mary stuffed it into her rucksack. As she jogged to the sports complex, she assessed her situation. Gabriel was a dick. Eli had acted like a dick. They both had to be taught a lesson. If her life "exploded into smithereens," so be it. Righteous indignation and anger roiled in her heart. It was a dangerous combination.

\*\*\*\*

They'd texted all weekend but that morning. Mary didn't respond to any of the five messages he'd sent her. Everything felt so right and natural when he left her bed on Saturday morning. Why the cold shoulder now? Had she lost her phone? She would've emailed from her laptop. Realized he was a coward for not standing up to Claudia and cooled on him? Maybe. But her version of manhood accepted cowardice as "sensitivity," and she'd reassured him that her firing didn't affect their relationship with each other.

"Wow!" A single, shrill syllable from behind the desk.

Eli broke his gaze from his phone, where he was searching for hints of where he'd gone wrong, and he looked at Felicity with faint curiosity.

"Remember the old guy who got beaten up at U of T last week?" she asked. "They've figured out who he is."

A vise of terror clenched Eli's stomach. He went over to the desk and peered at Felicity's screen.

"Dr. Gabriel Silverstein," said Felicity. "A philosophy prof. I wonder if Mary knows him?"

"Maybe." Eli's hands shook too much to find the

story on his phone. "Do they know who attacked him?"

"Not yet. Or maybe they do and they're not telling anyone until they've arrested him."

"Yeah. Maybe. They wouldn't want to tip him off. He could be dangerous," Eli muttered.

"Says here that the victim is too traumatized to cooperate with the investigation. Must be horrible for him. Acute PTSD. He'll need intensive therapy." Felicity's words were unusually authoritative. Of course. She was a psych major.

"Do you think the prof will come round and talk to the cops?" he asked.

"Ninety-nine percent yes. They'll push him until he does. They can't let a scumbag prowl the streets terrorizing people."

"Maybe there's more to the story than meets the eye. Maybe the man had it coming."

"What? An elderly prof? No way, Eli. A senseless attack like that had to be random. The attacker is definitely dangerous. No one on campus will feel safe until he's locked up."

Eli's brain whirred like a skill saw. He should've thrown away the clothes he wore last Tuesday. Changed between dealing with Silverstein and being with Mary. Reinforced Silverstein's silence with some sort of blackmail and come up with a bulletproof alibi for the hour between eight and nine. At least now he knew why Mary wasn't returning his texts.

Eli flopped onto the sofa and sent another text. — It's not what it looks like. May I pick you up at school so I can explain?—

This time Mary replied right away. —We can meet. Roasters at four.—

\*\*\*\*

Eli waited in front of the café with a large Earl Grey in a take-out cup. Mary disembarked from the streetcar in a torrent of rush-hour commuters and walked toward him, her gait brisk and her shoulders back. She meant business.

She received the cup with a cold nod. "Thanks."

"Want to go for a drive?" he asked.

"No. It's warm," she replied. "Let's find a place in the sunshine to sit."

They settled on a bench in the garden next to the art gallery. Eli didn't dare touch her. Didn't dare speak till she'd revealed the lay of the land.

Mary took a single slurp of tea through a jagged hole in the plastic lid, then set the cup aside. "Maybe you should begin by telling me what happened last Tuesday morning. Around eight thirty-four."

"Let's see." Eli shuffled his shoes in the dirt. "Uh, I was out on my bike, getting some exercise, and I ran into your prof, Gabriel Silverstein, and...uh...I made his acquaintance. We discussed things. He mentioned how sharp you are, and that you'd probably be a professor yourself down the road. I encouraged him to take a closer look at your proposal. I suggested that maybe his judgement was unduly harsh."

"Great story."

"Thanks."

"Except it's fiction and I'm into nonfiction today. Start again, Eli. From the beginning with no omission and no embellishment. And don't stop until the end when I turn up at your condo believing that my proposal is the best thing since *War and Peace*."

"I didn't lie."

"And somehow you haven't told me the truth either, so out with it."

Mary propped her feet on a rock and waited with a scary frown etched on her forehead. Short of spontaneous combustion, he had no escape.

"Well, uh…I saw how Gabriel hurt you on Easter morning. You'd already sent me your proposal and I read it. I'm undereducated but even I could tell it's brilliant. Then I got to thinking: how could I help Mary? Before you accuse me of having an ulterior motive, I want you to know that your vow had nothing to do with it. I asked myself, if you were my sister, what would I do? I wouldn't stand by and watch someone push you around.

"I figured out where Gabriel lives and noticed the path from his house to the philosophy building runs through a park. You were going to see him on Tuesday morning, so I intercepted him on his way to work. He's a snake, Mary. He had to be dealt with."

"A snake, is he? Stick to the facts, Eli. What happened next?"

"Isn't that enough?"

"No. There's a lot more to the story. For instance, you haven't explained how Gabriel ended up in the garden or why you were hitting him when he was down."

"What? You mean in the CCTV photo?"

She nodded.

"I was offering my hand to help him up."

"If you say so. It sure doesn't look like that. And that doesn't explain how he wound up there in the first place."

"We argued and I picked him up."

"Let me guess—by his tie?"

"It was the easiest thing to grab. He kicked me in the shin and I dropped him. He toppled over like a bowling pin and I wasn't fast enough to steady him."

"I suppose I can picture it," Mary conceded. "But why did you touch him in the first place?"

"He said some things that I found objectionable."

"Like what?"

"I can't tell you."

"The whole story, Eli."

"Well, uh, he said you were, um, a woman of easy virtue."

"You beat up a man who's weaker than you over a ridiculous taunt?"

"I told you, I didn't beat him. I only intimidated him and made him change his mind. Can't we stop? The guy's an asshole. You know that."

"No, we can't stop," she said with obvious exasperation. "Your story is mildly interesting but there are a few gaping plot holes. Things like, why didn't you tell me all this before? Why did you go behind my back? Why did you deceive me into thinking my proposal passed on its own merits?"

"Because it did. Gabriel would've made you dance like a puppet on a string, but he intended to approve it eventually. I saved you the trouble of jumping through his hoops."

"Oh, so now I should thank you?" she squawked. "After you lied to me?"

"I didn't lie. I just didn't tell you everything."

"You don't have to be a philosopher or a biblical scholar to know that amounts to the same thing."

"I was trying to help you by protecting you from a

cruel man."

Eli slumped on the bench. This wasn't going well. The harder he tried to reach her, the more firmly she dug in her sharply principled heels.

After a bitter silence, Mary said, "I was handling the situation in my own way. Now I can't gauge the strength of my scholarship. I've been deprived of the chance to solve my own problem. And I can't trust you."

"You can." She could! Why couldn't she see it?

"No, I can't, Eli. You were dishonest. We've been living under your lie for six days, and you had no intention of telling me the truth. You let me celebrate and prance around school with a shiny red ribbon that I didn't earn. A fucking participation medal. You know it and Gabriel knows it. You've made a fool of me."

"Mary, he as much as admitted your proposal was good enough. He was toying with you and I stopped him."

"Good enough." She sniffed. "'Good enough' is not good enough for Gabriel. He demands excellence and so do I. Now I don't know if I'm achieving that because he refuses to tell me."

"You give him too much power. Why does it matter what he thinks? You're a step closer to getting your PhD."

"'Getting it' is not the same as 'earning it.' Jesus." She crossed her arms and stared down a herring gull begging for food. "Anyway, this isn't about Gabriel. It's about you and me."

"I'm sorry."

She didn't break her focus on the gull. She refused to even glance his way.

"Really, Mary. You're right. I messed things up. I'm sorry and if there's anything I can do to regain your trust I'll do it in a heartbeat."

She took a mournful breath. "I don't know if we can fix this, Eli."

"Can't we at least try?" he pleaded.

She nodded slowly and turned to him, steel gray eyes glinting like gunmetal. "I've given the matter some thought. By the way Gabriel was acting, you must've nearly strangled him. You owe him an apology."

"I'll apologize today." Was that all? Thank God. He reached for her but she snatched her hand away.

"Also, Eli, you need to turn yourself in to the police."

"Uh-uh. No way. We're all better off if this blows over and no one ever finds out who we are. Gabriel agrees with me."

"So you've discussed it with him." She looked away again and muttered, "The shit pile keeps getting bigger and bigger."

"After the story first broke, I called him. No one can tell for sure that it's us in the photo. Not even Hilda Bainbridge. Isn't it better if we all keep quiet?"

"No, not at all," she said crisply.

"Why not? If I'm identified, it'll ruin my career. I'll be the notorious agent who beats up old men. Even if I'm not charged with anything, everyone will think I'm a criminal."

"And if you don't come forward, the community will live in fear. *The Meteor* has sensationalized the story to make it sound as if a psycho-killer is on the loose. The only way to relieve the public's anxiety is for you to confess to the police."

"I can't do that, Mary. If I confess, I might as well tear up my real estate license." She was trying to march him down a gangplank and he wouldn't go. No way.

"Eli, this is an opportunity to do the moral thing. The brave thing. To put others ahead of money and prestige."

"I do that all the time."

"When it's easy. When there's nothing of great significance at stake. Well, this time, there is. The well-being of the community, your integrity, and our future."

"Mary, if I confess, my income will dry up like that." He snapped his fingers. Mary stared at him, cold and hard as a marble statue, and he blundered on. "I won't be able to buy you nice things or help you with tuition."

"I don't want you to buy me anything." Her voice quavered with fury. "In fact, I'm going to pay back every cent you've paid me over and above my regular wage."

"Keep the money. You earned it."

"Every goddam cent, Eli."

"Don't, Mary. There must be some way for us to fix this. Yes, I lied. Yes, I screwed everything up. But I did what I did because I care about you. I care about us. I'm sorry. I won't lie to you again."

"Eli, your apology means nothing to me unless it's backed up by action. Even then...I don't know. I have to go."

He had a hideous feeling of losing grip on a rope, of weakening and being forced to let go of her, but he couldn't give up. "I'll drive you home," he said gently.

"I'll take the streetcar."

"Are you dumping me?"

"I need some space."

"You *are* dumping me. Mary—"

"Good-bye, Eli."

She threw her full cup of tea into a nearby bin and walked away. He was paralyzed with shock, adrift in an oarless boat with no haven in sight. He stayed on the bench, not knowing what to do or where to go next. Home? Work? Wherever he went, he'd think of her—his condo, his bed, Takamatsu, the sales office, Sugar Point, even his shower—there would be no sanctuary from his wretchedness.

Chapter Sixteen

Mary was back at square one in the snakes and ladders game of life. Jobless, alone, and broken-hearted, standing among strangers in a rolling sardine tin, breathing air humidified by bodies whose antiperspirant and mouthwash had failed with a long day's work. She couldn't have accepted a ride from Eli. She couldn't accept *anything* from him. Not his apology, not his money, not his goddam self-serving story. She'd done the right thing. She was sure of that. But why did the right thing have to hurt so much?

She pressed the back of her hand against her nose to stop her tears, a trick she'd learned in childhood. This time, it didn't work. Though she was hollow with grief, her tear ducts were brimming vessels and she couldn't keep from crying.

A liver-spotted hand waved a tissue in front of her face. She nodded to the giver, an old woman with kind, wrinkled eyes and the flawless smile of a denture wearer. "Thanks," Mary murmured as she wiped under her glasses.

"Honey, I have a granddaughter about your age. If you're in trouble and you need help..." The woman peered up, face radiating compassion.

Mary shook her head. "I'm all right."

"You don't look all right."

"I just broke up with my boyfriend, that's all," she

blurted. To a stranger on a streetcar. What the hell!

"You poor thing. Men are such trouble."

"He lied to me. I had to end it and now I feel so awful."

"Honey, it's hard but you did the right thing. A dishonest boy is like an unreliable car. He can be funny, handsome, rich, great in bed, doesn't matter. You can't trust a liar. If you want to find happiness, you have to trade up. Or take the bus. You know what I mean?"

"Yeah. Thanks. I suppose that's true."

"You have a tissue. You have my best advice. Now I'll give you one more thing."

"What's that?"

"My seat. I transfer at the next stop, honey."

\*\*\*\*

Eli lay on the sofa with a cold cloth on his head, a melancholy melody from one of Mary's playlists haunting his soul. She'd given him this, music, and he hadn't thanked her. He might never have the chance to thank her and the thought of that sucked at his spirit until he felt as if it were a shrivelled, dried-up pea. He'd head to a bar, or Takamatsu, but the Ikedas' sympathy would crush that pea into powder. The only company he could handle was his own. Barely.

What the hell. He wanted Mary back. He threw the cloth on the apple crate and called Silverstein, who actually answered.

"Silverstein? It's Eli Klassen."

"Ah, yes. Miss Rose's inamorato."

"I've been thinking—"

"Oh my. I hope it wasn't too taxing for you," snickered Gabriel.

"Not at all," said Eli. "Thinking gave me a little

thrill. I can see how you intellectual types get off on it."

"And these thoughts of yours?"

"We're cornered, Silverstein. We're like rats behind a diner fridge during the breakfast rush. The cops will dig and dig until the truth comes out. It might be better to be proactive. We could decide how we want this thing to end, then visit the police station together. As far as we know, all they have is a photo and Hilda Bainbridge's crazy theory. If we both paid a visit to the police, we could explain what happened last week and resolve their investigation once and for all."

"Now why would I want to do that?"

"To relieve public anxiety."

"I've never cared for the hoi polloi. I don't see any reason to begin doing so now."

"Then to call off the hounds at the *Meteor.*"

"Mr. Klassen, the hounds will lose our scent in due course. They are highly distractable animals. Tiny Tim will have his rollator stolen. The Tooth Fairy will catch rabies from the Easter Bunny. Any and all manner of calamity will elbow our story from prominence. Hold firm. In post-millennial parlance, that is how we'll manage the narrative. As we agreed."

"What if I told the cops you tripped and I was helping you up?"

"I'd call you a liar and inform the police you threatened to murder me by vivisection. I'm not a man who stumbles like a doddering, senile fool and relies on the aid of others. However, I am a man who sees merit in revenge, and I would press charges."

"Fine. If you change your mind—"

"I won't. I hope we shan't have occasion to speak again." Click.

Eli put his phone on the crate and sat with his elbows propped on his knees and his face buried in his hands. He couldn't go to the police alone. Not with a long-ago weapons charge, later reduced to trespassing, for forcing the return of a stolen snowmobile from the Klein farm by means of a hunting rifle. The cops would believe Silverstein over him.

His phone pinged.

Jesus Christ. Another message from Stephen: — I'm getting impatient. Twenty grand tomorrow morning or I talk.— appended with a photo of the frilly underwear he'd stolen.

—Those are Mary's. I don't think she can afford your ransom.— Eli texted back.

There. That took care of the Stephen Hill problem.

Eli lumbered to the balcony for fresh air and stood in the place where nearly a week ago Mary came to him. Where he'd held her in a cool morning breeze. He could throw himself over the rail, a dramatic end for a discarded lover. She'd be sorry she hurt him. What was he thinking? He wasn't a melodramatic teenage girl. He leaned over the rail and looked at the street below. A body falling from the seventeenth floor would splatter like a ripe tomato and put pedestrians in danger physically and psychologically. A suicide like that would be gruesome. Anyway, he didn't want to die. He wanted Mary back.

Vehicles and people moved through the street like blood cells in an artery. Amidst the controlled chaos, a taxi stopped at the curb and a round cloaked and bonneted woman got out, followed by a man in a dark jacket. The driver opened the trunk and the man heaved two huge suitcases onto the sidewalk and paid the driver. In cash? Had to be because it looked like the driver was making change. Holy shit. These people. Their clothing, body language, and the cash transaction. They were like people from Eden Springs.

It was Grandma and a male relative! Probably his own brother. Probably Jacob. Jesus fucking Christ. He couldn't say that out loud. Not in front of Grandma and Jacob. The intercom buzzed. Who the fuck used an intercom anymore? Klassens without a cellphone. That's who.

Eli tore from room to room, making his bed, wiping the bathroom mirror and fixtures with a skanky towel that he then threw in the tub, piling dirty dishes into the kitchen sink. Buzz-buzz. He took a deep breath and pressed the speaker button to welcome his family into his life on the seventeenth floor.

\*\*\*\*

"Did you bring popcorn?" Dominic called from the living room as Mary kicked off her shoes.

"Nope." She hung her jacket properly to delay her entrance for a minuscule moment. It was easier to talk to a stranger on public transit than to face Dominic, who liked Eli and would be disappointed.

When he saw her, he patted the sofa cushion. "Oh dear. Come to daddy."

She sat, he put a box of tissue on her lap and his arm around her shoulder, and she told him everything. When she ran out of story and tears—a heap of sodden, crumpled tissues her testament to that—Dominic said, "You did what you had to, Mary. Streetcar lady is right. Tricking you the way Eli did is a zero-tolerance offence."

"We were so happy. I can't believe it's over."

"It isn't over. You've given your Hercules a task. His motivation for acting the way he did was honorable, though the ends in no way justified the means. He thought he was rescuing his damsel, and you've corrected him. Severely…which he deserved. He might come through for you yet."

"I can't wait around."

"No. You shouldn't do that. You have to move on and fill your life with things that are important to you. But don't dive into the dating pool just yet. It's shallow and you'll hit your head on the bottom."

"Dominic, if you were in my situation, you'd be on Grindr the moment you left that park bench and were out of eyeshot."

"True. But I'm not you. For me, love is love and sex is sex. One-night stands are a thrilling hobby. Like philately or lepidoptery. You're different. If you shag some random guy to soothe your broken heart, it'll backfire. You'll think of Eli and feel ten times worse."

Mary hugged her knees to her chest and looked sideways at Dominic. "What hobby do you suggest for me?"

"Oenology."

"But we don't have any wine."

"I bought a box of Chateau Mouffette. It pairs well with popcorn. Which we don't have."

"Doesn't *mouffette* mean skunk?"

"Yes. Now don't be a wine snob, Mary. It's unbecoming."

"I'm not getting drunk with you, Dominic. I can't face tomorrow with a broken heart and a hangover."

"One glass? As a mild sedative?"

"One glass."

"*Un verre pour madame.*" Dominic sashayed into the kitchen, filled two fishbowl-sized glasses, and returned. Handing Mary her glass, he toasted, "Here's to moral rectitude!"

****

Grandma unbuckled the straps of the suitcase that Jacob had lifted onto the dining room table. She rummaged through jars and knitwear and paper-wrapped cheeses. "Ach. It's always the last place you look. First thing in, last thing out. Stands to reason, mind."

"The salve and tea can wait, Grandma. Let him suffer a spell. It serves him right," said Jacob.

"Hey, Jake. I'm right here and I understand English." Eli was back on the sofa with a cold cloth on his forehead at Grandma's insistence.

"Good," said Jacob. "No use hiding what I think and what everyone in Eden Springs thinks. You made an old widow worry and venture into Gomorrah to track down her prodigal grandson. She'll fete you with the fatted calf, but God sees everything and you'll have your reckoning on judgement day...." Jacob's voice trailed off. Expecting a lecture, Eli lifted the cloth and cocked an eye open. His elder brother had raided the pile of junk mail and was leafing through a flyer featuring discounted ladies' underwear.

"Something tickling your fancy, Jake?" Eli asked slyly. "Or someone?"

"Ruth needs a new nursing bra." Jacob puffed his chest like a peanut-brained rooster. "For little Ezra."

"Ah yes. The fruit of your loins. Poor Ruth. I mean, it's wonderful about Ezra, the miracle of a newborn infant, but what she must've had to endure on your wedding night—"

"You. Are. Sick. A sick sinner." Jacob dropped the flyer on the table and loomed over Eli with his eyes rolled heavenward. "Lord, if it be your will to punish—"

"Jacob! Eli! Enough!" Grandma grabbed Jacob's hand and stuck a fifty-dollar bill in his palm. "Walmart is open late." Then she turned. "Eli, is it safe for Jacob to go shopping at this hour?"

"It's only seven-thirty," said Eli.

"Yes, but what time do the gangs come out? The robbers and druggies and pimps?"

"Pimps?"

Unseen by Grandma, Jacob shook his head to signal she didn't know the meaning of the word and Eli shouldn't enlighten her. As if he would.

"Yes, Eli." Grandma's face was crinkled with worry. "All the bad men."

"This area's safe twenty-four hours a day, Grandma. You can borrow my car, Jake."

Grandma turned to Jacob. "Can you find a Walmart? Or a Food Basics?"

"The taxi drove by a grocery store called Price Chopper," said Jacob.

"All right. The prices won't be too dear with a name like that." She reached up, placed a gnarled hand on Jacob's shoulder, and bowed her head. "Dear Lord. Thank you for keeping us in safety and comfort during our journey today. We ask that you keep this child of Jesus safe as he conducts his errand. Amen." She opened her eyes and spoke to her oldest grandchild. "Eli doesn't have any milk, butter, or eggs."

"City people eat in restaurants," said Jacob. "They

think food comes from plastic packages."

"I've heard that too but your mama raised him so he can at least fry an egg. He can't have forgotten everything he was taught. Do you want a list?"

"No. I'll remember. Does he need anything else?"

"No, he doesn't," Eli muttered.

"Some nice pieces of chicken? Thighs with a good red color to them. You have to open the cellophane and lift the skin to check. Onions, carrots, and a cabbage, if it's not wilted," said Grandma.

"Keys are in my jacket pocket by the door," Eli said to a nervous-looking Jacob who detested city driving. "When you get on the elevator, press B2, and it's in a spot to the left of the door."

"Still the foreign car?"

"Yup."

After Jacob left, Grandma took a pillow from the bed and a crocheted blanket from her suitcase and commanded Eli to remove his shirt and lie prone. She pulled a chair next to the sofa, draped the blanket over his back, and massaged her special salve onto his forehead, temples, neck, and shoulders. The concoction was hot and cold on his skin and smelled spicy. She worked in silence, kneading the knots in his muscles with warm hands accustomed to hard work. "There," she said. "Now rest a spell while I make the tea."

He didn't listen. He never listened. Instead, he rolled toward her and asked, "Grandma, why did you come today? I'm happy to see you, but your surgery isn't till May and I would've picked you up. You didn't have to take the train."

"Why, to bring you medicine. Isn't that obvious?"

"How did you know I needed it?"

"Someone named Mary wrote to me and told me that your headaches are bad. She asked me to mail some salve and tea to you. I know you and I know when you get this way, you're up to some manner of mischief. You get headaches when you act against your conscience. Jacob's underfoot with the new baby and it's a couple weeks till planting so he could be spared to help me. I prayed and God told me you needed me, so here I am." She laid her hand on his arm and spoke softly. "Eli, it's plain you're a lost lamb and you're not happy. You don't have to tell me why. Not tonight. Unless you want to."

"Not tonight."

"That Mary must be a good friend to go to the trouble of writing."

"She is." The mention of Mary, by his grandmother of all people, made him sadder than he'd ever been. The dam broke, and he started sobbing like a boy who'd lost his dog. "Was," he choked.

Grandma put her arms around him, and he wept.

\*\*\*\*

Mary awoke in the night disoriented with loss. For over two months, Eli had been the center of her world. She thought of him as she drifted off to sleep, and she thought of him when she woke. She fought to break free from his hold, but try as she might, she couldn't jerk herself out of his gravitational field.

She turned on her side and hugged her pillow. If only she could lie in his arms again. Feel his breath on her forehead. Push her nose against his skin and smell him. Press her ear against his chest and hear the rumble of his voice. No. She flopped onto her other side. He lied. He was sneaky. He was prone to violence. Eli wasn't even her type. She had to expunge him from her life, beginning with his messages and photos and social media.

Mary reached for her phone and cleared their texts, though she left him in her contact list. She scrolled through her gallery...the selfie they'd taken in front of his car on Good Friday...a couple more photos from Easter. Was that all she had? Three measly photos? Not even worth erasing. Mary opened her social media to unfollow and unfriend, but Eli's activity only amounted to a few reposted articles on LinkedIn and Twitter. He wouldn't even notice her absence, so she didn't bother.

Surely it was part of the healing process and not too creepy to snoop on the Hill Realty website? There was Eli's headshot on the "Meet the Team" page. A dashing Eli in a row of smartly dressed people at a conference. A Disney prince Eli in black tie, accepting an award at the Toronto Real Estate Board gala. A laughing Eli, same event, between Jonquil and Lori, each with a champagne glass in hand. Claudia, his one-woman fan club, had more photos of him than she did. Claudia let herself love him—it was obvious in the way she fluttered around him picking imaginary bits of lint from his shirt. Why couldn't Mary give in to her feelings?

Because he lied to her, nearly garroted a weaker man, and made a fool of her.

Mary stuck her phone under her pillow and rolled over again. Darkness enclosed her in grief. She needed a life preserver. Something or someone to cling to until she could let go of him.

She hadn't used a dating app in months. Maybe Dominic was wrong. A date with a mature man would take her mind off things. No heavy expectations...just light conversation, a laugh or two, and someone to hold for a night. She'd do a little research, a mere dip of the toe in Dominic's metaphorical dating pool to test the waters.

****

At three a.m., Eli lay on his back with his arms crossed over his chest as if interred in a coffin. Next to him, Jacob snored loudly enough to raise the hair on his arms. Grandma had insisted on taking the sofa. "I'm weary from travel," she said. "You boys can talk and you'll both sleep better on a proper mattress." Tomorrow he'd order a couch that pulled out to a bed. The sofa was okay for naps, but too short for nighttime. Jacob would leave in a few days, then Grandma could take the bed and he'd take the pull-out.

Sleep was futile, so Eli opened his phone and checked his Tuesday schedule. Damn. Amidst the misery and chaos of the evening, he hadn't rescheduled his early appointment with a dowager and her rather large purse. He never dropped a ball and now he was fumbling like a last-chosen fielder on a slo-pitch team. He'd have to call her first thing in the morning, and if he couldn't reach her, text Felicity to cover for him. The thought of that should concern him, but he really didn't care. Grandma had promised her grandsons a breakfast of pancakes and sausage and he'd wallow in her kindness.

He didn't care to rush off, anyway. Mary's absence drained the sales office of color despite its bright red sofa and rainbow-hued prints. The irony of Mary's secret letter to his family wasn't lost on him, but he wasn't angry with her. Only sad, tired, and hollow with regret.

Chapter Seventeen

Unaccustomed to eating breakfast, Eli felt as if he'd swallowed an anvil as he drove to In-Spire. At least his headache was gone. Grandma stayed behind to wash, dry, and iron a pile of shirts intended for the dry cleaner, muttering under her breath that a laundry service was "a vain extravagance" and "it was time Eli found a wife." Pretending he didn't hear, Eli kissed her cheek and set off with Jacob in tow.

What would Felicity and the others—the City of Toronto—make of Jacob Klassen? Awkward Jacob, age thirty-six and finally a husband and father, dressed in his best navy bomber jacket and work pants, a Syngenta ballcap over his kitchen chair buzz cut. Fatherhood had catalyzed Jacob's smug religiosity to a feverish ecstasy. Eli was content to concede the moral molehill to him, if only he wouldn't blather on about Jesus when they got to the office. Which he would. Look up culture clash in a dictionary and you'd find a picture of a Bible-clutching Jacob with a goofy grin on his face next to a confused real estate agent. The propensity for spontaneous public prayer was encoded in the Klassen DNA, though the gene had skipped Eli, *praise Jesus*.

Jacob embarrassed him. Eli felt ashamed for feeling that way, and here they were on Lakeshore, minutes away from his mortification.

Jacob peered through the passenger window.

"Thousands of people on these streets and in these buildings and not one of them could feed himself if the trucks stopped coming and the stores closed. Without us, they'd all starve."

Eli swerved around a slowing Uber. "And without them, you'd be naked, getting around on foot, maybe dead for lack of medical care."

"I'll grant you that, Eli, but what is your contribution to God's creation?"

"Touché."

Jacob had made a valid point. In the grand economic machine, a farmer or a surgeon or a garbageman were essential cogs. A realtor was only lubrication, a facilitator in the movement of money. Might as well agree and move on.

However, Jacob had only warmed up. "You're like the tax collector in the temple. You take your cut and live high and mighty in a tower, though God knows your trickery." He stabbed Eli's shoulder with a knife-like finger. "Real estate agents can't be trusted. They're in business for themselves. Same as lawyers, insurance salesmen, and usurers."

"Usurers. You mean bankers? Jeez, you're hostile toward everyone in finance. Jake, if you're in money trouble, I can cover a payment."

"You laugh, but—"

"I'm not laughing. You have a family to support. You mentioned a new tractor, and if you're behind on a loan or whatever—"

"I don't need your money. We're getting by. I'm talking about your soul, younger brother. Toronto is a zoo. The people who live here, they're like exotic animals. All different and all jostling against each other and sleeping in pens and cages. A man can't be righteous here. There's no room for God. You don't belong here."

"I'm all right but thanks for the advice." Eli checked over his shoulder, then turned down a narrow alley to a lot tucked behind a nondescript building.

"How much do you pay for parking?"

"Three-fifty a month."

"Forty-two hundred a year?" Jacob's voice broke with incredulity and Eli predicted he'd share this shocking fact with all and sundry at coffee hour after Sunday service. "We could pave the lane or replace the roof with aluminum for that kind of money. All you get is the use of what, eighty square feet? A patch of pavement."

"Gotta spend money to make money."

Jacob whistled through his teeth. "If you didn't spend it in the first place, you wouldn't have to run in your hamster wheel and live in a cage."

"Judge not lest ye be judged," Eli deadpanned as he engaged the parking brake.

"'He that loveth his brother abideth in the light.' I say these things to you, Eli, because it's my duty as your elder brother to guide you."

Eli regarded his brother, now clambering out of the car. *Duty.* That's what made Jacob tick. He saw himself as patriarch-in-waiting and took the role seriously.

"We're late," said Eli. "When we get to the office, you can visit with Felicity, the receptionist, while I meet with my client. Felicity texted that she'd be happy to show you the project."

They walked in silence, Jacob a jumpy tourist, Eli dreading his meeting with the dowager, a formidable woman who disliked excuses. He checked his watch. Ten minutes behind schedule.

Eli opened the door and followed Jacob inside. "Where's Mrs. Humphries?" he asked Felicity, who stared vacantly at Jacob.

"Who?"

"My client. You were supposed to offer her coffee and my apology for running late."

"Oh, her. Uncle Stephen was here and told her she had better options. He offered to show her a two-bedroom in the Century project. They left five minutes ago."

"But she was all set to buy here. She only had to choose her upgrades and sign on the dotted line. She's my client." Who he'd buttered up for weeks.

"Don't tell me that, Eli. Tell Uncle Stephen."

"Holy shit." Felicity's eyes darted back and forth between the brothers. "You two look like freaking twins."

Jacob doffed his cap and dipped his head. "I'm Jacob Klassen. Older by seven years." His bashfulness lent him a down-to-earth charm that Eli had never seen before.

"No kidding." Felicity giggled. "I'll bet you have a ton of stories about your brother."

"I'm going for a walk," said Eli, making for the door.

Outside, he couldn't decide where to go. He didn't have another meeting for a couple of hours, so he wandered aimlessly down side streets, through churchyards and small parks, away from the construction projects and hubbub of the arterial roads. The rift with Mary had cracked him into pieces, and he didn't know who he'd be when he glued himself back together again, if he even could.

Eli should be furious with Stephen, but he found that he wasn't. At Hill Realty, Mrs. Humphries was a client of the brokerage, not the agent, and technically Stephen hadn't broken any rule, though he was in clear violation of decency and the salient unwritten rule, "thou shalt never steal a client from another agent." Furthermore, Stephen and Claudia took a generous cut on all transactions, though Claudia kept a tight grip on the purse strings to keep her husband on the straight and narrow.

On the other hand, Eli had it coming and he knew it. He'd slept with the man's wife and scooped his few investor clients while he was in rehab. Stephen was only evening the score.

Returning to the office, Eli walked through a garden blooming in forsythia and plum. Songbirds built nests and staked their territory in chirps and trills. However bereft and guilty he felt, the birds didn't give a damn about his feelings, and good for them. As Eli approached the door, Felicity's shrill giggle and Jacob's braying laughter carried through an open window. At least one Klassen was having a good day.

****

To pay Eli back without risk of financial ruin, Mary had to find a job to supplement her meager wage as a TA, so on Tuesday morning she sequestered herself in the dank basement office she shared with another doctoral student and rolled up her sleeves. Mary scanned the list of "opportunities" on the Kerry Workplace Solutions website. Receptionist, administrative assistant, file clerk...anything in that no-

217

fuss, no-muss category would do. She uploaded her resume and started filling out the Byzantine application form. The agency required three references, including one from her most recent employer, before they'd even offer an interview.

Two references were easy. Mary could ask Penny, the department people-pleaser, and Jim, a co-worker from her holiday serving job. But who could she ask at Hill Realty? Not Claudia or Stephen, and definitely not Eli. She didn't know Lori, Alex, or Bill well enough to ask a favor. That left Jonquil.

Mary texted her and seconds later, Jonquil responded with a phone call.

"Why, of course I'll be your reference, Mary," she enthused. "Only tell me, how are you? Really. I was utterly distraught when I heard you left us. How *are* you?"

"Not bad considering I didn't leave. I was fired."

"Yes, well, you'll be missed."

By whom, Jonquil didn't say, so Mary asked her.

"Well, I'll miss you and, umm, who else? That bicycle courier, the one with the handlebar mustache and all the tattoos—"

"Neither of us even knows his name."

"Not true. I know he's a Scorpio…it's Brendan. Or Brandon?"

"Brent," Mary offered as a lark.

"Brent! Of course. You've got a sharp memory, Mary, and that's what I'll say as your reference."

"Thank you, Jonquil. I really appreciate that."

"You're welcome. And some parting wisdom? When a door closes—"

"Another opens?" finished Mary.

"Yes. This may be the best thing that has ever happened to you. I know you were attracted to Eli, and you'll miss him, but you were chasing the impossible. Your auras aren't complementary. He's a shimmering, electric blue, and your aura, well, you're on a different wavelength."

"Oh? What color is my aura?"

"Well, before I say anything more, Mary, you should know that auras change. It's possible for anyone to nurture their spirit and develop their aura with meditation, breathwork, and other yogic practices. If you're interested in soul work, I can put you in touch with my healer. The art of reading auras is *extremely* complex, and I really should stay in my lane."

"There's no harm in sharing, is there, Jonquil? I am curious, and if you think I'd benefit from soul work—"

"It's beige," Jonquil blurted. "A dull fawn."

"That's not even on the color wheel," Mary whined. "That's camouflage."

"I also detect a hint of yellow," Jonquil said, back-pedaling furiously. "A subtle color. A nice warm beige is nothing to be ashamed about."

"You're saying my personality is boring beige."

"Not your personality, Mary. Only your aura. You're a very nice girl. It's a spiritual thing. Think energy. Chi. Magnetism."

"I'm a triple-A battery and Eli's a nuclear reactor?"

"I said nothing of the sort. Really, I shouldn't have stepped out of my wheelhouse. The science of auras is complicated. As I said, if you want the name of my healer—"

"That's okay, Jonquil. I won't trouble you for more than the reference. Thanks."

"You're welcome."

"Just out of curiosity, what color is Felicity's aura?"

"Felicity Hill?"

"Yes." Who else, for fuck's sake.

"Her aura is orange. A lively, adventurous, joyful orange."

"And orange is a complement to blue? On the color wheel?"

Jonquil replied slowly, "Yes, I suppose it is." Then, with artificial enthusiasm, she said, "It was lovely chatting with you, Mary. I'm sending you good vibes for your job hunt!" and she ended the call.

Their conversation bothered Mary for the rest of the day. Although Jonquil had spouted woo-woo nonsense, her crazy notions sat on a bedrock of truth. Dull, beige people didn't take risks. They stuck to the rules, kissed asses, double-checked references, and applied for the position of file clerk with Kerry Workplace Solutions. And they definitely freaked out when their boyfriend went all electric blue on them.

When Mary got home that evening, she asked Dominic, "Do you believe people have auras?"

"What?" He stopped watering his orchid and gave a small laugh. "Have you been hanging out in the drama department again?"

"I know it's silly. People don't have auras, but do you think it's possible to characterize people's personalities with color?"

"Sure. Why not? As long as I'm plaid. Or paisley. I wouldn't want to be pigeonholed."

"Let's start again. Assuming each person has an array of personality traits—"

"A sound assumption."

"And one or two of those traits are dominant—"

"A shaky assumption."

"What color would I be?"

"You?" Dominic rubbed his chin and took a long, appraising look at her. "That's difficult."

"Oh, come on, Dominic. It's not as if I'm asking you if I look fat in this dress."

"You're wearing jeans."

"Your literalism is unhelpful at present. You know what I mean. Use your intuition. The first color that pops in your head when you see me."

"Very well. Navy with gold chevrons."

"You're making fun of me."

"Because this is dumb. People don't have auras." With a shake of his head, Dominic picked a tiny clump of dust from a leaf.

"But if they did, would I be beige?"

"No, not beige. And not gray, puce, or brown either. You'd be a bold, primary color."

Mary smiled with relief. "Okay. How about Eli?"

Dominic gave Mary a scolding look. "I'm not answering that. You broke up with him yesterday."

"Just for fun and I won't ask any more crazy questions."

"Okay." Dominic sighed. "He's electric blue."

"Fuck. No kidding."

"Yes kidding. I just said the first color that popped into my head."

"That's the whole point, Dominic. You answered intuitively. I really am beige."

"No, you're not. Your imaginary aura is spectacular, Mary. You just don't have enough fun."

Dominic hugged her. "It's 'Reel Deal Tuesday'. Want to go to the cinema?"

Mary glanced at her messy desk. "Why not," she replied. "A little escapism might bring out my yellow."

\*\*\*\*

Used to cooking for multitudes, Grandma prepared a massive supper of roast chicken thighs, ham in case Eli preferred it to fowl, mashed potatoes, a rainbow of vegetables, a pickle tray, and a loaf of bread to round out the meal. Eli was mildly astonished that she'd pulled off such a feat given the paucity of cookware in the kitchen.

Grandma turned off the oven and said, "I'll leave the pies in so they're warm for dessert. Now go and sit at the table with your brother. Everything's ready."

Jacob had taken the chair at the head of the table, so Eli seated himself across from her.

"Jacob?" prompted Grandma. "Before the food gets cold."

They bowed their heads, though Eli didn't close his eyes, and Jacob cleared his throat as if warming up for the keynote address at a Toastmasters convention.

"Heavenly Father, we thank you for the bounty of this table, for the sustenance of flesh from animals winged and hooved, the nourishing leaves, seeds, and roots of your earth, and for the many people whose hands worked hard to bring us our supper. We also thank you for the blessing of family and for the shelter of Eli's home. Lord, with humble hearts, we thank you for our health that we may serve you in our labors."

Eli peered at Jacob and Grandma, whose eyes were clamped shut. The bounty of the table was cooling rapidly, but Jacob continued his blessing, voice rising in petition.

"Lord, we ask that you strengthen us to do what is right and good in service to you, and that you hold Eli, especially, in your tender and merciful care so that he may cut his way through the thorny wilderness of godlessness to a life of Christian devotion, justice, and grace. Help him turn away from darkness and false idols and direct him to your light. Deter him from the path of sin so that he may follow the path of righteousness. And help him mature into a Godly family man with a dutiful wife and obedient children. In Jesus' name, amen."

"Amen," whispered Grandma. She unfolded her hands and grinned at Eli. "'Bout time you ate a decent meal. Dig in!"

"Thank you, Grandma." Eli decided not to argue against Jacob's manipulative agenda cloaked in a prayer. "This looks and smells delicious," he said instead.

Jacob forked a thick slice of ham onto his plate, so Eli took a piece of chicken.

"You boys tell me about your day." Grandma pushed a heaping bowl of potatoes toward Eli.

"It was interesting," Jacob said through a mouthful of ham.

"You didn't leave the sales office," said Eli.

"Didn't have to. I saw plenty staying put in that portable. The receptionist, Felicity, she really likes you, Eli. And she's so pretty, not that it matters."

"Are you playing matchmaker, Jacob?" asked Grandma.

"Eli could do worse." He filled his plate from the bowls, licking a serving spoon before returning it to the coleslaw.

Grandma tapped Jacob's hand in rebuke. "What's her name?"

"Felicity," said Jacob. "Sweet disposition. Kind."

"And too young for me," said Eli.

"She's twenty-three," said Jacob.

"A young twenty-three," argued Eli.

"Even better," said Jacob. "At her age, you can still teach her. Mold her into a wife who makes her husband proud. She was keen on learning about farming and Eden Springs."

Grandma said, "I was eighteen when I married your grandfather. And your father and mother were both nineteen when they tied the knot. Worked out well for us despite our immaturity."

Eli stared at his plate. It hadn't worked out well for any of them. The Klassen men relished their self-appointed role as wife-molders, and Grandma, his mother, and Ruth suffered for it. Grandma corrected her children and grandchildren with moral authority, patience, and kindness, but Grandpa had relied on sharp criticism and a thick leather strap. This lesson in contrasts was lost on Jacob. Eli said quietly, "Felicity's a nice girl, but she's not the one for me."

"Eli, I advise you not to put off marriage. You're twenty-nine and a prolonged bachelorhood isn't good for men. It can lead to temptation," Jacob said gravely.

"Are you speaking from experience?" asked Eli.

"No. I know right from wrong," said Jacob, oblivious to Eli's sarcasm. "I delayed the joy of family life longer than I should have. I shouldn't have waited to marry."

"You didn't have a choice," said Eli.

"What's that supposed to mean?" Jacob protested.

"Boys! We shall have peace at this table." With a flash of her dark eyes, Grandma admonished Eli. "You should respect your brother. He's your elder and he only wants what's best for you." Then, she glared at Jacob. "And you—stop licking the serving utensils. If you want Eli to heed your advice, you can't behave as if you were raised by savages."

Chastened, Jacob stopped mid-slurp and lowered the gravy ladle into its bowl.

"Better." She smiled at her grandsons, then squeezed Eli's hand. "I looked through the furniture catalogue you printed, and I found a sturdy, wood-framed daybed. On sale, mind."

"Great," said Eli. "I'll order it after supper."

Preferring domestic goods over imported, Jacob asked about the furniture manufacturer, which sparked conversation on the economy and a cousin who made a decent living installing cabinets. Eli and Jacob set aside their differences and, at last, Grandma got her wish for a peaceable meal with her grandsons.

****

Even though the movie had its audience on the edge of their seats, Mary's mind strayed to thoughts of Eli. As Dominic munched on popcorn, Mary remembered how Eli had secretly paid for the apology cake. When the hero discovered he'd been double-crossed, Mary recalled how Eli comforted her after Gabriel's betrayal. And when the hero kissed the heroine, Mary thought of Eli's mouth on her own. So much for the escapism of film.

As the credits rolled, Dominic dabbed tears from his eyes with his monogrammed handkerchief and declared *What Love Demands* the most emotionally charged movie he'd seen in a decade.

"It was quite good," said Mary.

"Damned with the faintest of faint praise," said Dominic. "And it didn't take your mind off things, did it?"

"No," Mary admitted wistfully. "Maybe I should call him…discuss things."

"Mary, get a hold of yourself. Eli assaulted Gabriel and pretended nothing happened. You can't reconcile unless he does the right thing and demonstrates remorse with meaningful action. The ball is in his court."

"But I feel frozen, Dominic. I'm stuck in a state of suspended animation while I wait to see if he'll figure things out. The only way I can get unstuck is to assume it's over." They shuffled sideways down the row of seats. "I think I'll go back on Tinder."

"Can't you find some other Eli-substitute besides that icky app while you're in recovery mode?"

"I'm only going window-shopping. You know…fantasy land."

"Famous last words, Mary Rose. Famous last words," muttered Dominic as they strolled out of the cinema and into the night.

## Chapter Eighteen

Dominic's words were prophetic—a week later, Mary swiped right. Her date was a forty-two-year-old divorced clinical psychologist named Dr. Sidney Pounder, who informed her that she could call him "Sid" as he stood and shook her hand in Hooper's, a cocktail bar on the waterfront.

"I'm Mary, and you may call me 'Mary'," she joked.

Sid didn't laugh. Belying his profile, Sid didn't have a sense of humor, but he was polite, impeccably groomed, a skilled listener, and he resembled his Tinder photo. Over whisky sours, they commiserated on the sorry state of university education and the heartbreak of deceptive lovers, a grievance fest that continued after Sid paid for their drinks and they left the bar.

Though cool on the quay, it was a pleasant evening. Party boats and unrigged sailing vessels bobbed on their mooring lines. Across the harbor, the island glowed as its inhabitants switched on lights. Couples strolled hand in hand, and when Sid took hers, Mary recoiled slightly, then tried to appreciate his touch. He wasn't Eli. Sid's hand was soft, small, and womanish.

"It's good to walk," said Sid. "I sit too much at work and it's awful on my back."

Mary murmured her sympathy and Sid said, "I've

been to physio, massage therapy, two chiropractors, and even tried acupuncture, but the only thing that has helped is my waterbed. It's a lifesaver."

"They still make those? I thought waterbeds disappeared in the nineties," said Mary.

"They're not common, but you can still find them. I bought mine from a warehouse in Scarborough."

Mary glanced into the black water and shivered. "Isn't it cold sleeping on water?"

"The bed has a heating unit, so the water is body temperature. You can get away with a light blanket."

"Do you ever get seasick?" Mary laughed.

"No. I'm used to it," said Sid, missing his chance to reply with his own joke. "It's therapeutic. It supports the spine while relieving pressure on bony prominences."

Sid wasn't a bony person. In fact, he was round-shouldered and doughy. If Mary slept with him, she would be venturing into the territory of lesbianism. Another joke that no one would hear, and she felt rather lonely for it—and also guilty. Sid was serious, soft, and safe…an alliterative, embodied ode to the letter "S". He was also kind.

"Would you like to see the bed?" he asked. "I mean, look at it, not get into it. Or you could try it out, without me if you want, and experience it yourself. Unless you have another idea?"

Sid had presented door number one, two, and three: see his bed, think of something else to do together, or end the date. It was early and Dominic would be out. At home, Mary would have the houseplants and thoughts of Eli for company. She didn't want to go home. Neither did she see herself on a dancefloor or sitting close in a café booth with Sid. On impulse, she said, "I'd like to see your waterbed."

Sid smiled, and they walked to his place.

\*\*\*\*

Several blocks away, Eli changed into jeans while Grandma fussed with her bonnet. Jacob had left on the morning train, and Eli felt like celebrating his departure. When he asked Grandma where she would like to dine, she said, "Why, your favorite restaurant, Eli. Where else?"

"It's Japanese. Sushi."

"Raw fish?"

"Yes, but they have other dishes too."

"I'll have sushi," declared Grandma. "And a story for the ladies in my quilting circle."

They arrived at the tail end of the supper rush and Yuka jumped with surprise. "Eri-kun! And a special friend?"

"I'm Eva Klassen, Eli's grandmother." She bowed. "That's what you do in your country, isn't it?"

"Yes, it is, Grandma Krassen. Welcome!" Yuka smiled and bowed in return and Ikeda-san called, "*Irashaimase!* Best table in the house, Yuka!"

"Is it okay if we sit at the counter?" asked Eli. "That way Grandma can see how sushi is made."

Yuka pulled out a stool. "*Douzo.* I help you up?"

Grandma placed a hand on Yuka's shoulder, wiggled onto her perch, and arranged her skirt. "There. Thank you, Yuka."

In quick order, Yuka placed steaming bowls of soba and small plates of pickles in front of them along with tea and sake.

Grandma smiled her gratitude, then clasped her

229

hands, bowed her head, and prayed, "Lord, thank you for the food we are about to receive. Amen."

She took a chopstick in each hand and attempted to lift noodles to her mouth. Without a word, Yuka handed her a fork and spoon.

Meanwhile, Ikeda-san chopped and sliced with the flourish of a master. Grandma's face brightened in fascination. "Eli, I see why this is your favorite restaurant," she whispered. "I've never seen anyone handle a knife like that." Ikeda-san heard her and beamed proudly.

Grandmother and grandson ate and ate and when they were finished, Yuka asked the question that Eli dreaded but knew would come. "How's Mary?"

"I don't know," Eli winced. "I think she's snowed under with school. I haven't seen her in a while."

Yuka's eyes narrowed. "Then you'd better call her and find out how she is, don't you think?"

"I'd like to meet Mary myself," added Grandma. "What's she like, Yuka?"

"She's a pretty girl. Long, dark brown hair. Glasses from too much reading. Friendly, serious, and smart. Maybe smarter than Eri-kun. Shame to lose a girl like that." Yuka clicked her teeth disapprovingly.

Eli looked to Ikeda-san for support, but he shook his head with dismay and decapitated a fish with his cleaver.

"Dessert?" asked Yuka. "We have green tea ice cream."

Grandma loved sweets, and she patted her belly. "I have just enough room, Yuka. Yes, please."

Grandma marveled at the smooth, uniquely Japanese dessert, and they moved to the safer topics of exorbitant rents and the joy of having grandchildren. After Eli paid the bill and they left the restaurant, Grandma hooked her arm in his and searched his face.

"Thank you for a fine supper, Eli," she said as they strolled. "Now that your brother has left, it's only you, me, and the Lord. I'm a Christian woman but, at my age, I'm wise enough to leave judgement to Him. You may speak freely."

"You don't want to know."

"I do want to know. It's you who isn't telling. You might feel better if you do, mind."

Eli exhaled heavily. "Just between us?"

"Young man. Am I a taleteller?"

"No."

"Then unburden yourself. When we get home, I'll make real tea and you can say whatever it is you have to say. It probably isn't as bad as you think."

\*\*\*\*

Aside from his therapeutic bed, Sid's open-concept apartment was furnished by his landlord and had the ambiance of a tastefully decorated hotel suite. They kicked off their shoes and Sid excused himself to use the bathroom. Like a moth to a lamp, Mary went to Sid's bookcase and scanned the titles. He'd organized his books with the precision of a librarian with a mania for the Dewey Decimal System, and most of his reading related to his profession. Mary was leafing through a flipchart of Rorschach inkblots when Sid slid up behind her and peered over her shoulder.

"I keep those for historical interest mainly," he said. "They're a fuzzy assessment tool, but useful for opening conversations with patients. What do you see there?"

Mary stared at a symmetrical black blob with radiating smears. Eli with messy hair? "Um, a person?"

"There's no right answer, though that's a fairly typical response. People often see human faces and bodies in the images."

"I suppose I should be reassured. 'Typical' isn't suggestive of crazy psycho-killer cat lady."

"You'd be surprised." Sid padded across the room to a cabinet. "Wine?"

"Sure."

While he opened a bottle of Beaujolais, Mary took her turn in the bathroom. After she washed her hands, she texted Dominic. —I'm in his apartment.—

—Noooo! Save yourself, Mary Rose. Go home now!—

—He's nice and he has a waterbed.—

—Why didn't you say so?— Then, —I still think you should go home, but at least text me Sid's address. For safety.—

Mary did so, appended a smiley kiss emoji, then snooped. For safety. The plastic drinking cup and toothbrush were wet with very recent use. She opened the cupboard over the sink. Sure enough, Sid had boxes of Viagra and condoms, neatly stacked. What else? Robaxacet, an electric shaver, toothpaste, dental floss, a first aid kit, antiperspirant...nothing that screamed "danger." Quite the opposite. If Sid had an aura, it would be a placid, ultra-safe, porcine pink. Mary squeezed a pearl of toothpaste onto her fingertip and smeared her teeth with it.

When she emerged from the bathroom, she found Sid semi-reclining on his sectional sofa, cardigan off, top buttons unfastened. A perky pair of man boobs strained against the polycotton fabric of his shirt. He raised his glass to her with waterbed eyes. Her stomach flipped and she shuddered. She couldn't pretend she was attracted to him. Joining him on his waterbed was impossible. He simply wasn't Eli. It wasn't Sid's fault, but Mary just...couldn't.

"I'm...I'm sorry," she stammered. "I have an emergency."

As she shuffled her feet into her shoes, Sid came to her side and kissed her on the cheek. "May I call you?" he asked with a look of concern.

"You'd better not," she replied. "You're a wonderful man, but I'm still in love with my ex-boyfriend."

Sid's face crumpled with disappointment, and Mary rushed away. After she'd run three blocks, she texted Dominic again. —You're right. It wasn't right. I'm a cock-teasing jerk. I left.—

—I'm proud of you, jerk! If you promise to leave before the big boys come to play, I'll buy you a drink at the bar in the Peacock Club.—

—K. One drink to debrief. Thank you, Dominic.—

\*\*\*\*

"Thanks," said Eli, accepting a mug of milky tea. He sat back on the couch and propped his feet on a crate. "I don't know where to start."

"Start at the beginning." Grandma settled opposite him on her brand-new daybed, where she slept every night, preferring it to the queen-size bed in the bedroom.

"There's too much to say."

"Then start with Mary."

Eli blew on his tea, sipped and burnt his lip, then

set the mug on a hardcover book. "Mary. She's a twenty-six-year-old PhD student. Philosophy. She's brilliant, warm, funny, and curious. She's also beautiful and, to her credit, she doesn't realize it. And she's a terrible driver."

"You love her."

"Yes, but I haven't told her. I guess I was scared. She thinks she's tough, but she's not. She's vulnerable, and when I tried to protect her, I blew it."

Grandma nodded as if she knew how that could happen.

"Her supervising professor was giving her the runaround and blocking her progress in her program, so I confronted him."

"Oh, dear Jesus." Grandma laid her hand over her heart. "With fists?"

"No. I only grabbed his tie and threatened him. I swear, I didn't hurt him. Anyway, I didn't tell Mary, and when the prof changed his attitude toward her work, she was ecstatic because she idolizes him. A week or so later, she figured out the truth and she was devastated. And furious with me."

"Because you didn't tell her the truth."

"Exactly. She broke up with me immediately and said she'd reconsider if I turned myself in to the police and apologized to her prof. I've apologized."

"But you haven't gone to the police because of your record in Eden Springs," guessed Grandma. Forehead wrinkled in thought, she sipped her tea, then said, "Your hot head has caught up with you."

"I only gave him what he deserved."

"Who, Eli? Mary's professor? Johnny Klein? Jacob? That man who bothered Sarah behind the bleachers?"

"After I got the skidoo back, Johnny Klein never stole from us again. And Sarah was frightened and hurt. Someone had to do something."

"You have a pattern of losing your temper and taking matters into your own hands."

"I'm not a bully."

"No, you're not. You watch over the weak. But you're not God either. Violence isn't the Brethren way."

"I've seen plenty of violence in Eden Springs," Eli said bitterly.

"We correct our own. We don't presume to correct others. That's up to their own families and the Lord." When Eli didn't respond, she said gently, "You'd make a mighty noble cowboy, seeking vigilante justice like that, but this is Toronto. You love Mary and you want her back. She laid down the law and rightly so. What are you going to do?"

"I don't know."

"I think you do."

"I can't do it, Grandma. Mary will find out everything and she won't understand."

Grandma shook her head. "If she's the one, you'll have to tell her about your past sometime. Might as well confess to both her and the police."

"If I end up with a criminal record, I'll lose my career."

"Would that be so bad?"

"Pardon?" He sounded rude, but he was genuinely confused. How could Grandma even suggest it? Real estate gave him money, power, the very furniture she sat on. Sure, she chose the cheapest daybed in the catalogue, but he bought it without blinking. No one in Eden Springs could do that.

"Would that be so bad?" repeated Grandma. "The incident with Mary's professor is the tip of the iceberg, isn't it, Eli? Your greater sin is your greed. I think that's why you're getting headaches."

"Greed? No. I'm generous because I can afford to be."

"Your tea's getting cold. Why don't you drink it while I ask you some questions and you can think long and hard on your answers. You don't have to tell me them."

Eli nodded, picked up his mug, and swallowed without tasting.

"Have you done things you aren't proud of? For example, tricked someone? Took advantage?"

He had. He'd misled an investor who was scooping properties and renting them on Airbnb in a tight rental market. Also, arranged for an escort girl with kleptomania to seduce a shallow influencer who'd complicated a sale with last-minute conditions...though maybe that was a win-win. And then there was Stephen Hill.

"Have you done anything illegal?"

Did bribery for insider info at city hall count? A swindle on a double-ended deal?

"Are you proud of what you do?"

No. He wasn't. Lately, he dragged himself to work. He'd switch places with the cabinet maker in a heartbeat. Even Dino was less stressed out and contributed to the greater good by cheering people up. "Any more questions?" he asked with mild trepidation.

"No. I think those will do," Grandma said softly.

"One of my favorite verses might help you. Mark 8:36."

"For what shall it profit a man if he should gain the whole world and lose his own soul?" Eli quoted.

"Ach, that's it. You know what you have to do, Eli."

Grandma yawned as if bored with his confession, which he found oddly comforting. At seventy-five, she probably believed there was nothing new under heaven when it came to people. Only repeating patterns of sin, punishment, and redemption through the generations.

"It's time to rest," said Grandma.

Chapter Nineteen

Toil was better solace than casual dating. Now late afternoon, Mary hunched stiff-shouldered over her desk, marking exams and editing a trade manual, work she'd picked up through Kerry Workplace Solutions. At least her proposal had been rubberstamped by the committee. She'd completed her course work, and now she was officially "Mary Rose, PhD *candidate*". Ta-da! She'd celebrated this milestone with Dominic, Penny Wong, and a couple other philosophy students, even received Facebook congratulations from her mother and Candace Kaine, but the person with whom she wished she could share her joy for a job well done was Eli.

They hadn't spoken for three weeks.

Mary stretched and went to the kitchen for a glass of water. Four-thirty, according to the digital clock on the microwave panel. A change was as good as a rest. She decided to go downstairs for the mail.

There were flyers, a men's clothing catalogue for Dominic, and a letter in a plain, business-size envelope for her. From *Mrs. Abraham Klassen*. Mary's heart skipped a beat. She tucked the other mail under her arm and ripped open the envelope.

*Dear Mary,*

*I hope this letter finds you well. I'm staying with Eli because I have surgery at the Holley Eye Institute in about two weeks. It's what they call "elective surgery," which means I'm allowed to chicken out. (That's a joke, mind.) The Lord will see me through it.*

*I tried to use Eli's phone to call you, or at least find your number, but I couldn't make sense of the thing. Fortunately, I kept your letter with your return address. Thank you for letting me know about Eli's headaches. He was some surprised when his brother and I showed up in Toronto, but the salve and tea I brought him have done him a world of good physically.*

*I worry about his soul though, Mary. He misses you very much and he knows he did wrong. However, he's as stubborn as a mule and he's painted himself into a corner.*

*I'd be ever so grateful if you'd meet me. There's a coffee shop called 'Breaktime' on the corner and the prices are reasonable. Yesterday I bought a muffin there for $2.25! Eli doesn't come home till after five. Could we meet at Breaktime this Friday at two o'clock? My treat? By the time you get this letter, it will be too late for you to reply, so I'll pray and leave the rest in God's capable hands. Yuka told me what you look like, so I'll recognize you!*

*Yours truly,*

*Eva Klassen*

Mary jumped and squealed, "He's suffering, too." A tradesman passing through the lobby gave her a long, suspicious look. Mary said, "My ex-boyfriend." The man shook his head and walked off. She didn't care.

The logjam was shifting. Eli's grandmother didn't have to pray because Mary would be at Breaktime—early.

\*\*\*\*

Eli entered the office of Hill Realty. Everything

was the same on the surface. As always, abstract art adorned the bare brick wall, the smell of air freshener and burnt coffee wafted through the reception area, and *Feng Shui for Winning Realtors* sat on Jonquil's desk. It was he who had changed. The latest receptionist, a polite, efficient girl named Olivia, notified Claudia from the desktop phone that he'd arrived and he was called into the corner office immediately.

Claudia gestured to the sofa, but Eli took the chair at her desk, and she shrugged and returned to her chair opposite him. Same old Claudia, not a hair out of place, makeup photo-shoot perfect, military posture projecting success.

Eli met her eye, took a deep breath, and said, "I've decided to resign."

Claudia's mouth dropped open, then she shook her head and gasped, "Resign? Don't be absurd, Eli."

"I've given my decision a lot of thought and—"

"If it's money, we can renegotiate your split."

"It's not the money. You've been very fair and I'll always be grateful for that. I'm just tired. Exhausted with the hustle, the endless schmoozing, and I need to carve out some space for myself, away from real estate."

"Tired? Then what you really need is a vacation, Eli."

Claudia stood and walked around the desk. He felt like a diver in a flimsy cage being circled by a shark. She slid her hands over his shoulders and kneaded his muscles.

"You're tense," she crooned. "After the spring rush, you should take a break and Hill Realty will pay for it. A Caribbean resort? Perhaps a cruise? I know:

Europe! France is beautiful in early summer."

"I need more than a rest, Claudia." Eli shrugged and leaned away. "I've been doing some soul-searching, and I've decided to move on. I'm not going to another brokerage. You can reassign my clients after I've informed them. I thought I should tell you first."

Claudia stilled her hands. "How courteous of you." She stalked back to her chair and stared across the desk. "I don't buy your excuse. *Tired.* You're only twenty-eight."

"Twenty-nine."

"You're healthy. I know you have stamina. Sure, you've had a few health challenges, but you're not even thirty. You have years of high earning potential ahead of you and you're good at the game. I don't want to lose my top agent." Her lip quivered. "My friend."

"Claudia, we *are* friends and I hope that won't change."

"Is it because of Mary's dismissal?"

"No."

"No? Okay, then level with me. I've known you since you were a gawky, runaway teenager and I've mentored you and treated you well. Now you're dropping a bomb on my business...a business I built from scratch. I deserve to know why you're doing this without your vague excuses."

Eli shifted in his chair and considered how to lay out his cards without revealing the crucial one. He cleared his throat. "Back home, in Eden Springs, I did some things I shouldn't have. My bad habits followed me here and now my past is catching up with me."

Claudia's face froze in horror.

"Nothing sexually deviant," Eli rushed to add. "I

241

only righted wrongs in a way that the law doesn't appreciate. You could call it 'hillbilly justice.' If I wind up in the news, I don't want my name to damage Hill Realty."

"What did you do?"

"I can't tell you."

"You have to. I'll need to prepare a statement in case I have to protect the Hill name." Pleading, Claudia reached across the desk with an open hand. "Please. Tell me. What did you do that was so bad?"

Reluctantly, Eli took her hand. Claudia wasn't the type to make a scene, but she was under tremendous stress—dealing with a reckless husband and an irresponsible niece—and he'd thrown a bale of straw on the camel's back. He had to end their meeting before she tried to guilt him into changing his mind.

He spoke slowly and clearly to avoid misunderstanding. "I can't tell you what I did *yet*. I'm planning to confess to the police. The things I will tell them have nothing to do with Hill Realty, but it's better for you and the team if I'm no longer associated with the brokerage when I do it."

With a bewildered expression, Claudia shook her head. "When will this happen?"

"In a week? Maybe two? I'll wrap things up with my clients first."

She withdrew her hand, sat back, and stared across the desk. In a blink, she changed gears to cool, hard-as-nails business mode. "Could you stick around until the model suite is installed and the hydro and plumbing are working? Jonquil and Siobhan will decorate it."

"Yes, of course."

"And send me a draft of your letter to your clients

before you communicate with them. I want to vet everything that comes out of Hill Realty in your name."

"You can trust me, Claudia."

"Can I? Eli, we've both bent the rules and we've worked closely. You're about to dump your dirty laundry into the public square. Some of mine could be mixed in with yours. You want to hoist yourself onto a stake and let the world set a fire under your feet? Go ahead. But don't you dare drag me into your martyrdom."

"I won't. It'll be a clean break. First I'll deal with the model suite, then I'll draft the letter. I won't discuss any of this with anyone unless you want me to."

"Just keep your mouth shut. I'll handle it."

"Thank you, Claudia. For everything." He stood and said quietly, "You've been like a mother to me."

"A *mother*? Fuck you, Eli."

Perfect. Her rage would see her through the worst of the next few weeks.

Chapter Twenty

Dressing to meet with a septuagenarian Klassen was more difficult than dressing for a Tinder date. Mary hadn't taken this much time with her appearance since her second day at work with Eli, way back in February. Today, the weather was warm, and she decided on a print dress, her denim jacket, and slip-on sneakers. Hair fastened into a braid, she hoped she looked sensible yet feminine, wholesome rather than flaky.

Although Mrs. Klassen said, 'her treat', Mary bought two teas and seated herself at a corner table with chipped Formica and a view of the street. At 1:59, a short, plump, slightly stooped woman wearing a navy bonnet, a plain ankle-length dress, and Velcro running shoes appeared in the doorway and looked about.

Mary stood and stepped forward. "Mrs. Klassen?"

"Yes. Mary!" She walked over, round face beaming. Her dark eyes, an older female version of Eli's, twinkled in greeting. She seized Mary's hand and shook it in both of hers. "You may call me 'Eva' or 'Grandma'. That's what Yuka and Takeshi call me, 'Grandma', and I rather like it. Makes Toronto feel more like home."

"All right. Grandma," Mary smiled in return. "I took the liberty of buying you tea and there's milk and sugar on the table."

"Ach. This was supposed to be my treat. They bake

nice muffins here, though they could be from a mix, mind. Which do you like best, raisin bran, morning glory, or blueberry?"

"Morning glory, but—"

"Me too!" Grandma was at the counter before Mary could tell her she wasn't hungry.

Seated at last, Grandma accepted Mary's thanks for the softball-sized muffin she'd placed before her and said, "You're just as I expected, Mary, based on what Yuka and Eli told me. I feel as if I know you already."

"Oh? But I don't know you."

"Well then, let's see…I'm seventy-five years old, that's three-quarters of a century, and I have twenty-seven grandchildren. I've lost track of the great-grandchildren because Eli's generation is busy," she prattled. "I have to keep all the children's names on a calendar so I don't miss a birthday."

"Eli told me you live on his father's farm."

"That's right. Eli's father is Isaac, my oldest. It was his oldest who brought me here and that's Jacob. The Klassen men are good men, but they tend to get their blood up when they think they're right and someone's crossed them, and unfortunately, they don't bat a thousand where judgement's concerned. Takes a special woman to make a happy marriage with a Klassen man. She has to be smart to match his wits, strong to match his spirit, and even-tempered to steer him, because a meek, wishy-washy woman is like a green light for his worst impulses. Listen to me! I'm talking too much. Let me say a quick word of thanks to the Lord for the muffins and tea and then you tell me all about yourself." Grandma bent forward with clasped hands and mouthed a blessing, then looked up and nodded.

"Well?"

"Eli might have told you I'm a student of philosophy, born and raised in Toronto."

"Yes, and he said you're an only child of divorced parents, but I shouldn't feel sorry for you because things are different here. He said friends replace kin with all the coming and going in Toronto." She waved over the table. "We should eat!"

Mary popped a piece of muffin into her mouth and washed it down with tea. Grandma broke off the top of her muffin, took a big bite, and closed her eyes as she chewed the gummy mass. "Hmm," she mumbled. "They're so moist. They must use a lot of oil…"

"I'm surprised Eli spoke of me," said Mary. "We were close friends—"

"Dating," said Grandma. "I found your toothbrush and deodorant in his bathroom and your clothes in his bedroom."

"Yes, we were dating, but we broke up."

"And how do you feel about that?"

The nosy question was delivered so skilfully that Mary answered without thinking about her answer. "Sad. Heartbroken. I really liked Eli."

"*Liked* him?" Grandma said through another mouthful of muffin. "I see…"

"Perhaps he didn't tell you what happened…why we broke up."

"Oh, he told me about Mr. Silverstein."

Mary smiled inwardly at the 'mister' and pictured Eli confessing under his grandmother's interrogation.

"Eli hopes to win you back," Grandma continued. "On the other hand, he wants to preserve his reputation, and that's an error of pride. We can't control what others think of us; we can only do what is right. 'But if ye suffer for righteousness' sake, happy are ye.' That's from the Book of Peter."

"A wise Greek slave named Epictetus said much the same thing."

Grandma's brows rose in a look of delight. "Wisdom is like that, isn't it? From the Bible, or the mouth of an innocent child, or the sayings of the learned, truth is eternal. If Eli repented, corrected his behavior, and atoned, would you take him back?"

"Yes, if that's what he wants too. I don't care about his reputation."

Grandma sipped her tea, then chuckled. "You did the right thing, cutting him off like that. He needed a stern lesson. He's like a horse with the bit in his teeth. The best thing to do is to corral him—the horse, I mean—and firmly correct him. Now people are more complicated than horses, that's certain, but Eli deserved a swift kick, and you delivered it. Mind, a man likes to think he's a king, but a woman has her ways. Mary, that muffin won't eat itself, and you're awfully thin. Very pretty, but thin. Please eat."

The flattery was untrue and embarrassing. Blushing, Mary nibbled her muffin while Grandma continued.

"I believe he's turned a corner. He's less aggressive on the phone, taking time for breakfast instead of rushing into the fray, but that's not enough. Stopping doing wrong is only a start. He has to take the next step."

"I set clear conditions. Eli knows what they are."

"Yes, he told me about that. I think he needs some encouragement. A nudge. He's like a child standing at the end of a dock, toes curled over the boards, hesitating, afraid to jump. If you saw him in person and told him you'll wait for him in the water, that everything will be all right…" Grandma took another giant bite and, chewing, peered at Mary.

Mary gazed through the window. A bag lady pushed a shopping cart laden with her tattered belongings against a bump in the sidewalk. Other pedestrians gave her a wide berth, though Eli wouldn't have if he were there. He'd have pulled the front wheels of the cart onto the next slab of concrete. He was a living contradiction of the Hobbesian hypothesis that humans are inherently despicable and require governance. Eli was fundamentally decent, and Mary loved him for it.

However, she wondered if Grandma wasn't pushing her into a fool's errand. "Why did Eli leave Eden Springs?" she asked, meeting the old woman's earnest, chestnut eyes.

"Lots of reasons, I suppose." Grandma brushed crumbs onto her serviette and dumped them onto her plate. "He was a bright boy, but impulsive. He had a penchant for finding trouble…fighting unwinnable battles…and going with the wrong girls. The Brethren cure for immaturity is scripture, prayer, and a simple life of marriage, children, and hard work. He did his share workwise, no question, but he pushed against our ways. I do believe he found more use for the Bible as a paperweight than in its Holy words. His elders couldn't contain him, so he had to leave Eden Springs. That was his wish, anyway."

"A lot of boys chase girls and rebel. What did Eli do that was so wrong?"

"First, he got expelled from school for questioning the Word of God without relent. I helped him with his schooling as I could, but mostly he went to the library and taught himself. Next thing you know, he's finding evidence for evolution in basic plant and animal breeding." Grandma frowned and shook her head at the memory. "By the time he was sixteen, he was out of Isaac's control. Eli took his father's best hunting rifle and forced a neighbor to return a stolen item. A few weeks later, he beat up a man who was under the thrall of satanic perversions and had bothered three young girls. One of those girls was Eli's sister."

"You mean the man sexually assaulted them?"

"Yes, I'm afraid I do. The fellow left town in a hurry and I don't blame Eli for acting outside of the law because the girls felt safer after that. Then one day, Isaac slapped Eli's mother in front of the younger children, and Eli demanded his father apologize. When he refused, Eli punched him. Everything could've been forgiven if Eli had prayed and repented, but undermining his father's authority as head of the family and not acknowledging the error of his ways could not be. Eli went willingly."

Mary sipped her tea as she grappled with Grandma's revelations. "Is he allowed to return to Eden Springs?"

"Ach, yes. Isaac eventually forgave his son. Eli can return for visits...weddings and funerals and Christmas and such. His nieces and nephews are thrilled when he comes home. When he finally decides to walk with the Lord, he can return to live with us permanently. He's a Klassen, but he's making a choice to stay away, Mary. He's stubborn."

"I don't understand how I fit in with what you're telling me. I'm not a Christian. My father is a secular Jew, my mother was baptized Catholic but now she's a Unitarian, which is the church of everything and nothing, and I'm an atheist who doesn't know a psalm from a hymn. I'm the Klassen family's nightmare. Why are you trying to bring us together?"

"Why? Because I prayed on it and God told me He'd rather Eli be happy than for the family to keep at him to obey. From what Eli has told me, you're a good person. You stand up to him and you can help him stay out of trouble." Grandma laid a gnarled hand over her bosom and gazed upward, to an imaginary heaven beyond the stained tile ceiling. "Even if you don't believe in Him, God sees what's in your heart." She smiled and squeezed Mary's hand. "That's enough for me."

Mary was fascinated by this unusual woman. Despite her age, Grandma wielded her moral certainty like a weapon. She simply consulted 'God' and claimed authority without nuance…without considering gradations between black and white. Though she seemed wise, anyone with a philosophic bent wouldn't charge headlong into a course of action without exploring its tints and shadows.

Mary said, "I'll think about everything you've said. All your advice."

"That's all I may ask of you," Grandma said brightly, as if everything would unfold according to a divine plan. "Talk to Eli. Encourage him."

The subject was closed. Mary swallowed the last of her tea. "You mentioned you're having an eye operation?"

"Yes. At the Holley Eye Clinic. My doctor said I'm a special case, so he referred me there instead of locally." Grandma frowned, and Mary sensed the old woman was worried about the procedure despite her faith. "Eli's been on his computer, reading up on cataracts and such, and he says he can give me the eye drops if I have trouble with them. The doctor agreed to fix both my eyes, so I only have to make one trip to Toronto. A lot of my friends have had cataract surgery and they tell me they see much better after it. The world comes back into color and such. I'm as ready as I can be."

"God will see you through it?"

"He will," Grandma declared. "I hope the doctor will let me say a short prayer, mind."

Mary couldn't imagine a doctor refusing such a request and said so. "Are you enjoying your stay in Toronto?" she asked over the din of the increasingly busy coffee shop.

"Ach, yes. And do you know what I like best about the city?" Grandma didn't wait for Mary to answer. Instead, she seized Mary's hand one last time and said, "The people. So many languages and skin tones and ways of dressing...it's like that Norman Rockwell painting of the people of the world. We have the print hanging in the Sunday school classrooms to remind us that everyone is a child of God. And it's true! Even though you don't believe it, you are, too, Mary."

And on that sentiment, the two women rose from the table and Mary carried their dishes to the counter. On the street, Grandma reached up, encircled Mary's shoulders, and gave her a squishy hug and kiss. "Not a word of this to Eli?"

"Not a word," agreed Mary. "If I contact him, I won't mention a thing."

After their goodbye, Grandma walked off, then paused, turned, and called to her. "*When*, not *if,* Mary. Eli may not know it, but he's counting on you."

\*\*\*\*

Eli watched for Felicity, who was attending the "Young Women in Business" luncheon at the Coronation Club. He checked his phone and drummed his fingertips against the steering wheel, as if the rhythmic sound would bring her marching through the revolving doors. With her high heels and a newfound, aunt-pleasing work ethic, she'd asked him to pick her up at three o'clock so she could return to the sales office—the time confirmed with an exchange of texts only an hour before. Rush hour started early on Fridays, and Eli was impatient to wrap up the day's business and tie off some loose ends ahead of his resignation. Women streamed onto the sidewalk, but no Felicity.

This would be one of the last favors Eli would do for the Hills. Next week, he'd meet the lawyer and turn himself into the police. That was the plan, anyway. Grandma called it repentance, and he called it *fucking scary*.

At half past three, a mini-skirted, makeup-smeared Felicity stumbled through the door with two girls behind her. They looked drunk. Felicity grabbed the arm of one of the girls, pointed to him, and laughed. He waved back. Clinging to each other, the girls careened across the sidewalk and splat! Felicity fell face forward.

Eli exited the car and hurried to her side. Felicity had already pushed herself up onto her hands and knees. The contents of her purse were scattered over the sidewalk, and she clumsily scraped at them, giggling and cursing like a toothless sailor. Her new friends staggered off to their Uber. Wallet, cellphone, lipstick, vape pen, tissues, a tampon...Eli helped gather the items before assisting an ungainly Felicity to her feet. Aside from a scraped knee and a broken high heel, she was uninjured. Even her sense of dignity escaped her fall unscathed, for she didn't display an ounce of shame, let alone apologize for being late and making a scene. Eli packed Felicity and her wayward purse into the passenger seat.

"I'll see you home safely," he said from the driver's seat without meeting her eye.

"Uh-uh-uh, Eli. We're going back to work. Me and you!" She pawed his arm with pointy, striped fingernails.

"You're in no condition to work, Felicity. You've skinned your knee right through your stocking. Your shoe is broken. Just tell me your address."

"Nope! Shales Offish. I can work. I'll take off my shtockings and change my shoes." She saluted like an eager recruit and broke into a peel of giggles made shrill with alcohol.

"Felicity, you're too drunk to work. I'll take you home and you can sleep it off," Eli insisted.

"Your home?" she leered.

"No, yours." He shook her hand off his arm. "Just tell me your address."

"Nope."

"I could ask your Aunt Claudia."

"Don't you dare!" Felicity's giggles morphed into a maudlin blubbering. "You don't want me, do you? After all I've done for you, you wanna jus' get rid of me."

"That's not true," he said as if calming a skittish horse. "It's Friday afternoon. You could start your weekend early."

Felicity responded with a blood-curdling cry, followed by body-shaking sobs. Eli put the car into gear and pulled into the street. It was a fifteen-minute drive to the plastic-covered furniture in the rooms of the new model suite. When they got there, he'd put her in a chair with a cup of coffee and close the door until she was sober enough to cooperate.

As Eli negotiated the busy downtown streets, Felicity played with the buttons of the stereo until, by some miracle reminiscent of monkeys typing the works of Shakespeare, she managed to find a song she liked featuring a high-pitched, crystal-shattering voice. Felicity turned the volume high enough to rupture their eardrums, and when Eli turned the music down, she began to cry all over again. Next week couldn't come soon enough.

****

Considering the gradations between the black and white of Grandma's advice took all of a minute before Mary followed the will of her heart to the sales office. She took the streetcar to Lakeshore and walked toward Navy Street, where she spotted Eli's car parked at the curb. Experience informed her he was coming and going when he didn't use the lot. Maybe after she apologized for rejecting him, he'd ask her to ride along. Mary's heart thumped in her chest, and she felt lightheaded and queasy with butterflies in anticipation of seeing Eli for the first time in nearly three weeks. Surely she could trust Eli's grandmother to know what was best. This felt so right. She couldn't wait a single second longer to see the man she loved, so she quickened her pace to a dash and gained the front step to the door.

No one was in the office, but the door to the new model suite was open. That's where he'd be...getting everything ready for a busy weekend. Why not surprise him? Mary crept through the small foyer to an open-concept space. The room smelled of new paint and all the furniture, still covered in plastic, had been left in the center. He had to be somewhere nearby. Was that giggling she heard? Coming from the bedroom? Mary tiptoed down a short hallway and froze.

**** 

Maneuvering Felicity into the sales office had been no mean feat. She'd passed out as they neared Navy and Lakeshore, so Eli texted Claudia to get Felicity's address but Claudia didn't reply, which wasn't unexpected given their last conversation. He couldn't let Felicity sleep alone in a parked car. What if she vomited and choked? In the end, he half carried her, purse and all, into the office, managing to unlock the door to it and the model suite with his free hand.

Though Felicity perked up, Eli decided to put her on the plastic-covered queen-size bed. After an awkward tango, she lay supine, arms open and extended like a demented angel, slurring an appeal for him to join her. Instead, he went into the model kitchen, dumped the plastic fruit from a ceramic bowl into the sink, and returned to the bedroom to leave the bowl on the bedside table.

Despite severe inebriation, Felicity was shockingly quick. In the sliver of a second, she grabbed his wrist and pulled him toward her with the strength of a pro wrestler. Caught off guard, Eli tipped into a bent-limbed arabesque and fell face-first onto Felicity's heaving chest. As Felicity locked her arms around his head, he struggled to free himself without hurting her. The more he wiggled, the more tightly she clamped her arms. "Take me, Eli!" she gasped, smothering him between her breasts.

As he fought for air, he heard a blood-curdling yelp that hadn't come from his opponent. With the noise, Felicity loosened her hold only enough for him to glimpse Mary standing in the doorway, a look of abject horror on her beautiful face. Mary turned and ran, and Felicity tightened her hold. By the time he extracted himself, Mary was gone.

Eli looked up and down the street in vain. He couldn't guess which way she'd run and no one on the street knew either. He took a chance on west and ran several blocks only to realize he'd chosen the wrong direction. By now she could be anywhere...on a streetcar, in a taxi, sobbing on a bench in a park. Frantic with the thought of what she'd witnessed, Eli tried to contact her, but his calls bounced off some ethereal wall. If he thought his misery would never match the day she'd walked out of his life, he was wrong. This was far, far worse, because her pain would exceed his.

****

Doubled over from the effort of running and shocked with grief, Mary slumped against a wall. She couldn't get what she'd seen out of her head. All she could think of was Felicity, sprawled on a bed, skirt scrunched up and legs splayed, and Eli on top of her with his face buried in the deep cleft of her boobs. If

Grandma imagined Eli was depressed from the breakup, she was very, very wrong. Evidently, Eli was perfectly fine and ready to perform.

Drained of all hope for reconciliation, Mary slid to a crouch and opened her phone. She deleted Eli from her social media and contact list and then she blocked him. After a long, hard cry, she called Dominic and told him everything.

\*\*\*\*

Stephen picked up Felicity from office daycare at six p.m. using Claudia's car because his was under repair for a fender bender. Eli locked up and drove directly to Mary's place. She couldn't block an actual, in-the-flesh person. She'd have to listen while he explained. As he drove, he thought of what he'd say that would convince her that her eyes had deceived her.

Someone moving had propped open the utility door, so Eli ducked through it into the building and climbed the stairs. The corridor was dim and smelled of comforting, multiethnic suppers. He knocked.

Dominic opened the door and promptly slammed it in Eli's face. Eli heard the jangle of a chain lock and he knocked again. Dominic slowly turned the knob and opened the door a crack. If he thought the chain lock would keep anyone with a strong kick from entering their apartment, he was woefully naïve, but Eli had no intention of forcing his way in.

"Dominic, I have to speak to Mary," he said to half of Dominic's scowling face. "Please."

"She won't see you. You should leave now."

"If she would give me five minutes, I can explain—"

Dominic abruptly closed the door, so Eli knocked

again.

This time Dominic's words were muffled by the closed door. "Leave or I'll call the police."

"I'm leaving," Eli called. "Could you tell Mary to call me?"

Loud, bass-heavy music carried through the flimsy door. They'd blocked every avenue of communication. So be it. Eli didn't blame them. Not one bit. Mary believed she had irrefutable evidence that he was involved with Felicity, and if he were in a similar circumstance, he'd do the same thing. He'd have to think of some other way to get through to her.

Chapter Twenty-One

The beginning of spring term had always been an optimistic time of brand-new notebooks and fresh reading lists. Undergrads played frisbee on the commons lawn, romances blossomed on sunny benches, but Mary felt as flat as a cardboard cut-out. On Monday, she descended the stairs to her basement office to discover that her officemate had accepted delivery of a dozen red roses on her behalf and placed the bouquet on her desk.

"I didn't tip the delivery guy," said Sophie. "I hope he wasn't too disappointed. Anyway, cheer up. Someone loves you."

"Thanks," replied Mary. "I'll try."

When Mary failed to indulge Sophie's curiosity by opening the card or commenting further, Sophie pushed her books and laptop into her bag and said, "I'm teaching Phil 219, Collectivist Ideologies, for that sweet old communist bear, Igor Ivanov. Pray for me!" With a mischievous laugh, she bounded off.

Mary looked at the perfect, velvety-petaled roses and shook her head. She pulled a small envelope from its perch on a plastic stick and opened it. As expected, the note was written in Eli's angular scrawl, though he'd made a serious effort to write legibly.

*Dear Mary Rose,*
*I've made mistakes, but what you saw on Friday is*

*not what you think it was. Please give me a chance to explain. Text me or call me. At least unblock me. Please.*

*I miss you.*

*Love,*

*Eli*

A big, fat, hot, salty tear formed in Mary's eye, spilled over its eyelash dam and rolled down her cheek. The first tears were followed by trickles and then torrents of tears. She loved Eli but she'd seen what she'd seen and she'd never unsee it. She hated the term "gaslighting", but what Eli was doing was its very definition. She'd never heard him lie outright, but she'd heard him embellish or downplay the truth in his dealings often enough to know what she had to do to survive this awful episode in her dismal, crappy life.

Mary tore the note in half, in quarters, in eighths, and on, until it was a handful of confetti. Then she grabbed the bouquet, marched to the washroom, and threw it and the confetti into the bin.

## Chapter Twenty-Two

With deceptively dull, droopy eyes, Franklin E. Thoms, LLB, peered over his half-moon glasses at Eli. "John and Jill Q. Public feed like lions on a case like this, but if we avoid a charge, there's nothing to report in the *Daily Muckraker*. The cops can't keep you if they don't have evidence besides the security tape and your statement, so unless Silverstein comes forward, they've got nothing on you. Do your homework, and we should be finished by late morning. Then you can go on with your anonymous life and sleep like a saint."

"Silverstein said he'll press charges if I go to the police," warned Eli.

"Guy like that, he's yanking your chain. You're doing the right thing and down the line, he won't be able to blackmail you. Forget about him. Tomorrow we walk into the police station, you say your bit, humor their questions like we practised, and we leave. Easy-peasy." Thoms yawned as if Eli's case were as routine as buying milk. "I get paid by the hour and it's your money, but we can go over everything one more time if you think it'll help."

Eli shook his head. "No, I've got it. Dress like a banker, memorize my script, keep my answers short and simple."

"And don't talk to anyone except me and the cops." Thoms pushed his pen and legal pad to the side.

"By the way, how're the Hills?"

"They're fine, as far as I know. I resigned from the brokerage three days ago."

Thom's laugh bordered on a snicker. "Claudia's the brains in that operation, am I right?"

Eli nodded. "She's shrewd."

"They're members at Royal Oaks. He's usually poolside with a stiff drink and dark glasses, taking in the view. Now she's a horse of a different color. Got a nose for blood...a hound's sniffer for who's divorcing, ladder climbing, and what have you. She's extra friendly with people who're in the thick of a life transition and could use some timely advice on real estate."

"That's Claudia," Eli said half-admiringly.

Thoms pointed a knobby thumb at his legal pad. "They know about any of this?"

"Only that I did something wrong,"

"Not wrong. A mere misunderstanding."

"And I chose to resign because of it."

"Jesus. Bet that's put a twist in Claudia's thong." Thoms stretched, signaling the end of the meeting. "We'd better make sure she doesn't wind up in a full-on wedgy," he said ominously. "Wouldn't want to see that bird angry."

"I know what I have to do," Eli said with unconvincing conviction.

"Atta boy. Eight a.m. Look sharp."

Eli left the office of Thoms, Finkel, and Harrison and walked in a misty drizzle to the car. If Franklin Thoms knew the nature of his next errands, he'd choke on his Cuban cigar.

Eli sent a hasty text, then got behind the wheel of

his roadster for the last time and drove to Fountain Street where Stephen waited on the sidewalk. Eli stopped illegally in front of a hydrant, got out, and tossed the keys to Stephen. "You might as well drive," he said.

Stephen moved like a little kid who was about to take the wheel of a go-kart. Eli got into the passenger seat and buckled up. More than a fender bender, Stephen's recent accident had led to the lack of a vehicle when his Saab was written off and his insurance claim remained in limbo due to reckless driving. Stephen needed wheels and the BMW was just the ticket.

"A-One Pre-Owned, you said?" Stephen disengaged the parking brake.

"Yeah, over on Weston, just south of the 401."

"I've heard of it. Wide inventory." Stephen frowned at the gearshift, but Eli wouldn't undermine his dignity with coaching. Stephen wiped his palms on the thighs of his trousers, then played with the gearstick, found first, and the car lurched forward. "I'm a little rusty," he admitted.

"You'll have the hang of it in a block or two," said Eli, and Stephen did. They cruised northward, Stephen with a childish yet demonic grin, Eli gripping the armrest handle on the door.

Confidence evidently increasing with each mile, Stephen eased his seat back slightly and sped up. "What are you buying?"

"A 2018 Toyota Corolla. Silver-gray, automatic."

"What the fuck?" Stephen shot a surprised look at Eli. "You leaving real estate to teach fucking school or something?"

Eli laughed. "It *is* the kind of car a teacher would drive, but no. I need a basic, no-frills car for a friend to learn on. The Corolla is a good car for that."

"No offence, Eli, but if I was learning, I'd rather do it in this one." Stephen patted the dash, then geared down for slow traffic. "This 'someone'…it's Mary, right?"

"Yeah, though she doesn't know it yet. That's where you come in."

"I gotta tell you, Eli—and I'm not complaining— you're a fucking pansy at negotiation. This bee-yoo-tee of a car for playing messenger? Down the line, if you ever need an errand boy…" Stephen pounced on the horn to warn a woman pushing a baby buggy that he wasn't stopping for her, even on a rainy day. Same old despicable Stephen.

"If everything goes to plan, our deal is worth it to me," said Eli. He'd sworn off intimidation and violence, but if Stephen Hill crossed him, he'd make an exception.

****

Not a block from home, Mary walked down St. Dunstan Avenue with her rucksack slung over one shoulder and her umbrella propped on the other. The weather matched her mood. Keeping to the right side of the sidewalk to avoid being splashed by vehicles, she spotted a sporty BMW…Eli's car? Had to be. She lowered her umbrella to hide her face and ducked into an alley.

Shit. The BMW stopped. She'd tell him to lay off and she'd keep walking…enter a café and go into the ladies' room if need be. Except the man who got out of the car wasn't Eli; it was Stephen Hill. Mary's heart sank with dread. Why would Stephen drive Eli's car unless something bad had happened...unless Eli was hurt...or in trouble...or worse.

Mary stepped out of the alley and called, "Stephen?"

Stephen skipped over the curb and smiled, the same wide leer as on last winter's transit ad, only white and bright thanks to cosmetic dentistry. "I wondered where you went, Mary! Got a minute?"

"Sure. Is everything all right?"

"Yeah." Stephen palmed his forehead theatrically. "The car! You thought I was Eli, didn't you? You'll never believe it, but he drives an old lady car now. A fucking Corolla."

"Oh." She couldn't think of a better word.

"Listen, it's kind of wet out here. Do you mind joining me in the car? I have something I have to show you."

A creepier set of sentences had never been uttered, but despite his faults, Stephen had never done anything to scare her, so Mary closed her umbrella and did as he asked.

"First, I want your promise that you'll read every word of what I'm about to show you, beginning to end," said Stephen. Sensing her hesitation, he added, "It's rated 'suitable for all ages', but I can't tell you what it is. You have to read it yourself."

Mary nodded. "Okay. I promise. Beginning to end." Brows raised in confusion, she accepted the proffered cell phone.

"It's mine," said Stephen. "Please note the date and the times."

She squinted at the screen, then enlarged a series of

texts. "Last Friday. Starting at four p.m.," she murmured.

—Hi Stephen. I picked up Felicity from her event. She was overserved and I have to get her home. Can you give me her address?—

—Ask Claudia.—

—I have, but she's not answering my texts.—

—Can't chat. Client.—

—Help me, please. Felicity is not cooperating, there are a thousand Hills in Toronto, and she lost her ID somewhere in the Coronation Club. Just give me her address and I'll take her home.—

Then, five minutes later.

—For her safety, I'm putting her to bed in the model suite, but she's very aggressive and she needs her family. When can you pick her up?—

Then twenty minutes later.

—Answer your phone! Something urgent has come up. I have to go, but I can't leave her here alone. She's so drunk it isn't safe.—

—I'll be there in ten.—

Mary returned the phone to Stephen. "Thank you," she said quietly. A lump that felt like a sand-covered golf ball formed in her throat. She pulled the door handle, but Stephen caught her sleeve.

"That's not all," said Stephen. "Now listen." With a thick thumb, he navigated to his voicemail and played back a message from the same date.

Mary heard Eli's clear, semi-panicked baritone over high-pitched weeping. "Stephen. Call me as soon as you get this," he said while a histrionic Felicity slurred, "Don't you want me, Eli?"

Stephen closed the screen and put his phone in his

jacket pocket.

"I've got to go," said Mary.

"It's raining. I can drive you."

"I need to think...fresh air. Thanks, anyway." Mary gave Stephen a weak smile and escaped the strangling humidity of the car formerly owned by the tragically misunderstood Eli Klassen.

As she walked away, the BMW inched along the curb beside her. Stephen rolled down the window and shouted, "I forgot to tell you. He said you shouldn't call him today. Wait a day or two, and then decide."

Chapter Twenty-Three

After an hour-long interview, Franklin Thoms and Eli left the police station and debriefed on the sidewalk.

"I'd buy you a drink, but it's only ten in the morning," said Thoms.

"I appreciate the sentiment." Eli shivered. "I'm sure glad that's over."

"You were as nervous as a nun in a whorehouse, but you spoke well," Thoms chortled.

"Thanks."

"Gotta love a rookie cop. I couldn't believe our lucky stars she let slip that they only have ten seconds of video. Whatever Silverstein does, you got there first and we're well-positioned to shoot down whatever half-truths he spews. Squint and it really does look like you're trying to help an old man."

"I was."

"I know."

"Thank you. For everything, Thoms. You made the occasion way easier than it might've been."

"Only doing my job." They shook hands before parting ways. "What are you going to do to celebrate?"

"Take care of some business, and if that goes well, hopefully reconnect with a friend."

\*\*\*\*

Whatever the reason for the request to wait to make contact, Eli had to know what he was doing, and Mary had to trust him, but all this not knowing was breaking her to bits. Multiple theories coalesced, burned like super novae, and fizzled in her brain. Distracted with speculation, Mary trudged home from a long but unproductive day in the Toronto Reference Library. As she left the apartment stairwell, she heard the strains of her favorite love song, an ancient Led Zeppelin tune, leaking around the door of Number 210. Dominic. He never missed an opportunity for drama. On the contrary, he'd transform any random happening into an event. He had his reasons for playing that song, and she was in for a ride.

As soon as Mary had kicked off her shoes, Dominic greeted her with a kiss on the cheek and a searching look. "You really don't know?" He grasped her shoulders and playfully shook them. "I can't believe you don't know."

"Don't know what?"

Dominic clucked his tongue. "My dear, you are of another century entirely. How is it you miss every viral, crazy story in the very city you live in? In your hometown? Including the stories that affect you! Or should I say infect? Get it?"

"Yes. Virus, viral story, infect. I get it. But what are you talking about?"

Dominic steered Mary by her shoulders to the living room and turned off the music. "I predicted your glaring ignorance, so I've warmed up the TV and adjusted the bunny ears so we can watch the show together. Drinky-poo?"

"No thanks. Not until I know what you're talking about." Mary sat on the couch in front of Dominic's laptop, which was open and elevated on a pile of books on the coffee table.

Dominic joined her and leaned forward to click on a *Meteor* video article, open and waiting to be viewed. He looked sideways at Mary and paused with his hand over the keyboard. "Ready?"

"Just play it," Mary snapped.

A preamble and a "this just in-exclusive scoop" sound effect introduced a clean-shaven, angelic-looking Eli dressed in a plain, dark suit. Seated on standard studio furniture across from him was senior journalist, Tracy DeLillo.

"What the hell?" muttered Mary. Dominic shushed her, and she sat back, mouth gawping.

After introducing her interviewee and setting up the story, Ms. DeLillo asked, "Why now? Why come forward to the media at this time, Mr. Klassen?"

"Call me Eli," he said with a boyish smile. "I realized the release of U of T's CCTV image and the media coverage around it has caused some members of the community to become frightened and concerned for their safety. After some soul-searching, I decided to go to the police and explain what had happened, but it wasn't enough. I thought your viewers and readers should know the truth as well."

"Take us back to that day, Eli. Who is the man in the garden? What actually happened?"

"The man is Dr. Gabriel Silverstein and he's the advisor of a talented doctoral candidate in the philosophy department. It so happens that his student is a woman, and I don't have to tell you that toxic sexism persists to this day when certain men act as gatekeepers, whether in the arts, or business, or academia. That's especially true when the man's power is waning, and the young up-and-comer is brilliant and threatens to eclipse him."

"Are you saying that Dr. Silverstein is another Harvey Weinstein?"

"No."

"It certainly sounds as if you're insinuating it."

Eli shrugged. "The young woman, my friend, is brilliant. I'll leave it at that and suggest to you that there's a fascinating story in the public interest within U of T's philosophy department."

"All right, Eli." The interviewer leaned forward, as if speaking confidentially despite a rolling camera. "How did Dr. Silverstein find himself on his back in a flowerbed at the university's western gate first thing on a Tuesday morning in April?"

Eli tented his fingers and hesitated.

"Come now. He wasn't gardening...or hunting for Easter eggs." She gave Eli a tight, knowing look.

With a pained expression, Eli answered, "He was there because I put him there, unintentionally."

"Unintentionally?" Ms. DeLillo shook her head in a disbelieving scold.

"Yes. Where I come from, a man is duty-bound to act when he sees injustice. I asked Dr. Silverstein to behave as a man ought and respect his female students. Our conversation became heated, and I took hold of his tie. He kicked me and toppled over. When I tried to help him to his feet, he swung at me."

"You physically assaulted him."

"Yes. I grabbed his tie. I've informed the police of my actions and I take full responsibility for what I did. I'm told that Dr. Silverstein is within his rights to press charges. That's up to him."

Ms. DeLillo's nose twitched. "Don't you worry about ending up with a criminal record? You're a real estate agent and you could lose your career with this revelation."

"Was. *Was* a real estate agent. I'm currently unemployed."

"With nothing to lose?"

"And everything to gain."

"What do you mean by that?"

"I've lost my career and my sales income. I'll probably lose friends over this incident. On the other hand, I've gained self-respect. I've changed. And I really hope that beautiful, brilliant PhD candidate recognizes that I'm a better man than I was. I hope she gives me another chance because I love her."

"Aw," purred Ms. DeLillo. "What's her name?"

"I won't say, but she knows who she is."

Ms. DeLillo straightened her papers. "Is there anything else you'd like to share?"

"Yes. I'd like to apologize to Franklin Thoms. I'm sorry I couldn't follow his advice. Mr. Thoms is a great lawyer and I'm a lousy client."

Ms. DeLillo smiled stiffly. "Thank you for agreeing to this interview, Eli." She turned and peered at the camera. "And thank you for watching. We look forward to pursuing this story in the coming days."

Dominic closed the laptop, then paused and looked at Mary. "I'm sorry. Did you want to see that again?"

"No," she replied. "I want to call Eli."

"Then call him!"

Mary was already searching for her phone.

****

After supper, Eli sorted bottles of various eye drops

to help Grandma prepare for her cataract surgery. He wrote out the instructions in bold, large letters with a sharpie while Grandma chuckled that soon she'd be embroidering pillowcases for her granddaughters' hope chests. Eli was still tense after two difficult interrogations, though he tried to hide it, and Grandma was doing her best to distract him with cheery conversation. They both jumped every time his phone rang, his heart lurching in the hope of seeing Mary's name and number on the display. After several nuisance calls from reporters, it was finally her.

"Well?" asked Grandma.

"It's Mary."

"Then hurry up and answer it!"

Eli fumbled with his phone as if it was a radioactive grenade, and finally managed to connect.

"Hey. It's me," she said.

"Hey, you." He turned away from Grandma's nosey gaze and shuffled to the balcony.

"I'm sorry, Eli," Mary said softly. "I'm sorry I doubted you."

"Me, too." He propped his elbows on the balcony railing and waited for her lead.

After a torturous silence, she said, "Do you think there's any chance we could—"

"Go for a drive?" he finished.

"I was going to say talk, in person, but okay. Sure. Go for a drive. I heard you have new wheels."

"I do. A sensible, unremarkable, gray Toyota."

"And fantastic cover," Mary joked. "I'll bet the media is chasing Stephen all over town in his new sports car."

"Probably. I give the BMW a week to live. A

month at best. He's a terrible driver."

"Worse than me?"

"Well..."

"Never mind. Do I have time for a shower?"

"Definitely not." As Eli stepped inside, Grandma pushed the car key into his hand.

****

After Mary ended her call with Eli, Dominic announced he was leaving early for dance class. "And I think I'll go out for drinks after," he added.

"You don't have to do that," said Mary.

Dominic was already buttoning his jacket. "Yes, I do, my dear." He danced off before she could object.

Thirsty from a long day, she padded into the kitchen for a glass of water. The microwave blinked the time, a little past six. She was hungry too, so she ate an apple and a handful of walnuts. Eli wouldn't arrive for at least fifteen minutes. She had time. She went to the bathroom, slipped out of her clothes, ran a hot shower, and stepped into the tub.

How good it felt to lather up and wash away the grime of the city. As she shampooed her hair, water cascaded over her shoulders and streamed over her skin. She hummed then sang the Zeppelin tune Dominic had played, her soft voice echoing off the porcelain tiles.

Through the semi-transparent shower curtain, Mary glimpsed a presence in the doorway. An Eli-sized presence. She sang quietly and pretended she didn't see him as he, too, shed his clothing. Seconds later, Eli stepped into the shower behind her.

"Hey." He folded her in his arms and nuzzled her neck, his body warm against her back. "You left the door unlocked."

"So I did."

"I could be Norman Bates."

Turning, Mary took a long look at Eli and laughed. "You are the opposite of Norman Bates. I've never felt as safe as I do right now."

Front pressed against front, Eli bent and kissed her. Their mouths danced in an ecstatic reunion, and when at last the kiss ended, Eli said, "I love you."

"You love me." Mary's lips brushed the wet skin of his collarbone. "What a coincidence? I love you, too."

"You said we should talk."

"We've talked."

Eli slid his soapy hands over her back from shoulder to bottom. A hot, urgent need for his touch burned within her. As he kissed her, she ran her own soapy hands over the contours of his shoulders, his chest, and his abdomen, her fingers circling in his hair ever lower until she found him, hard and ready.

She caressed him and he groaned. "Bed."

Mary turned off the tap with her toe, and they toweled each other off. Like the first time, Eli scooped her up and took her to bed.

The setting sun cast the room in an ethereal glow as Mary gazed into Eli's dark brown eyes. She couldn't look away. She watched his serious face as he parted her legs and drew himself along her. He shifted position and entered slowly and smoothly, and she cried out with the feel of him, with the intense sensations of his firm, slow thrust. Their eyes remained locked in wordless communion, in the giving and receiving of love. He kept his rhythm slow and close, mastering himself and mastering her.

Mary felt the first ripple deep in the center of her being, and the ripple surged into a wave, then crested and broke. She gripped him, arms and legs, and in her deepest place. Joyful energy built and crashed over her being, and through it all, she held him in her gaze. Eli's breath quickened, his muscles tensed with raw power, and he took her as high as he could, meeting her ecstasy with his own.

"Eli," she whispered hoarsely. "Eli." Only his name. Only him. He was enough.

Spent, he eased off, and they rested, limbs entwined and bodies melded. Night was falling. At first, they didn't speak and they didn't move except for the rise and fall of their breath. Eli's exhalation tickled her neck and, guessing he'd fallen asleep, she moved to give him space. His arm tensed to hold her, and he teased her nipple with his fingertips.

She spoke first. "You're awake."

"Well, on the phone you said you wanted to talk, Mary Rose." His voice was husky in the darkness of the room.

"Yes, I did. But I think you cleared up everything when you told me you love me."

He gave a low, unsure laugh. "There's still something we have to discuss."

"Yeah?"

"Yeah." He rolled onto his side, his eyes and teeth shining in the darkness. "Remember when I said, 'no other men. Only me'?"

"Yes, I remember."

"When we were, uh, broken up, did you keep our promise?"

"We were 'broken up' so I don't have to answer that, but yes, I kept our promise because, deep down, I never lost hope for us." With the fiasco at In-Spire with Felicity, she didn't dare ask him the same question and she found she didn't care to.

"I'm glad," said Eli.

"What if I'd said 'no'?" asked Mary.

"I'd get over it eventually."

They held each other and drifted off to sleep.

A couple of hours later, Eli startled awake and sat up. "I have to go," he exclaimed. Before Mary could ask why, he said, "My grandmother's visiting. She'll be worried if I don't come home."

"Go then," Mary urged with a warm laugh. "You really must."

"When you meet her, you'll understand."

"I already do understand."

By the lights of the city, she watched him pull his boxers and jeans over his slim, athletic hips and tuck carefully before zipping his fly. She would never tire of watching him move.

"Could you leave me your T-shirt?" she asked.

"Pardon?"

"Your T-shirt, please. You could wear only your sweater, or take one of Dominic's shirts, but I want to keep your shirt so I can smell you after you leave."

"It's kind of sweaty...."

"Even better."

Eli bent, found his shirt, and tossed it to her, sinewy muscles moving under his skin. "I won't steal from Dominic."

"He won't mind. We trade clothes all the time."

"Like sisters," said Eli.

277

"Like roommates," Mary corrected.

Sweater on, he bent over the bed and planted an intentionally sloppy kiss on her forehead.

"We still haven't taken our drive. Can I pick you up at school tomorrow?"

"Four. In front of the library."

This time, he kissed her lips, a tender, lingering kiss. He said, "I'll be there," and then he disappeared into the night.

Sitting cross-legged among the rumpled sheets, Mary bunched up Eli's shirt, buried her nose in the cotton fabric, and took a long appreciative sniff, inhaling its musky odor. She pulled the T-shirt on, drew up her knees underneath it, and hugged herself. Her three-week nightmare had ended. She'd come very close to losing a man whose depths she'd only begun to fathom, and the very thought of it sent a current of ice down her spine.

$$****$$

A steady rain broke through the clouds as Eli drove through nighttime streets. The wet weather reminded him of Eden Springs. Every year, just ahead of planting, Dad and Jacob walked along the pine windbreak, discovered small ponds of standing water in the backfield, and wondered if they should lay tile come fall. And every summer, during a dry spell, they decided against the idea. The seasonal rhythm of the land swept the people who depended on it into a yearlong cycle of work and rest, hardship and celebration. They were soul-bound to the earth, and they were lucky for it. Jacob crowed about the superiority of rural life, but he'd never lived in the city and his beliefs were untethered from experience. Eli knew it as fact.

And here was the trouble. Mary was like Jacob in that very same way. Toronto was her universe in the way that Eden Springs was Jacob's.

When Eli and Mary had rested together, her hair damp on his shoulder, her bewitching softness against his body, and her sweet breath warm on his chest, he'd longed to say, "Forever. Promise me forever." He stopped himself. After mustering his courage all day, with the police and the *Meteor* interviewer, he'd blinked with Mary. It was cowardly. The worst she would've said was "maybe," and he could live with that and hope for more. In his heart and soul, he knew he'd eventually need "forever" from her, but some strange force held him back from seeking it, as if he didn't know what he was offering her.

Maybe the key to their future was hidden in the past, in a reckoning he'd put off for too long. He would never be an obedient disciple of the Brethren Church, but he wasn't a hyper-materialistic, big-city hustler either. He'd lived in two versions of himself, one imposed and one adopted, and they were both traps.

With a swoosh of puddle water under the car, his mind returned to Eden Springs and the creek-fed pond at the edge of the farm. People were teachers and so were animals. Snakes shed their skins, and deer their antlers. He'd even seen a painted turtle basking on a rock in August sunshine with its shell flaking off like potato chips. If he went back to that pond, he could sit on a rock, shed pretense, and work things out.

Eli turned into the garage and parked. Grandma would be asleep by now. Used to her room in the quietest corner of a rambling farmhouse, she'd awaken even if he tiptoed. He wouldn't discuss the situation with her. Her advice was predictable anyway: pray and bring Mary to Eden Springs to meet the family. Prayer was impossible, but returning to Eden Springs was not. In fact, it was necessary.

## Chapter Twenty-Four

Eli stopped the Corolla behind a streetcar, and Mary scurried across the bike lane and hopped in.

"Like it?" he asked.

"It's certainly less complicated," she replied.

"This is the car you'll use to learn how to drive," he announced as they followed the streetcar at a snail's pace.

"I don't know, Eli. Our first lesson didn't go very well." She peered through the window as cyclists whooshed by on their right and an oncoming delivery van came inches from clipping the driver-side mirror. Even as a pedestrian, she felt intimidated by Toronto's traffic. "When you were my teacher, you ended up with a terrible headache, remember?"

Eli shrugged. "I don't seem to get those anymore."

"Really?" She stared at him and wondered what else had changed in three weeks.

"Really." He grinned. "At least not debilitating ones. Grandma brought me medicine. But you wouldn't know anything about that…"

"Um, I might. I wrote to her without telling you and asked her to send you some."

"I know, and she decided to deliver it herself. She thinks you're an angel because of that letter. I told her you're into godless philosophy and unchurched, but she won't change her mind. You're an angel."

281

"I'm flattered, but of course, you know better," said Mary. "Where are we going?"

"Belgrave Park for a walk? And then we'll pick up Grandma and go to Takamatsu. She has surgery tomorrow and she can't have anything to eat or drink after midnight. She's very excited to meet you and going out for supper will take her mind off her procedure."

"Eye surgery would make me nervous, too."

Eli tensed his grip on the wheel and steered through a gap in the traffic. "What did you say?"

"Her cataracts. They say it's routine, but the idea of someone cutting into your eyeballs would be scary."

"How do you know she's going for eye surgery? I didn't tell you or anyone at Hill."

"Didn't you?" Mary asked innocently. When Eli didn't reply, she said, "Oh, I suppose you didn't." Damn. A stupid, unnecessary secret was ruining the afternoon.

A frigid silence enveloped the car for the rest of the journey. Eli backed into a tight space at the park's boundary. They got out and he paid the meter. He was clearly annoyed, but he took her hand anyway and they walked on a footpath to an ornamental lake noisy with birdsong.

They found a bench at the water's edge, and she squeezed his hand. "Eli, I'm sorry. I know about your grandmother's surgery because I met her at Breaktime last Friday. That's when she told me about it. We should've told you we met, but we agreed to keep it a secret."

"Why?"

"Why what? Why did we meet? Why didn't I tell

you?"

"All of it."

"Your grandmother wrote to me and asked me to meet her because she was worried about you. When we met, she asked me to talk to you. I told her I'd think about it, but I ended up going directly to the sales office because after what she said, I had to see you. You know what happened after that."

Eli shuddered. "Yeah, I do know. And it's too bad because, by then, I'd already told Claudia I was resigning, and I'd lined up a lawyer for advice on going to the police. I didn't need an intervention."

"Is that what you think it was? An intervention?"

He responded with a shrug that came across as dismissive. At once, she felt a frisson of anger and she took a deep breath to push it away. "Eli, I went to In-Spire because I love you and I wanted to see you. Your grandmother said you were suffering and, believing that to be true, I couldn't stay away from you any longer, so I went to you. I guess it was a mistake."

"Do you think so? What happened at In-Spire was a misunderstanding. Your mistake was freezing me out in the first place and then plotting my rehabilitation with my grandmother."

"I didn't have a chance to tell you that we'd met."

"Yes, you did, Mary. Last night you pretended you didn't know she was in Toronto."

"Okay. Fine. That's true. But the way you dealt with Silverstein behind my back was a way bigger lie, and I had to 'freeze you out'. I have my standards and I won't apologize for that. I've forgiven you for your big lie. Why are you being so hard on me for this small one?"

"Because it feels like a betrayal of trust."

"I *am* sorry, Eli. Yes, it was sneaky and wrong of me, but I didn't mean to hurt you."

"I know." He encircled her shoulder, pulled her close, and kissed the top of her head. "I'm being too hard on you. I just want honesty. That's all."

"I want that, too."

They sat together, deep in their thoughts, so quiet and still that a large bird landed in a rocky shallow. Mary looked up at Eli to see if he'd noticed it. His sharp eyes were focused on the bird.

"That's an interesting bird," she said. The majestic creature flapped its wings and flew away.

"The heron we've scared off by talking?"

"I scared off." Hoping the answer would be 'no', she asked, "Have you hunted them?"

"Herons?" Eli smiled. "Nah. That's illegal, and they probably wouldn't taste very good anyway because they eat fish and frogs."

"Oh." She cuddled under his arm and gazed over the water, hoping the heron would return. Here, in the middle of Toronto on her home turf, she felt disadvantaged by Eli's easy answer. He knew the species of the creature, its habits, and whether one might hunt and eat it, while all she saw was 'a really big bird'.

"Did you and Grandma talk about Eden Springs?" he asked, eyes scanning the lake.

"Yes."

"Did she tell you why I left?"

"Yes. She mentioned your run-in with the law, your free-range curiosity, and the fight with your father. Stuff like that."

"And here you are, next to me. She didn't frighten you away from me with an account of my sins?"

"Your 'sins' as you call them, seem rather noble to me, and consistent with how you've conducted yourself in Toronto."

"You sound as if you're grading me like a term paper."

"Sure. Why not. I've watched you, Eli, and you've done the same with me. As for your sins...well, if I were a man, I wouldn't want to be your enemy. Everyone has a weakness, and a hot temper inflamed by a primitive sense of justice is yours."

"Primitive?" The color rose in Eli's cheeks. "I guess I can't refute that."

"Fair's fair, so tell me—what are my weaknesses?"

"You, Mary Rose, have a narrow range of experience. Yes, you've partied and experimented in ways that if God existed, He would surely smite you for. You've read every book in the library...attended all the concerts...but I'll bet you've never caught a fish and pan-fried it over a fire or woken up to a rooster's crow."

"That's true. I've led a sheltered life," she joked, though his criticism cut close to the bone. "If I didn't know better, I'd say you're angling to take me on an educational field trip to Eden Springs."

He nodded. "Highly educational. You need experience in the field. Literally."

"Finally. Someone who uses the word 'literally' correctly. Yes, I'd like to experience the fields and the barns and meet the Klassens and observe you in your native habitat. I think it would be educational."

"This weekend? I have to take Grandma home,

anyway."

"It isn't too soon? I mean…with us…"

"Mary, I've been running from myself. I have to reckon with my past, make peace with it, and you should know where I come from. I want you with me."

"Okay. In that case, I'd be honored." She smiled and he drew her even closer and kissed her forehead again, though she knew he wouldn't go further. He thought kissing in public distasteful.

She said, "I'll have to bring some work with me, though. Does the farm have Wi-Fi?"

"Yeah, and a brand-new icebox and even a laundry mangle."

As Mary laughed and punched Eli's shoulder, he added, "My dad keeps tight control on usage so it might be better to use your phone to make a hotspot." His own phone buzzed a message. "It's Yuka. Grandma walked to Takamatsu. She says we should head straight there to avoid the media who've shown up outside the condo."

"Sounds like you're famous."

"Or infamous." He shuddered as his phone pinged again. "Yuka also says that Grandma brought her a homemade cake to go with green tea ice cream."

"Is your grandma being kind or competitive?"

"Likely both." Eli chuckled.

****

The next day, Mary kept her phone on even while lecturing in case Grandma and Eli needed her. Fortunately, they didn't, as God answered Grandma's prayers and her surgery went smoothly, or so Eli had texted her when they returned to the condo just before noon. He spent the remainder of the day administering eye drops, blocking calls, and deleting email from reporters, and ordering pizza for each shift in the building's security concierge.

In the evening, he phoned Mary with an update and added, "Grandma's follow-up appointment is at nine fifteen tomorrow, and assuming Jesus comes through for her again, she'll be free to go home. When can you be packed and ready to go?"

"I have a seminar in the morning. Is one o'clock early enough?" asked Mary, suddenly struck with anxiety over meeting Eli's family.

"Yeah, sounds good. We'll beat rush hour and be there by supper," he replied. They said their goodnights and the call ended.

Now she stood by her empty duffel bag that lay open on the bed and she peered into her closet.

"One must never underestimate the importance of that crucial first impression," Dominic drawled from the doorway. "Overdress and they'll think you're a snob. Underdress and they'll think you a wanton, worldly harlot who's corrupted Eli, the innocent, runaway farm boy hypnotized by the glittery temptations of the city. You, my dear, must walk en pointe upon the tightrope of fashion."

"Gee, thanks for the reassuring advice." Mary opened her top drawer and transferred three pairs of underwear and socks into the duffle bag. "The question is, how do I strike that balance?"

Dominic sidled to her side. "If clothes make the woman, or offer a mere hint of who she is, do not pack any band T-shirts or torn jeans. You are not a groupie."

"Okay. There goes half my wardrobe." She rummaged through the second drawer for pajamas.

"Yes, those are perfect," gushed Dominic. "A

pattern of ladybugs on brushed cotton. Ideal for a slumber party with the Klassen girls."

Mary startled at the words 'slumber party' and stared at Dominic. "You don't think—"

"I do. They won't even consider letting you sleep with Eli. You're not married. The family is large, perhaps underhoused for their numbers, and unlikely to have a guestroom. You, my dear, shall sleep in the girls' room."

"Eli didn't say anything about that," Mary stammered. "If, *if* that were true, he would've mentioned it, wouldn't he? I'm going to call him."

"Don't bother." Dominic arched his brow in a knowing expression and Mary realized he was right.

"Jeez. I was only packing pajamas in case I had to get up during the night," she muttered. "I guess I should pack an extra pair."

"Those with the penguin and igloo pattern are cute."

Mary put the pajamas in the bag. "What next?"

"*Grand-mère* wears dresses. Mother and sisters likely also wear dresses. How about a couple of full skirts, nothing above the knee, and your prettiest blouses? Also plain T-shirts and jeans for the barnyard."

Mary riffled through her closet and pulled out various garments on hangers while Dominic gave each a thumbs-up or down. After much frowning, chin rubbing, contemplation, and discussion, the duffel bag was full.

"'One o'clock,' you said?"

"Yes. One." Mary zipped up the bag and lugged it to the front hallway. "I think I'm more nervous than when I delivered my proposal before the committee."

"You don't say...."

"I wish you could come with us, Dominic. For my sake. You know...safety in numbers."

He roared with laughter. "*Moi*? The Klassens would eat me alive. I'm a defenseless sodomite and I'd be absolutely no help to you." He pinched her cheek affectionately. "Eli loves you. I love you. Grandma loves you. Just be yourself, and you'll win their hearts, too, Mary Rose."

"I hope you're right," she sighed. "Besides petting zoos, I've never been on a farm before."

"There you go. That's your *entrée*. Disarm them with your humble naivety and you'll do just fine," Dominic said sagely.

"What if I can't remember all their names?"

"You remember your students' names, don't you?"

"Yes, but judging by Eli and his grandmother, the Klassens look alike, and they all have Old Testament names. You know...Eli, Ezra, Esau, Esther..."

"Elijah, Enoch, and Ezekiel," finished Dominic.

"Uniformity adds a marked level of difficulty," said Mary.

"Then devise a system of communication with Eli and he can remind you of their names in a discreet way. You're a smart cookie, Mary. Remembering names should be the least of your worries."

"Oh? And what should be the most?"

"Nothing. You shouldn't worry. By the way, I forgot to ask: how did Gabriel react to Eli's interview with Tracy DeLillo?"

"With no reaction at all. At least not on campus. He's in Chicago at a conference and probably waiting till he's back to say or do anything."

"Hmm...Interesting." Dominic shrugged and straightened a book on its shelf.

"What's interesting about that? He travels a lot."

"Oh, nothing. Forget I mentioned him." Dominic smiled. "Go away. Have the time of your life and come home with stories, Miss Rose. On Sunday evening, I want to hear every detail of your trip to the country."

Mary agreed to try to have fun, though Dominic's throwaway comment about Gabriel bothered her well into the next day.

****

"You remind me of your father on the eve of his wedding," said Grandma as Eli squeezed a tiny bottle of medicine and yet another drop missed its target and rolled down her cheek. "Why don't you give me the bottle? I can do the drops myself now."

"Sorry. I don't know why I'm so shaky." Eli did as Grandma asked and dropped onto the couch.

"Young man, you've got a case of the nerves is all. I find that reciting the sixty-second Psalm is calming when I'm all wound up and out of sorts." Grandma dabbed her eyes with a tissue. "Also, prayer. But there I go, repeating like a broken record."

"I appreciate your advice, Grandma, but prayer has never helped me. I'd go for a walk to work off some energy, but the media hounds are baying at the door."

"You've tipped the doorman to keep those hounds outside, and they won't bother you inside the building. Didn't I hear you brag to Jacob that there's a pool and a gym downstairs?"

"Brag?"

"Yes. Brag. Go work off some energy before you

get a headache."

"But you just had surgery. What if you need me?"

"Ach. It was like going to the dentist. Go on. I'm quite content to pack my suitcases and putter without a nervous audience."

"All right. If you're sure you'll be okay, Grandma, I'll go for an hour." Eli rose from the couch, changed into shorts, a T-shirt, and sandals, grabbed a towel, and ventured to the pool he'd rarely used.

Heeding the "shallow water" warnings, he hopped into the pool. The air was practically green with chlorine fumes, yet the water was cool and refreshing. He kicked off the side and glided underwater, then surfaced into an easy front crawl. As he sliced through lengths of the pool, he lost himself in the rhythmic cadence of his own breathing and the tranquil solitude of the pool with only his thoughts for company.

As usual, Grandma had unceremoniously named exactly what was bugging him. It was Mary. They weren't getting married, but their journey to his past felt equivalent…as if he was taking a mail order bride from a foreign country to Eden Springs. He shouldn't have invited her, he should be going home alone, but it was too late to change the plan. They were in for a wild ride on a rickety roller coaster he'd built with his very own hands, and he'd just have to trust her to hold tight through all the crazy.

Without the protection of goggles, Eli's eyes started to burn. He swam a final lap and pulled himself onto the deck. He was tired enough to sleep, though only fitfully given the stakes of the weekend ahead.

Chapter Twenty-Five

Grandma snored in the backseat while Eli drove at precisely one hundred kilometers an hour, hands glued to the steering wheel and eyes glued to the road.

"Since you bought this car, your driving personality has changed," Mary teased from the passenger side.

"What do you mean?" Eli said irritably. "I'm driving safely."

"Yes, at precisely the speed limit in the slow lane. In your old car, you slalomed down the highway at one forty."

"We're not in a hurry."

"I've noticed," Mary said with artificial cheer.

Damn, Eli was moody. Inwardly she debated asking him to take the next exit and drive her to a train station, but Penny and Dominic had texted that reporters had descended and were circling both the philosophy building and the apartment like sharks. For better or worse she was trapped with Mr. Grumpy and she'd have to make the most of the weekend. They lapsed into a suffocating silence broken only by the noise of vehicles speeding by on the left and a rhythmic snuffling as Grandma "rested her eyes."

After an hour and a half's drive, they exited onto a secondary road that ribboned over hills and valleys, through meadows and forests and tiny towns governed by single traffic lights. Determined to enjoy her weekend away, Mary took in the view. Fluffy white clouds floated in an azure sky over verdant pastures and chocolate-colored fields. Farm equipment added bold punches of red, green, and yellow. The colors were so vivid, the countryside looked like a Kodak ad.

"How much farther?" she asked.

"Another two hours," Eli replied. "We have enough gas to get to Eden Springs, but we can stop if you need a break."

"I'm okay."

Back to oppressive silence. Eli opened his window and let his right hand drop onto his tensed thigh. Mary peeked over her shoulder. Grandma's head lolled back on the headrest and a rivulet of drool ran from the corner of her slack mouth. Definitely asleep. Eli would never admit to suffering such a vulnerable emotion as anxiety, let alone fear. But if she approached obliquely and claimed those feelings as her own, she might get to the bottom of what was bothering him.

"This is my first time meeting your family and I'm super nervous," Mary said matter-of-factly. When he responded with a shrug, she said, "Maybe you could give me some tips so I know what to expect and how to behave."

At last, Eli looked at her properly. "You, Miss Rose, do not need lessons on how to behave. It's my family that worries me."

"Are you worried about how they'll behave toward me or toward you?"

"Both." His frown deepened, and he shifted in his seat, glancing in the mirror to check on Grandma. Slouching back, he said, "I can handle them. More you."

"Eli, I'm in love with you, not your family. Whatever they say or do, you are not guilty by association."

"Okay, but you have no idea what they're like…all together in a big mob." Back to eyes forward and stony silence.

"Then tell me—what are they like?"

"Like brainwashed sheep in a cult led by an obnoxious, stupid man. The current leader is my great uncle Gideon, who believes he can tame snakes and heal broken bones with prayer. The family blindly follows wherever Gideon's madness leads them. Since they live in isolation, they've lost touch with the wider world. With reality."

"Wow. You're making me think we'll be paddling down a river in a canoe to the sound of banjos and we might not make it out alive."

Eli regarded her quizzically. "That's dramatic."

"Actually, it's cinematic. Maybe if we have a strategy…."

Eyes back on the road, Eli slowed, then overtook a tractor pulling a gigantic machine.

"What's that thing?" she asked.

"What thing? Oh. A planter."

"What does it plant?"

"Corn, maybe soybeans."

"Of course." Mary nodded, feeling intimidated by all the things she didn't know about rural life. "Eli, never mind your family. I was raised by a certifiably batty mother, so I can draw on experience to cope, but I don't have a freaking clue what to do on a farm."

Finally, he smiled, only a tiny little grin, but it was

something. "Well, it's a busy time of year. We'll help out with chores on Saturday and on Sunday—"

"Church." Mary gasped.

"No. Everyone will go to church except us. We'll go for a walk in the woods or whatever and go back to Toronto after lunch."

"Right. Sounds good." They passed a sign announcing that Eden Springs was twenty kilometers away. The countdown was on. "I still think I need more information."

Eli shrugged. "You know Grandma. Mama and my sisters will treat you the same way she does. Just try to be helpful in the kitchen and the garden and nod along with their religious bullshit."

"Go with the flow down the path of least resistance. That's useful advice."

"And I'll deal with the men," he said gravely.

Eli signaled and turned down a gravel road. With the change of surface under the wheels, Grandma woke and stretched. "Almost there, Mary," she chirped with evident pride. "Watch for a white frame house with green trim, an orchard, and a barn with three tall silos."

After a couple more miles, Eli turned down another gravel road and Mary spotted the Klassen farm, trees blossoming in clouds of pink and white, the house nestled into a hollow on a sheltering hillside dotted with cattle. The place was so pretty she could scarcely imagine there was anything to dread.

They drove by a pond and up a narrow avenue of evergreen trees and Eli parked next to two passenger vans, a couple of big, old cars, and a trio of dirty pickup trucks.

"Praise the Lord, we're home!" exclaimed

Grandma.

Spotting Mary, a barefoot boy abandoned his miniature gravel pit and yellow digging toys and ran into the house through a side door.

"That's Seth," said Grandma.

"He's shy," Eli added. "He won't say 'hi' because he doesn't talk, but he'll let the others know we're here."

Eli pulled the lever to open the trunk, and they got out of the car. After an afternoon's journey, Mary was glad to stand. A brown and white long-haired dog bounded to Grandma and wagged its tail. "I think Rex missed me. Didn't you, Rex? There's a good boy," Grandma crooned as she patted his head.

As the dog ran around the car to sniff Eli and Mary, dark-haired, dark-eyed people, tall and short, young and old, fat and thin appeared—women from the house, men from the barn, and children swinging to the ground from limbs of trees and riding up on bicycles and scooters. The people resembled Eli in all but one respect: they were tanned and Eli was pale from his indoor lifestyle. Strong hands seized bags from the trunk, little hands grabbed the skirt of Grandma's dress and clung to Eli's legs. Mary was surrounded by Klassens.

The crowd parted as an old, gray-bearded man stepped forward, shirtsleeves turned up and work boots clotted with dry mud.

"Uncle Gideon." Eli nodded, his expression inscrutable.

"Eli." Gideon extended his hand, and they shook. Then the old man tilted his head back and eyed the stranger in their midst. "You must be Miss Rose. Sister

Eva phoned to warn us you were coming. Welcome."

*Warn?* At once, Mary didn't feel welcome at all, but Grandma clasped her arm and said, "The Lord has brought us home safely, Gideon. Perhaps you could offer our thanks."

Upon Grandma's prompt, Gideon scowled but Grandma's request was righteous and clearly designed to give him an opening to lead his flock. "I shall," he growled.

In a gesture of protection, Eli stepped next to Mary while the Klassens formed an irregular ring around the newcomers and bent their heads. Doing likewise, Mary watched Gideon from the corner of her eye.

The patriarch raised his arms skyward and spoke fervently. "Lord Jesus, we thank you for conveying your daughter Eva home to the bosom of her loving family. We also thank you for guiding Eli to his rightful home and bringing this...uh...Pharisee from the city with him. We pray that you will enter their hearts to remind Eli and to teach Miss Rose to walk with you, our Father, on the path to salvation. May all who are present obey your commands with steadfast virtue and give us the strength we need to welcome them to Eden Springs. May you rid them of Satanic notions so they may become faithful members of your flock. Amen."

"Amen," echoed the crowd.

So she was guilty of crimes unknown before they'd even met her. Mary shifted her focus to Eli, who was scuffing the toe of his shoe in the gravel of the lane. He squeezed her elbow in solidarity and they both looked up.

"Hi, Mama," he said as a woman with a careworn smile stepped toward him from between two men.

They embraced in a warm hug, and then the woman turned to Mary. "Never mind Uncle Gideon," she whispered. "You are very welcome here, Mary. I'm Miriam."

In seconds, the Klassens swarmed them, slapping shoulders, shaking hands, and hugging the newcomers according to a set of arcane rules of greeting that Mary couldn't work out. The last to greet them was Eli's father, with a wordless nod of his head and a reserved handshake.

Gideon cleared his throat, and everyone froze in place. "I believe the women have prepared a feast. Is that correct, Miriam?"

Eli's mother nodded. "Yes. We've only to lay out the food."

"Then let us proceed to the table," he thundered.

The men followed Gideon to a hand pump to wash up outdoors as the women hastened indoors. Three teenage boys carried their bags and peppered Eli with questions about the replacement of the BMW while a boy of about four rode on Eli's foot and a little girl perched on his arm.

A young woman bounced up and linked her arm in Mary's. "I'm Esther, Eli's youngest sister. You'll be sleeping in my bunk tonight. Our sister Sarah used to have the bottom, but she's married now and home with her baby who's sick with chicken pox. Anyway, welcome!"

"Thank you, Esther," said Mary. "You may kick me if I snore."

Esther flattered Mary's lame joke with a belly laugh and said, "Tonight, you can tell me about Toronto. I'm trying to convince Dad to let me move to the city for university, but Uncle Gideon's dead set against it. Oh-oh. Now look; we've only met and I'm spilling my guts already."

With that pronouncement, Esther was replaced at Mary's side by a woman who carried a fat, adorable baby in a sling. "I'm Ruth, Eli's sister-in-law. Uncle Gideon has decided you should sit on my bench at supper."

"Thank you, Ruth." Mary meekly followed her into the house and watched with dismay as Eli was swept away in a tide of men and boys.

"We usually eat together in the kitchen, but kin have come from other farms, so we girls will be in the kitchen and the men will eat in the dining room tonight," Ruth explained. "We'll serve them first."

Long-skirted women had already started filling bowls, cutting meat, and buttering vegetables, while young girls conveyed platters brimming with food to the dining room. As usual, Dominic's fashion advice had been spot-on, and she didn't stick out from the Brethren women too brazenly in her skirt, blouse, and braided hair.

"Is there anything I can do to help?" asked Mary.

"Ach, no," said Ruth. "You've had a long journey, Mary. Rest your feet."

"I've been sitting all afternoon and I'd like to help."

"Could you cut the bread?" Ruth placed the handle of a long knife in Mary's hand. "Slice thick and thin, but squarely, mind, so the boys can take what suits them."

Mary was grateful to have a task, and though her slices were crooked by any objective measure, Ruth and

Esther praised her skill with a knife, as if she was a child in need of encouragement.

At last, male Klassens served, the women and girls surrounded the kitchen table with bowed heads and Grandma said grace, expressing gratitude for wholesome food and her safe deliverance from the moral desert of Toronto, and requesting strength for the travails of life. As if choreographed and rehearsed, the youngest girls each picked up a plate and filed past pots and pans for their supper. They were followed by the older girls, Grandma and the other elders, and finally women Mary's age, who took their supper last. Esther and Ruth ushered Mary first into line within their cohort.

In Toronto, Mary had believed that Eli must be Grandma's favorite grandchild by the way she doted on him, but little girls vied to sit next to their beloved matriarch, who bestowed on them the same tender affection she'd given Eli. Evidently, every child was Grandma's favorite child.

The food tasted as rich as it smelled, and Mary thought she'd never eaten beef so succulent, or potatoes so sweet and creamy. Before she'd swallowed her third bite, a pointy-nosed girl of about fifteen asked, "When will Eli marry you?"

"Delilah!" Miriam hissed. "Spare Mary such questions! Your cousin will announce his engagement when he deems the time is right to share his news."

*Engaged.* Face burning, Mary stilled her fork and looked around the table as several pairs of dark eyes goaded her to answer Delilah's question. "We, we haven't set a date," she stuttered. *Or established that we ever intend to marry. Holy crap!*

"A June wedding, when the roses are in peak bloom, is beautiful," said a round-faced woman from across the table. "Mind, late summer is better for the meal."

Ruth said, "Jacob and I married in spring and—"

"A winter baby followed," teased Esther.

"Isn't Uncle Eli's birthday in August?" asked a young girl.

"Ach, yes, Becky, and he'll be turning thirty," Miriam answered through a mouthful of food.

"So old to start a family," said a skinny, cross-eyed girl. "Oh, my. I'm sorry, Ruth. I forgot. Jake was what…thirty-four when you married?"

"Thirty-five on their wedding day," corrected the girl next to her, "and thirty-six when sweet baby Ezra was born."

"Some men are late bloomers, but they're worth the wait," Ruth said defensively. "Don't you think that's true, Mary?"

Before she could reply, Gideon's voice boomed from the dining room. "We need more potatoes and gravy!"

"And meat," called another man.

At once, several women who were unburdened with babies stopped eating and hurried to replenish the bowls and platters in the dining room. When Mary moved to assist, Esther grasped her sleeve and kept her back. "Next time the men call, we'll go," she said. "And you don't have to answer any prying questions." She shot a theatrical scowl at the giggling girls. "They don't understand that things are different in the city."

"Thanks, Esther," Mary said quietly.

"Mind, you'd best not enlighten them. Uncle

Gideon doesn't like it if we know too much," she cautioned. "Especially if you're a girl."

****

After supper, Eli's brothers gave him a tour of the new milking shed while interrogating him on Mary's background and character. The sun was low on the horizon when he broke away from their company to check in with her. He'd spotted her with Esther, Leah, and the girls feeding a carrot to Shylock, the Shetland pony. In the mellow evening light, Mary's hair shone like a halo and her blouse and skirt clung to her curves. She looked like a radiant goddess. Leah placed a hand on Mary's shoulder, and they all laughed. Oh, to be a fly on Shylock's back and hear their conversation. He'd rejoined the men on the porch and listened instead to their speculation on the weather and commodity prices.

Now it was after ten and the house was in darkness, his nephews fast asleep in their bunks. Eli texted Mary, and she replied she was still awake. They met on the porch swing, Mary bundled in a quilt against the chill as he'd suggested. Rex lumbered up from his mat for a scratch behind his ears, then turned two circles and lay down again with his snout tucked under a back paw.

The quilt was big enough for both of them, and they snuggled under it. Eli's arms wrapped around Mary as spring peepers serenaded them from the shrub-ringed pond at the bottom of the lane and the floral scent of the pasture wafted in the air.

"How's everything on the girls' side?" he asked.

"Everyone's asleep except Esther, who's wide awake in the top bunk, but she promised she wouldn't tattle on us if you and I met in the night."

Eli chuckled. "That's Esther."

"She admires you, Eli, for leaving Eden Springs and, in her words, 'making something of yourself.' She wants to go into nursing…so she can travel."

"It's too late for that. Esther's already twenty-two and she'll marry soon. Uncle Gideon and Dad found a man for her, though she's been too stubborn to meet him."

"Jesus, Eli. You're starting to sound like you never left this place. As you're well aware, twenty-two is not too old for university. There's no such thing as 'too late' and she's very curious about life in Toronto."

"What are you suggesting?"

"That you help her. You have enough money to give her a start and—"

"I'll think about it."

"That's it? You'll think about it?"

"Yup."

Mary crossed her arms and said nothing. Her shoulder blade dug into his rib. She didn't know the hardship of leaving a close-knit community and family, of making a start in Toronto, especially for a Brethren girl who was sheltered by controlling men. He had to talk to Esther himself and come to his own decision. "I didn't say 'no', Mary," he said gently. "Things aren't as simple as they appear. I'll talk to her."

"Thank you." She said the words as if any discussion with Esther would come with a foregone conclusion and paid-up tuition.

Mary's body softened against him and he nuzzled the crown of her head.

She laughed lightly. "Your aunts and sisters think we're engaged. They're angling for a wedding date."

"Oh, no. The horror," he replied with a trace of

sarcasm. "It's outlandish."

"I think it's funny."

"If you take their perspective, it's not funny at all. I've never brought a girlfriend home before. I've been watching you and you're doing your best to fit in—which I appreciate more than I can say. They view marriage as normal and natural."

He turned to her and held her close. The barn's floodlight cast Mary's face in mysterious shadows, and though he couldn't read her expression, he felt her warmth. "I love you," he said in a low voice. "Even more than in Toronto."

"And I love you, too. Even more than in Toronto because I understand you better. The more I learn about you…"

As Mary's voice trailed off, their mouths came together in urgent passion. Eli desperately desired to be naked with her, inside her, flesh with flesh, but he could only permit himself to unbutton her pajama top, slip his hand over her heart, and kiss her. As he slid his fingertips over her breast, Mary sighed, and he felt her breath hot in his mouth. Their tongues mingled, and Mary moaned. If only—

Someone flicked on the porch light. They broke apart and sat straight, holding hands and stifling giggles like naughty Sunday school pupils. They had to get through Saturday. Then, on Sunday morning, they'd go fishing and they'd be alone, and he would have her. He'd open her blouse, take her skirt up over her luscious thighs and he would have her as a man was meant to have a woman.

"Sunday," she whispered, as if she'd read his thoughts and agreed with him completely.

Chapter Twenty-Six

After a breakfast of rolls and cheese—the post-church dinner being Sunday's principal meal—Miriam shooed Mary out of the kitchen. "There're only a few dishes to do and the weather is perfect for your adventure. Mind, Uncle Gideon will be furious with you and Eli when he discovers you've skipped church, but Grandma says God dwells in the rushes as surely as in His Holy House and we must give you our blessing to live as you wish. If the two of you change your minds, Eli knows where we are."

"Thank you, Miriam."

Mary felt guilty for provoking Gideon's ire—it seemed that if the dour uncle wasn't happy, ain't no one in the family could be happy—and her feelings must've shown because Miriam smiled broadly and added, "You worked hard in the garden yesterday, Mary, and you deserve a rest."

"I planted an entire row of onion bulbs upside down! I made extra work."

"And then you planted them right side up."

"With help."

Miriam clucked her teeth. "Forget about that. The onions have forgotten and now they're planted properly, happy as can be, roots down." With firm hands, she turned Mary toward the door and nudged her onto the porch. "The bass will be biting. If you get a fair catch, we can fry them for dinner."

Mary found Eli playing in the sandbox with his nephews. He tipped the box of a toy dump truck onto a miniature mountain, and the boys scooped the dirt with the excavator he'd given them the previous day, his small nieces having received dolls. Eli ruffled Seth's hair and they smiled at each other. He told the boys he'd see them after church and stood to join her.

They found two rods, a tackle box, a net, and a bucket in the driveshed.

"We could take the car so you can practice driving on the lane." He pointed toward a track that followed a row of trees. "Or we could walk to the pond."

"How far is it?"

"See that field?"

Mary shielded her eyes with a flat hand, judged a distance of about three or four city blocks, and nodded.

"It's one field further than that."

Recalling their last driving lesson, Mary said, "It's a beautiful day. Let's walk."

And indeed, it was a beautiful day, with nary a cloud in the sky and bees buzzing around dandelions and other flowers she admired but couldn't name. Eli was quiet but not moody. In one day, he'd tanned to a healthy nut-brown and he moved with an agile ease, as if farm work had reacquainted him with his body. This was as good a time as any to broach a tricky subject.

"Did you have a chance to speak to Esther?" she asked.

"No. I looked for her, but Leah said she left for church early. I told you I'd talk to her, Mary. You don't have to nag."

*Nag?* She was only asking a question. Jeez. They

walked in a pensive silence. If he was going to be sour, he could be the one to restart their conversation. The sunshine warmed Mary's bare arms, pterodactyl-like birds circled overhead, and Toronto seemed a million miles away. They'd return to the city that afternoon, and till then she'd do with the day as Grandma suggested—*rejoice and be glad in it.* They passed over a culvert, through a copse of trilliums and huge trees breaking into leaf, and emerged in the corner of the next field.

"I'm sorry, Mary," Eli said gently. "You weren't nagging. You sounded like my own conscience, the voice I keep trying to ignore, and I snapped at you."

"It's okay."

"No, it isn't. You're not a punching bag." He kicked a stick off the lane, seemed to hesitate, then spoke guardedly. "Here's the thing. I grew up with arbitrary rules...with strict lines between right and wrong within the nutty world of the Brethren Church, but I couldn't obey. I ran away and never got around to replacing the old rules with better ones, so I make mistakes. I do selfish things."

"You've been generous with me."

"Because I love you and it's easy to be generous. The situation with Esther is different. I know what I have to do, and I know what basic decency demands, but I don't want to deal with all the complications with helping her leave Eden Springs. Uncle Gideon, Dad, and my older brothers won't take it well, and she'll be vulnerable when she leaves. She'll need a lot of support and not just with money. She's only twenty-two and she'll need a guardian."

"You left unaided. As a teenager."

"She's a girl."

"Eli, you're disparaging half of humanity with that comment. Esther's capable and strong and she can stand on her own two feet. She's a female version of you in many ways. Don't underestimate her—or the good you'd do by helping her."

Eyes dark under furled brows, he said ominously, "She's been promised. They might come after her."

Mary met his frown. "What if they do? You know them. Toronto's your turf. You can handle them."

"Maybe, if I'm there to intervene. I'd be outnumbered."

"Kidnapping is illegal. Esther's capable of calling 911 if you give her a cell phone."

"Calling for outside help is not the Brethren way." When Mary sighed with impatience, he said, "You're right. That's a cop-out. I'd protect her. But you have to understand, if they know I'm helping her, we won't be welcome back here for a very long time."

With the stakes laid bare, Mary felt his dread. "You might be sacrificing your connection to your family and Eden Springs."

"Yes, and it sucks. Even though I left, I still love my family—even Uncle Gideon, Dad, and Jacob—and I want to see the kids grow up. You've won over Mama and my sisters, and I felt as if we were building a bridge this weekend."

"But helping Esther will destroy the bridge."

"It might. And trying to avoid helping her makes my head pound."

"Eli, whatever you say about rules, your moral compass points to true north. You have to do the right thing and let go of the outcome. You can't control that."

"The words of a famous philosopher?"

"Not so famous, but a philosopher nevertheless. They're the words of Grandma Klassen."

Eli rubbed his chin. "Hmm. I think I've heard of her."

They followed the lane through a thicket of scrubby bush to a clearing with a pond and a forest beyond it. Hands occupied with fishing gear, they shuffled and picked their way over loose rock to a level area near the forest. The pond hummed with life. With happiness. That is what Mary felt in this place. "Does the pond have a name?"

A confused smile passed over Eli's face. "Does it need one?"

"No."

"We call it 'the big pond', 'the small pond' being the one near the house."

"Some places are so beautiful a name won't do them justice," Mary declared. "This is one of those places." After they set down the fishing tackle, she turned to Eli. He took her in his arms and swung her in the air like they were kids on a playground.

\*\*\*\*

Mary easily learned to bait a hook and cast, but they only caught sunfish, which Eli released. When he blamed their lack of success on a late start, she laughed and said, "I'd rather the fish swim away than land on a plate, anyway."

After an hour of catch and release under an unseasonably warm sun, they waded barefoot at the pond's edge. Their toes sank into mud and their feet ached in the cold water, so they decided against swimming and instead retreated to the shade with only chipmunks and chickadees for company. The forest floor was as soft as a bed and the air was scented by the cedars and hemlocks towering above. Eli had fantasized about bringing Mary to this place, and here they were, Mary lying in his arms, Mary gazing up at him with her wide, gray eyes. He wanted her now, and he also wanted this moment to last forever, to etch the simple happiness of this morning in his memory. She was content to follow him and he would take his time with her.

Eli brushed his fingertip over the cinnamon dusting of freckles on Mary's cheeks and nose.

"I don't tan very well," she said.

"I see that. Your freckles look nice, Mary." It was true and that is all he had to say.

Her lips were full from sunburn and he kissed them, top lip and bottom, and then both at once, and she kissed him back, mouths moving slowly as if it were their first nervous kiss. He ran his hand down her back and over the rough cotton of her skirt, cupping her round bottom and pulling her close. She clung to him as he pressed against her thigh. She invited him into her mouth with a flick of her tongue on his teeth, and he deepened their kiss. They pulled their bodies together and kissed until they were dizzy with arousal. They then broke apart, their hands fumbling to unbutton and unzip each other's clothing.

"Leave your skirt on." The words came out as a husky command. "And ride me."

Mary nodded and he rolled onto his back, cock hard over his lower belly. She did as she was told, the wet heat of her against his balls, her skirt draped over their bodies, hiding everything from view. Astride, she looked down at him, and her eyes pierced through to his soul. Her hair cascaded over her shoulders, obscuring her full breasts, revealing only enough to drive him insane with lust.

Mary slid her hand from his chest down his torso, lifted the hem of her skirt, and ran her fingers round his base and the length of him. His skin sizzled with her touch. She was ready, breath rising, body aquiver, thighs gripping his hips, pussy moving against him.

"I need you," he groaned. "Now."

"Now?" She gripped his shaft and raised herself over him, pressing him against her opening, and she stopped. "You want it now?"

If she didn't listen, it would be over before they'd started. "Now!" he growled, fighting for control.

Teasing, she guided him in partway, and stopped. He took her hips in his hands and he impaled her, deeply and smoothly. Eyes rapt, she looked skyward and moaned as he dug into her as high as he could. Fallen needles rubbed harshly on his back, but he didn't care. There was only the raw sex of this woman, this sun-kissed, round-breasted goddess, and he edged toward oblivion with each thrust.

"Now?" She gasped and fell onto him, pressing her forehead against his neck. She angled herself and rode him, taking the length of him, taking all she could. "Eli." She whispered his name, her voice filled with longing, and then she called it out repeatedly, as if desperate for rescue. "Eli!"

Gripped inside her, he bucked and she cried out, her body swaying and shaking with the pleasure of him. He buried himself in her depths and stayed with her, both lost in ecstasy. And then it was over. For a long time, they held each other as closely as they could.

Mary rolled off him and nestled in close at his side. He dozed, enveloped in her scent, her leg curled over his thighs, her arm across his chest, and her pubic hair wet against his hip. This was paradise.

****

Mary didn't nap. Trying not to disturb Eli, she turned over, found his jeans, and made herself a pillow. Eli roused and embraced her, his front snug against her back, his soft cock sticky against her bottom. "Pillow?" she asked, reaching for his shirt.

He balled the shirt up and snuggled against her once more. "If we did this in June, we'd be eaten alive by blackflies and mosquitoes."

"Well, today is perfect."

"Eden before the apple incident," he murmured into her hair, tickling her scalp and giving her goosebumps.

"What time do you think it is?"

"Does it matter?"

"We shouldn't be late for lunch."

Eli propped himself on his elbow. "About eleven, judging by the sun. We've got an hour."

"Not long enough."

"You like it here?" He ran his hand from her hip, along the valley of her waist, and cradled her breast.

"Like it? That's an understatement," she replied. "Belgrave Park is spoiled for me now. The noisy people, the dog shit and litter. Here even the birds are better. They fly around without begging or stealing, courtly and aloof." She inhaled the scent of pine and soil, and then slipped her hand over his. "You were really scared to bring me here. To Eden Springs."

"I didn't know if you'd like it…if you'd get along okay with my family. If it went badly and they rejected you, they would be rejecting me—just when I've finally stopped blaming them for being who they are."

"What if that had happened? What if they hated me?"

"I'd have taken you away and I wouldn't come back."

She swallowed the lump in her throat. "When you're finally reconciling, you'd leave again?"

"Yes, for you I would." His chest moved against her back. "I'd give up everything for you."

"Everything is too much, Eli."

He slipped his hand between her breasts and pulled her close against him and kissed her temple, took a wayward lock of her hair in his teeth, and tugged playfully. Mary wasn't fooled. He was gathering his courage to say something.

"Remember when you agreed, 'No other men. Only me'?"

This again. Why did he have to keep asking that? "Yes, Eli, I remember. Nothing's changed."

"Would you agree to it forever, Mary?"

Forever? Her heart jumped. "What are you asking?"

"To marry me."

Yes…of course…but no…what the hell? She loved him with all her heart, but she couldn't be "Mrs. Eli Klassen." Her mind flitted to Dominic in a tux with an ostentatious boutonniere leading her up a church aisle like a cow at an auction—or a human possession—and she recoiled. "What if I said 'yes', but I'd rather let time marry us, not a ceremony. No wedding, no justice of the peace or officiant, and definitely no minister. We'd live together and our lives would merge organically."

"I'd be cool with that. If we agree we're forever, then we're forever, right?"

"Right. Then you have your answer. Yes to forever." She'd never been more certain of a 'yes' in her life. Her next "Yes!" echoed over the pond and through the glade.

"Mary?"

"Eli?"

"This is the weirdest engagement ever. And I am so unbelievably, fantastically happy, I don't know what to do."

"That's easy," she laughed. "Fuck me."

"Such language! Mary Rose, you swear like a sailor, and as your forever man, I shall have to discipline you."

Now she was shaking head to toe with laughter. "If you think that's what I deserve."

Eli's cock pressed hard against her rear and his breath quickened. She rolled onto her front, cushioned her face in his jeans, and wiggled her ass in the air. He slapped her there, hard enough to make a thwack but not hard enough to hurt .

"You can do better than that," she teased.

And he did. He covered her with his body, pushed himself between her legs, and twined his fingers in her hair. "You want me to have you?" he whispered in her ear, a three-day-old beard scraping her skin.

"Yes." Mary arched her back to lift her hips and he slid into her pussy with a gentle thrust.

When she moaned her pleasure, he released her

hair and pulled her onto her knees to take her deeper.

"This feels so good but I can't...I can't..." She panted. "You go."

Eli filled her, gliding in and out, giving her the length of him. He came fast and, with a final thrust, he broke away. "Your turn." He rolled off her, gasping for air.

He knew exactly what she wanted. Mary flipped onto her back, skirt damp with sweat and ringing her waist. Eli pushed her thighs apart and knelt before her. With the stroke of his finger, he bared her clit, slid his finger into her, and licked her tenderly. She sighed and laid back and let herself be loved under the evergreen bower.

****

They did their best to brush the detritus of the forest floor from each other's clothing and hair and then washed their faces and arms in the still water of the pond. Tadpoles and minnows darted in the reeds and a turtle sunned himself on a rock. They would leave this place and the creatures would remain, living out their lives in the ancient rhythms of days and seasons. Mary watched Eli as he examined tracks in the mud a few feet away.

"Bear." Muscles tensed, he spoke in a low voice and his gaze darted left and right. "About a half an hour ago. Took a drink right here."

"When we were...oh my God!" Mary's mouth formed a shocked O and her stomach somersaulted. "A bear?!"

Eli laughed. "Nah. They're only muskrat tracks. You should see your face." He imitated her and laughed harder. Jesus, he was beautiful, especially when he was

315

happy.

She laughed, too. There would be a next time in this place, wouldn't there? A next time whether Esther moved to Toronto or not. Mary pushed her wet feet into her slip-on sneakers and noted with relief that her skirt covered the scratches on her knees. They gathered up the fishing gear and headed back.

Miriam, Leah, and Ruth already had dinner on the table when they entered the house—ham, two kinds of soup, corn bread, cheese, pickles, salad, and a row of pies on the counter for dessert.

Miriam smiled at Mary, then peered fondly at her son. "No fish?"

"We only caught sunfish. It was too bright for bass by the time we got to the pond," answered Eli.

"You keep city hours," she scolded, smiling all the while. She flicked a tea towel at him. "Wash your hands please and sit."

"Where's Esther?" Eli asked, hands already under the tap.

Leah shrugged. "She was at church, but she took off alone on her scooter. Said she wanted time to ponder Uncle Gideon's sermon."

Ruth, who was nursing Ezra in a rocking chair, snorted. "He spoke on the evils of distracting and lascivious amusements…chiefly dancing…and she dozed off and didn't hear a thing."

Eli started humming a lilting waltz. Taking her turn at the sink, Mary looked over her shoulder at him in fascination. It was the first time she'd ever heard him express himself musically. He carried on, singing in a rich baritone. "On a hill far away…"

Joining him with a tap of her toe, Leah sang along,

"Stood an old rugged cross, the emblem of suffering and shame…"

Laughing, Miriam raised her hand like a stop sign. "Careful, you two. Uncle Gideon will hear you and you both know he banned that hymn."

Eli grinned at Mary. "Grandpa Klassen liked that tune and Grandma *adores* it, but Uncle Gideon thinks it tempts people into dancing. You know, having fun and moving their feet in time to music and other terrible things."

Storm clouds gathered in Miriam's face. "Don't make trouble, Eli. Soon you'll leave, and we will remain, and we must have peace among us." She went to where he sat and hugged his shoulder, giving his body a shake with her arm. "Please, for me, follow the rules through dinner, and you can sing *The Old Rugged Cross* at the top of your lungs when you're on the highway."

"I'm sorry, Mama."

He did look sorry, like a boy who'd batted a ball through a plate glass window. Seated to his other side, Mary rubbed her ankle against his and he squeezed her knee.

Miriam kissed the top of his head and mussed up his hair the way he'd mussed up Seth's. "You're a good son, Eli. I only wish you'd try harder to convince Uncle Gideon and your father of it." With an impatient huff, she went to the door to call the family to prayer and dinner.

Gideon's gloomy mood cast a pall over the meal, and conversation was confined to requests for the saltshaker and the passing of butter. A half hour later, the family began drifting from the table to the porch, where Isaac would read the day's scripture to all assembled.

"Jacob tells me the traffic is bad if you leave your departure too late," Gideon said to Eli.

Hoping to make time for Eli to find Esther, Mary said, "I'll help with the dishes before we go."

"Your help is not needed," boomed Gideon. "You'd best pack, if you haven't already."

"We packed this morning and I want to help," said Mary.

Leah shot Mary a hopeless look and shrugged. "It's okay, Mary. These won't take but a few minutes. Mind, your leaving comes far too soon, but Uncle Gideon's advice is sound. Jake told us the cars and trucks crowd the roads so tightly, you'd walk as fast as you drive when it gets to supper hour in Toronto."

Gideon glared at Leah to warn her that he didn't welcome her jollying, her unrequested support evidently nipping at his ultimate authority. She curtsied contritely and scraped a crust into the compost bucket.

In a bid to cut the tension, Mary said sweetly, "Jacob is right about the traffic."

Gideon roared, "You be silent. It's for Eli to speak on the rightness of Jacob's observation, not you."

The older children scrambled from the kitchen and the younger children hid in their mothers' skirts. From her vantage by the stove, Grandma glared at the back of her brother-in-law's head, then cast Mary a zipped-up smile. Mary got the message, and at once she realized how helpless Eli must have felt when Gabriel abused his power. Being a muzzled party in a family drama was torture, and there was nothing she could do to relieve her anger.

Eli was holding Ezra to give his mother's arms a break. He passed his nephew back to Ruth and said evenly, "We'll go, Uncle Gideon. And you will not speak disrespectfully to Mary again."

Face red with rage, Gideon pounded the table and spewed spittle with his venom. "I shall not speak to Miss Rose again, for I haven't cause nor wish to. You didn't attend church this morning, Eli. As you are not behaving as Christians, I have no duty to treat you as Christians."

Eli clenched his hands into fists and the cords stuck out in his neck. He glanced toward Grandma and his mother and sisters and took a slow breath to calm himself. Mary watched as he held Leah's eye, and Leah shook her head in a resigned way. Looking at the patriarch again, he spoke with barely controlled fury. "You're right, Uncle Gideon. You have no duty to treat me as a Christian because I've renounced my faith. I'm still a Klassen, though. You could try treating me as your nephew and Mary as your guest. Grandma, Mama, and the girls understand the difference between church and family, but it seems lost on you and that's a choice you've made. You've chosen condemnation over love."

Tears flooded Miriam's eyes, and Mary wanted to hold her and cry with her, but fear and pride held her back. She vowed never to let Gideon get the better of her again.

Gideon scowled at Miriam as if she was a whimpering dog beneath his contempt. "Sister Eva, you should quiet her. I'll see Eli and Miss Rose off," he said tersely.

There was nothing more to say or do. With Gideon's declaration, Mary and Eli's trip to the country ended.

Chapter Twenty-Seven

The weekend wasn't supposed to end with him scuttling off like a beaten animal while Mama bawled her eyes out. Now he was crying, tears stinging his eyes and streaming down his face like twin creeks fed by springs. He gripped the wheel and drove fast, very fast, away from his humiliation. Eli stole a cowering look at Mary, and she stared directly back with puffy eyes through steamed-up glasses. She was crying, too.

"Pull over," Mary pleaded. "Stop somewhere and take a break. You can't drive like that."

"Like what, Mary? Like a coward who lets his uncle mistreat his family?" he sobbed. "In the morning you agreed to forever, and by noon I blew it. You saw the real me. They all did. I let them down."

Mary spoke firmly despite her tears. "There's a cemetery on the top of this hill. We can park there."

Shoulders heaving, he wiped his face with the heel of his hand. Mary was right, as usual. Women were better with hard emotional stuff like this. He jarred the car into a gated lane and slid to a gravel-grinding stop under a chestnut tree.

"Turn off the car," ordered Mary.

First, he needed air. He opened the windows all the way and turned the key in the ignition.

Mary reached across from her seat, and he leaned over, and she held him. There was nothing to say. She'd witnessed his weakness. He hadn't even reached out to Esther. If they'd gone to church, everything might have come out differently, but he couldn't capitulate to his psychopathic uncle and his ass-licking father and brothers or what was the point in leaving in the first place? Fuck!

That bloody hymn echoed in his head. Jesus fucking Christ. He was so distraught he was hearing things, too. Except it wasn't in his head. Mary wasn't singing. She didn't even know the words to *Jesus Loves Me* let alone *The Old Rugged Cross.*

A muffled girl's voice came from the back of the car. "So I'll cherish the old rugged cross..." It was Esther!

At once, Mary and he broke apart and looked at each other, mouths agape. Quickly as he could, he pulled the lever for the trunk latch and jumped out of the car.

Esther was already pushing the lid up by the time he got to her, and her sock and sandal-clad foot was searching for the ground. Eli's sorrow transformed into relieved happiness at the sight of her.

"Aren't you going to help me, elder brother?" she asked as she unfolded her long limbs.

"Esther!" He took her hand to pull her close and he hugged her. "Jesus!"

"Yes. I'm a stowaway. Feel free to take the Lord's name in vain, Eli. I won't tattle. You should see your face." Esther laughed. "Hi, Mary." She waved.

Their hands instinctively intertwined, and they danced in a three-person ring, laughing until their stomachs hurt. Eli was the first to face their new reality.

"We can talk in the car," he said gravely to Esther.

"They'll soon discover you're missing. We'd better put some distance between us and Eden Springs."

"Ach, my dear, favorite brother," she replied. "Leah will keep them at bay for hours yet. She has a million excuses for my absence and they won't worry overmuch until supper."

"And then what?" Mary asked with a shiver.

The siblings shrugged. "I guess we'll find out," said Eli as he closed the trunk.

"We can go to my place," said Mary. "Dominic will want to meet you, and they'll look for you at Eli's. Grandma has my address, but I have a hunch she'll pretend she doesn't know it."

"Is Dominic your roommate?" asked Esther.

"Yes," said Mary.

"And he's a man?"

"Yes again."

Esther's voice rose an octave. "You're okay with that, Eli?"

"Sure. Why not? Dominic cares for Mary like a brother."

"How can you be sure he thinks—"

"He's gay."

"I'm meeting a real, live sodomite?" Esther squealed.

"I wouldn't call him that," said Eli.

"Right. 'Gay'. Toronto is sounding more interesting all the time!"

After Esther did a few jumping jacks to loosen her limbs, the trio got back in the car and drove eastward into the future.

****

At her insistence, Mary took the backseat so she

could check her messages, having neglected her phone and her work since Eli's text on Friday night. Brother and sister had much to discuss, but she couldn't hear their conversation over the wind from their open windows, and she was content to remain blissfully ignorant of their scheming. Restored to function, Mary's phone burst into a series of rattles and pings. Toronto was newsy, and the more she read, the more she both dreaded and relished their return.

The first message was from Candace Kaine, who'd sent a link to Eli's interview with Tracy DeLillo. "Is this your boyfriend, Mary? If so, he's a keeper! BTW, are you coming up to Laurentian for the Spinoza conference?"

Mary replied with, "Yes, he's my bf, and probably. Are you speaking at it?"

Next were two missed calls from Penny and a voicemail. "Hi, Mary, I hope you're having a restful weekend. It's Saturday morning and things are, um, topsy-turvy here. The Dean is on the warpath and apparently Gabriel is having a meltdown in Chicago. Monday will be chaotic. I told the Dean I'd reach out to you. Want me to take over as your advisor? Talk soon."

Mary couldn't face a lengthy conversation, so she texted back, —Yes, please be my advisor, Penny! Thank you! May I call you tomorrow morning? I don't teach till Tuesday.—

Mary looked up as they sped by a loud transport truck swaying under a heavy load in the center lane, then refocused on her phone.

Interspersed among prying queries from journalists and other grad students, Dominic's messages warned of a growing media presence on St. Dunstan Avenue and offered style tips for tell-all interviews. Sent that morning, his latest text informed her that Oprah had chased him to the laundry room for an exclusive tête-à-tête, but he fended her off with a spray of collar starch. Mary chuckled, and messaged they'd be back before supper and there would be three of them.

As Penny warned, Gabriel communicated in full freak-out mode. His texts began with a deluded, —We must meet for a drink next week, Miss Rose, and discuss our misunderstanding. How about Tuesday?— And descended incrementally to the nadir, —That was your last chance to answer me. You'll be hearing from my lawyer, you antifreeze blooded, slanderous, libelous, phallus-chewing bitch.— Mary copied and pasted his texts and emails into a Word document titled, "The Screwball's Letters", as a tribute to C.S. Lewis whose writing she'd adored since childhood. She massaged her temples, disappointed but not surprised at his outbursts. If Gabriel pressed charges against Eli, the document might come in handy.

And finally, there was a text from Claudia: —I've been trying to get ahold of Eli for three days. Please tell him to contact me.— This Mary erased. After all, Eli would have Claudia's messages on his own phone.

Mary was so engrossed in her virtual return to Toronto that she only realized they'd turned off the highway when the Corolla juddered to a halt. The Klassen siblings peered over their shoulders from the front seats. "Rest stop, Mary," said Eli.

"My bladder's bursting. I desperately need a toilet," Esther said frankly. "You coming with me, sister?"

*Sister?* Mary grinned so widely she thought her

cheeks would split. She closed her phone and tossed it onto the seat, then ran to catch up to Esther, who hustled to the building. The parking lot felt like a DMZ between the surreal world of Eden Springs and the real world of Toronto. She'd left the city with a pile of work on her desk and she'd return to the same, but she'd gained a *sister* and a profound respect for Eli.

****

After waiting in a long Sunday queue in the food court, they returned to the car with coffee for each of them. Eli had bought gas and now he leaned against the hood, fixated on his phone.

"Any interesting news?" asked Mary.

Eli smirked. "Stephen texted that reporters keep tailing him. He wants to sell the BMW back to me."

Mary handed him a takeout cup. "Are you going to take him up on his offer?"

"Nah. The Corolla's better for a beginner driver." As he slurped from his cup, Esther chimed in, "I'll teach you how to drive, Mary."

"Thank you, Esther," said Mary. "I'd like that."

Ignoring their conversational diversion, Eli added, "To Stephen's credit, he's telling them I traded up for a black Jaguar convertible."

"I liked your BMW," muttered Esther.

"Any other news?" Mary asked, curious about Claudia's messages.

"Yuka messaged that she wants Grandma's sponge cake recipe. I'll send Grandma the address to Takamatsu. It's probably better if we lay low and use Uber Eats if we want sushi."

"I refuse to hide from Dad and Jacob," said Esther. "You said you'd get me a phone for safety."

326

"It's not just them. It's the media I'm concerned about," said Eli.

"Why? You think we're rockstars or something?"

"Kind of."

"It's a long story, Esther," said Mary. "Eli's like a darkly complicated superhero." She set her cup on the hood of the car and fetched her phone from the backseat while Eli explained his infamy. Mary found the DeLillo interview in Candace's message and gave her phone to Esther.

The more Esther saw, the higher her eyebrows climbed. When the clip ended, she returned Mary's phone and gaped at her brother. "Wow! Jacob told us your life is boring and pointless, but you're not boring at all!"

Eli bowed with fake modesty. "Aw, shucks. That's so sweet of you to say, darling Esther."

Before Esther could make a retort, Eli's phone rang. "Hello? Yeah, everything's fine...We found her and she's riding up front...Okay...A half hour ago?.. We're almost in Toronto. Bye, Leah—and thank you. Tell Mama we love her and everything will be all right."

"They know!" Mary and Esther said in unison.

"Yup. I'll feel better when we're at Mary's. We're sitting ducks on the road."

"Eli, I have an idea," said Esther.

"Oh, oh," said Eli.

"It's ingenious, and Mary will appreciate its merits even if you lack the imagination required for full understanding." Esther beat her hands in a drumroll on the roof of the car and paused for dramatic effect. "I'll drive."

"That's it? You'll drive? Uncle Gideon's so-called school has been very damaging to your mental develop—"

Esther play-kicked Eli in the shin. "Listen. When we get to Toronto, you need to hide from the paparazzi, right?"

"We're not movie stars but whatever. Yeah."

"And I'm a good driver. You said so yourself when you taught me."

"Yes, but you've never driven on a multi-lane highway."

"I've been watching you. It doesn't look hard. Fast cars to the left, slow to the right, signal and check before you make a move."

"Okay, but you've never driven in the city."

"The rules are the same everywhere, aren't they?"

"More or less," Eli conceded. "You have to watch for cyclists and transit—"

"They're like horses and tractors." Esther rolled her eyes. "Anyway, do be quiet and listen to the rest of my plan. I brought along the blanket Grandma crocheted for me, and it's in the trunk. You two sit in the back and when we get near Mary's, hide underneath it, and I'll smuggle you in. Street, parking lot, backdoor, all under the blanket. Ta-da! It's a great idea, isn't it?"

Eli scratched his chin. "Well, it's an idea," he hedged. "Though its greatness is debatable. What do you think, Mary?"

Mesmerized by the siblings' banter, Mary startled at the sound of her own name. "Who, me?"

Their brown eyes fixed on her, Eli and Esther nodded.

328

It was a ridiculous idea. Two people shuffling into the building under a blanket like a pretend pony would attract attention, not deter it, but there was no harm in cooperating, and she didn't want to hurt her new sister's feelings. "I'm game."

And with those two words, the decision was made.

\*\*\*\*

Eli had to admit that Esther was a good driver, and he had to talk to Mary before they got to St. Dunstan Avenue, so he squeezed into the backseat with her holding hands across the bench seat like a nervous suitor in the back of a taxi. The feel of Mary's warm, smooth hand in his reassured him. Prepared to coach, he watched Esther merge onto the highway in a manner that would make any instructor proud, then turned his attention to the love of his life.

"When we get to your place," he said, "we won't use a blanket for cover. Let's just walk into the building. Dominic and Stephen are given to drama, and I doubt we're as interesting to the media as they say."

"Yeah, I think you're right, Eli. With Dominic, a single 'a moment of your time, sir?' from an easily dissuaded novice reporter transforms into a media mob on the replay. They both like to embroider their stories."

Eli glanced at the speedometer, noted their moderate speed, and looked back at Mary. She'd pushed her glasses on top of her head, and her cheeks were pink with sunburn. With a single weekend of fresh air and wholesome food, she glowed with health. They'd have to get out of the city more often. Even with Uncle Gideon's theatrics, the weekend away had done her good.

"Claudia's been trying to contact me," he said casually. "When I didn't answer her texts or calls all weekend, she left me a long voicemail this morning."

"Oh?"

"Apparently, the sales office is in chaos since Stephen took over at In-Spire and Synergy is breathing down her neck for a personnel change. And she thinks the incident with Gabriel is good publicity for Hill. You know, the folk-hero thing."

Mary nodded. Her mind moved chess pieces several plays ahead, but he'd take his time and give his reasons.

"I could help her," he ventured. "I mean, with a few conditions."

"Eli, you got horrible headaches when you were in the thick of things at Hill. You're better now."

"I got horrible headaches when I went against my conscience. If I go back, if *we* go back because I'd want you with me, I'd do things differently. Straight shooting only."

"You seemed happier when you were helping your brothers on Saturday than you ever did with Hill."

"That's true. It's satisfying to put in an honest day's labor with a tangible result."

Mary ran her thumb over the roughness of his palm and peered at him with concern. "I wouldn't think any less of you for taking on a construction job in Toronto. As an example. Anyway, what's the rush to return to work? You can live on your investments for a while and think about things."

"I can't be idle, Mary. I'm not Brethren, but I was raised by them, and work is like oxygen for me. I'd go insane if I had to sit twiddling my thumbs and contemplating my future."

"Okay. I get that. I'm the same."

"Thank you. Now listen—" He briefly looked through the windshield at the looming tailgate of a pickup. "Esther! Three-second rule applies here, too!"

"I do thank you for your unnecessary advice, dear brother," Esther called back. "He merged in front of me and, as you can see, I'm slowing to make space."

"Okay, good," Eli shrugged and returned to his plan. "I, *we*, have enough money for us. And Esther too. But I'd like to be in a position to help Leah, and down the road, my nieces and nephews—any Klassen who wants to leave Eden Springs and needs help to do it. For that I need more money and real estate is the fastest way to get there."

"You'd hustle for a higher purpose," Mary said with a weak smile.

"Hustle?"

"Sorry. You're right. 'Hustle' has a nefarious connotation and that's not fair." She shook her head in apology and tried again. "You'd work for Claudia but keep your hands clean and fill a war chest."

"Exactly. And if you were there part-time, I think we could do well and then move on, after In-Spire is sold out and you've finished school." Recalling Mary's radiance as they fished in the pond, he added, "Wherever you want to go."

"I'd help you—you know that. You're okay working with Claudia again, after everything that's happened?"

"Well, if Felicity's at the Fountain Street office and I dictate terms, I think I could make it work. If you think pragmatically—"

"I'm an idealist."

"You're a pragmatic idealist," he countered. "Claudia is offering a golden olive branch and I'd like to accept it."

"No fighting with graphic designers?"

"Only if Brad Stefano deserves it." Mary's eyes shot darts of recrimination and he said, "For you, I swear off violence and I'll trust in my uncompromising reputation to back up our interests."

"No manipulating Stephen Hill?"

"Who's driving the BMW, Mary? He manipulates me."

"Oh, so now you're a lamb," she said, brows arched.

"The wolf and the lamb shall feed together," he said with smooth sarcasm.

"And they shall not hurt nor destroy in all my holy mountain," called Esther.

Eli smiled with affection at his sister. "Eyes on the road?"

"As ever, elderly brother," she sang in reply, "because I'm driving."

"Good. Do not, under any circumstances, look over your shoulder," he said.

Though unchurched, Mary recognized Eli's Biblical reference and handed him the key component to Esther's harebrained plan. Then, she leaned in close, and Eli threw the crocheted blanket over their heads and they kissed, long and slow, to seal the deal.

**A word about the author...**

Renata North is a registered nurse by profession and a writer by passion. Her short stories have been published in the anthologies "Dark Secrets" and "Murder! Mystery! Mayhem!" She is the author of two novels, a spicy Victorian romance novel, "What Love Demands", and an award-winning satirical suspense novel, "Elmington", published under her everyday, non-romantic name, Renee Lehnen.

Renata lives in Stratford, Ontario with her husband.